"A man. A man nam

He's checking in. By himself."

Maisie's blue eyes glowed as she looked at her granddaughter.

There was nothing for Meg to feel defensive about. She knew that. Which didn't explain why her shoulders stiffened and her stomach tensed. "So you're telling me this because..."

"I'm telling you this because we don't often get single men at the Hideaway. It's a romantic spot. Our guests are usually couples. And when couples check in, they usually have their minds on—"

"What they have on their minds isn't what I want to have on my mind," Meg reminded Maisie. "I told you, Grandma, I've given up waiting for Prince Charming. Prince Charming has left the building. And I'm pretty sure he's left the island, the state and the continent. Besides..." It didn't look as if Maisie believed her protests any more than Meg did, so she decided to change course. "Just because this Gabriel Morrison is here by himself doesn't mean a thing. He might be meeting someone."

"I don't think so. He tried for a room at the hotel near the park. They're booked. Christmas in July, you know." Maisie's eyes twinkled. "If he was bringing a woman, he would've asked for a room for two."

"You asked."

"Of course I asked. It's my duty as an innkeeper!" *And as your grandmother* went unsaid.

CHRISTMAS AT CUPID'S HIDEAWAY

Connie Lane

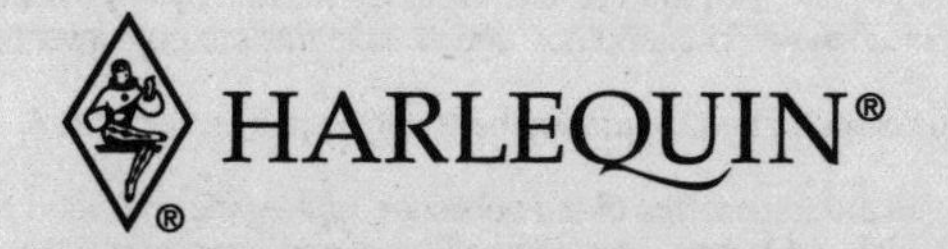

TORONTO • NEW YORK • LONDON
AMSTERDAM • PARIS • SYDNEY • HAMBURG
STOCKHOLM • ATHENS • TOKYO • MILAN • MADRID
PRAGUE • WARSAW • BUDAPEST • AUCKLAND

ISBN 0-373-16996-5

CHRISTMAS AT CUPID'S HIDEAWAY

This edition published by arrangement with Harlequin Books S.A.

Visit us at www.eHarlequin.com

Printed in U.S.A.

Dear Reader,

Welcome back to Cupid's Hideaway, the wonderfully wacky bed-and-breakfast inn where anything romantic can—and does—happen! In *Stranded at Cupid's Hideaway,* you met Laurel and Noah, two doctors who couldn't agree about anything except that they were in love. In *Christmas at Cupid's Hideaway,* a handsome guest checks in. Gabriel Morrison has his eye on Meg, the Hideaway's sexy chef, but his mind is a thousand miles away. Gabe is a successful advertising writer with a serious case of jingle-writer's block. But don't worry—Cupid's Hideaway will work a little magic on Gabe. He's about to find out that inspiration comes from unexpected places. Just as Meg will learn that you can't hide from love—even on an island in the middle of Lake Erie.

While Cupid's Hideaway is a figment of my imagination, South Bass Island and the town of Put-in-Bay are real, and it's one of my favorite vacation spots. The island is only three miles from the Ohio mainland, but as soon as I set foot on the ferry, I leave my everyday life behind. The leisurely place and friendly atmosphere are perfect for a little R and R. I love walking along the rocky beach and exploring the cottage-lined streets. My favorite thing? Driving one of the golf cars that residents and visitors alike use to cruise around the island.

If there's one thing I've learned on South Bass, it's that you can celebrate the holidays any time of the year. Because the weather's often too harsh in December to allow for visitors, the island has a special Christmas-in-July celebration, complete with a visit from Santa in his Bermuda shorts and Hawaiian shirt!

Happy holidays! Enjoy this visit to Cupid's Hideaway, and let the spirit of celebration live in your heart—all year long!

Connie Lane

P.S. Readers can reach me at connielane@earthlink.net.

Prologue

Tuesday, Noon

''Gabriel? Hey, it's me, Latoya. You haven't checked in since you left the office last week and I've got a stack of messages for you. It's just after noon here in LA and if you're driving and heading east—well, I'm not even going to try and figure out the time zones. I only know it's got to be sometime in the afternoon wherever you are. It's a beautiful July day, but I'll be eating lunch at my desk. As usual. Give me a call.''

Tuesday, Late

''Gabriel? Latoya. Haven't heard from you. Dennis says that means you found either a car or a woman you couldn't resist. Which is it? When you're done—ah...whatever it is you're doing—give me a call. There's plenty of messages here, including a couple from the Tasty Time Burger folks in New York. They're anxious to talk to you.''

Wednesday Morning

''Me again. Bright and early. At least it is here. That means you can call anytime.''

Wednesday Afternoon

"I know you're picking up your messages, Gabriel. You never let an hour go by without picking up your messages. Whatever time it is where you are, I can tell you one thing—they're still working in New York. The folks over at Tasty Time Burger world headquarters have already called three times. And that's just in the last couple hours. I'm running out of excuses, so do me a favor, will you? *Call me.*"

Thursday, Very Early

"Gabe? Dennis here. Dammit, Gabe, you're making me nervous. And Latoya's practically having apoplexy. She says you've never been away this long without checking in. Even that time you headed to Mexico with that what's-her-name. You know, the one who had her own TV sitcom for a while. If you can check your messages when you've got a blond bombshell on your arm, you want to explain why you haven't done it all week?"

Friday Afternoon

"Dennis again. Why do I feel like I'm talking to myself? They've started a pool at the office. A What-Happened-to-Gabe pool. The odds-on favorite is that you've been abducted by aliens. Can't imagine why they'd want you. Stop playing games and give me a call, will you? The Tasty Time Burger folks are riding my tail. I'm running interference for you, buddy, but it's getting tougher every day and they're getting antsy. I'll tell you what, let's keep this simple. Call them directly. Hum a few bars of the new jingle. Give them some idea of the lyrics. I know, I know, you artistic types, you don't like to be bothered while you're working. But there's only so much I can tell them. I explained that you'd decided to drive to New York—you know, to clear your head and give yourself plenty of alone-time to concoct the best advertising campaign in the history of greasy fast food? I assured them that you're writing up a storm. I guaranteed them that you're going to write the greatest jingle you've ever written. You *are* going to do that, aren't you, Gabe? Gabe?''

Chapter One

He didn't save the voice-mail messages. Why bother? The last thing Gabriel Morrison needed right now was the all-time roughest, toughest tag team of Dennis and Latoya. Instead, he tossed his cell phone down on the passenger seat of his Porsche, and, anxious to get his mind on anything but work and the office back in LA, he flicked on the radio.

Love my Tenders.
Love them lots.
Shaped like little steaks.
Love my Tenders.
Eat them all.
They're not fried, they're baked.

Gabe dropped his head against the steering wheel and groaned.

Bad enough he was stuck in a traffic jam that looked to be a couple miles long.

Worse that his air conditioner was on the fritz, he was almost out of gas and he was driving (or more specifically, idling) in the center lane between two eighteen-wheelers that dwarfed his car and cut off any chance of getting a breath of fresh air, even with the top down. Way worse when every time he checked, there were more and more messages from the office. More and more messages it was getting harder and harder to dodge.

And now he had to listen to the Love Me Tenders commercial?

Insult to injury.

Gabe clicked off the car radio and drummed his fingers against the dash that was quickly heating up from the intensity of the afternoon sun.

Funny, he'd always thought of Ohio as a cold place. If he was still in Ohio.

As if it would give him some connection to reality, Gabe craned his neck and looked around. He didn't see a sign that gave him any hint about where he was, but up ahead, he did see a break in the traffic. Not much to go on, but it was something. And right about now, something was better than nothing.

The next time the huge truck in front of him started to crawl forward, Gabe waited for his opportunity. He let the space between the vehicles widen and while the truck on his right was still grinding into gear, he punched the accelerator and shot into the open space. It turned out to be an exit lane and once he was off the freeway, he took the opportunity to look for a gas station. Easier said than done. By the time he saw a familiar red-and-yellow sign up ahead, he was in another line of traffic. This one wasn't moving any faster than the last.

At least there were no eighteen-wheelers around.

Gabe glanced over at the late-model minivan next to him. It was packed to the gills with luggage, and while the adults in the front seat seemed resigned to the fate of waiting in line for who-knew-what, the three pint-sized passengers in the back had obviously had enough. Too keyed up to sit still, they bounced in place and tossed a stuffed animal back and forth between them.

"Hey, dude!" The kid on the passenger side couldn't have been older than seven. He rolled down the back window and waved a toy stuffed bulldog in Gabe's direction.

Gabe cringed. He recognized Duke the Dog immediately. Then again, he suspected most people would. Whether they wanted to or not.

After just six weeks on the air, the Love Me Tenders dog-food commercial had become a cultural icon of sorts that had taken on a life, and a cult following, all its own. A lovable, cuddly Duke, star of the commercial, was available full-size in toy stores everywhere. A miniature variety was being given away in record numbers along with the kids' meals at a popular fast-food chain.

The kids in the minivan had the Cadillac version: an almost-life-sized Duke, complete with sequined jumpsuit and black ducktail wig, the outfit he wore in the commercial as he crooned the now-famous words to a tune that was just catchy enough to have the country singing along. And just different enough from the original to avoid any nasty lawsuits.

"Hey, dude! Look!" The little boy wagged Duke in Gabe's direction. "It's the Love Me Tenders dog. Isn't he cute?"

"Love Me Tenders! Love Me Tenders!" his little sisters sang next to him.

And Gabe was sure that somewhere between LA and wherever he was sitting now, he must have died. Died and gone to hell.

Not ready to accept his fate—or maybe just to get away from his own past and his own thoughts—he pulled onto the shoulder and shot past the waiting traffic. He took the first turn-off he came to and drove as fast as the state (and he knew for sure it was Ohio now because he saw a State Trooper) allowed.

A few minutes later, he found himself at the entrance to a ferry dock.

"Islands? In Ohio?" It was news to Gabe but he didn't stop to question it. He didn't hesitate, either. It looked like the ferry was just getting ready to leave the dock and he joined the last of the cars waiting to get on.

At this point, he didn't much care where he was headed. Anywhere was better than nowhere.

And for the last week, he'd been headed nowhere fast.

"WHAT DO YOU MEAN, a new guest?" Meg Burton pulled open the oven door and drew out a tray of cookies sprinkled with red-and-green sugar. She set them on the rack she'd left on the counter in the Cupid's Hideaway kitchen before she turned back to her grandmother. "You can't have a new guest checking in. You're completely booked. It's Christmas in July week, and the tourists are everywhere. You've been booked for months."

Maisie Templeton breathed in the aroma and gave the cookies an approving smile. "I was booked," she said. "The Crawfords." Maisie was the least inhibited person Meg had ever known. Her grandmother was over seventy, but that didn't stop her from pursuing her life's passion: Cupid's Hideaway, an island bed-and-breakfast inn known for its unique decor, its loyal clientele and the fact that the fluffy little old lady who owned it didn't just encourage romance, she aided and abetted it.

But at the mention of the Crawfords, even Maisie's cheeks went a little dusky under the coating of pink blusher she wore. "You remember them. They visited last summer, around this time. They were the ones who—"

"The ones we had to call the police about!" Meg rolled her eyes. She remembered the Crawfords, all right. So did everyone else on South Bass Island. The Crawfords and their exploits were already legendary in the annals of island gossip. Medium-aged. Medium-sized. Medium-temperament people. Bland as TV dinners. Or at least that was what Meg had thought when she'd seen them arrive.

Who would've guessed that a little game they'd been playing with a pair of furry handcuffs and a bottle of peppermint-flavored massage oil—which they'd purchased from the Cupid's Hideaway gift store—would result in not one but both Crawfords getting stuck in the closet of the Love Me Tender room?

Meg stifled a laugh, but only because she remembered how upset Maisie had been by the whole incident. Not that she was embarrassed. It would take a whole lot more than Mary and Glenn Crawford's wild imaginations to embarrass Maisie. No, her grandmother had been honestly distressed. After all, she believed that as innkeeper, it was her duty to make sure her guests enjoyed their stay at Cupid's Hideaway. And the very idea that they'd had to call not only the island police but half the volunteer fire department just to get the Crawfords unstuck....

Meg hid a half smile by turning back to her cookies. She tested the temperature with one finger and carefully lifted each one off the cookie sheet with a spatula. "What, they got arrested somewhere for something they were up to?"

"No. No. Not arrested." Behind her, she heard Maisie pour a cup of coffee. "They had to cancel. Something about appearing on a TV show. 'Life's Most Embarrassing Moments.'"

"More power to them." Meg finished with the cookies and wiped her hands on the apron she was wearing. She leaned against the counter, accepting the china mug of coffee Maisie offered. "So how many more for breakfast tomorrow?" she asked.

"Just one." Maisie poured a mug of coffee for herself. Using sterling silver sugar tongs, she added three lumps, then enough cream to make an ordinary person's cholesterol jump at least a dozen points. But if there was one thing Meg knew about Maisie, it was that she was far from ordinary. As if she needed further proof, Maisie grinned at Meg over the rim of her cup.

Meg had seen that look before. All twinkles and smiles. All sweetness and light. She knew it meant Maisie was up to no good.

"A man," Maisie said. Her blue eyes glowed. "A man named Gabriel Morrison. He's checking in. By himself."

There was nothing for Meg to get defensive about. She knew that. Which didn't explain why her shoulders stiffened and her stomach tensed. "So?" She sounded defensive, too, and she gave herself a mental kick in the pants. "So you're telling me this because..."

"I'm telling you this because it isn't often we get single men here at the Hideaway. It's a honeymoon spot, a romantic spot. Our guests are usually couples. And when couples check in here, they usually have their minds on—"

"I know exactly what they have their minds on." The exact same thing Meg had been trying *not* to have her mind on since she'd returned to the island after trying life on the mainland. Rather than explain it to Maisie, as she'd tried to explain it so many times before, she headed to the refrigerator. She counted the eggs, made sure there was enough butter, did a quick survey of the pecans, raisins and cream she'd bought to make a batch of her famous sticky breakfast rolls. Satisfied that she was all set, she closed the refrigerator and turned around.

Of course, Maisie didn't back down an inch. She was stationed next to the marble-topped table where Meg made bread, and she had the nerve to look as innocent as the baby goldfinches that chirped their heads off in the nest right outside the kitchen window.

"What they have on their minds isn't what I want to have on my mind," she reminded Maisie. "I told you, Grandma, I've given up waiting for Prince Charming. Prince Charming has left the building. And I'm pretty sure he's left the island, the state and the continent. Besides..." Because it didn't look as if Maisie believed her protests any more than Meg did, she decided to change course. "Just because this Gabriel Morrison is coming here by himself doesn't mean a thing. He might be meeting someone."

"I don't think so. He tried for a room at the hotel over near the park. They're booked. Christmas in July, you know."

"And that means he's not meeting someone because..."

"Because he would've asked for a room for two. And when Janice from the hotel called to see if we had any rooms available—"

"You asked."

"Of course I asked." Maisie pulled herself up to her full five-foot, one-inch height and threw back shoulders that were just this side of scrawny. "It's my duty. As innkeeper. I have to know who's staying here. And if a man's bringing a woman, it's my duty—as innkeeper—to remind him that we have a wide selection of products in the Love Shack designed to please them both.''

''Yeah.'' This time, Meg couldn't help herself. She had to laugh. ''Like they pleased the Crawfords?''

''They were smiling when they left here.'' Maisie's eyes twinkled. ''But that hardly matters. The Crawfords were the exception to the rule.'' Her grandmother glanced from Meg's brightly painted toenails peeking out of her sandals to the curly red hair she'd wound into a long braid. ''Kind of like a beautiful woman who refuses to get out and try to meet a man.''

''Grandma, I told you. I'm just not ready. Not yet. Someday maybe I will be. Someday, when I find someone different.'' Although it was ancient—and best forgotten history—Meg felt the familiar pang of emptiness. ''Someone who isn't Ben.''

Before Maisie could respond and remind her, as she always did, that the past was past and the future was what mattered, the little brass bell inside the front door rang, announcing their guest. How she'd timed it so perfectly, Meg couldn't imagine, but Maisie chose that exact moment to hurry into the wide pantry on the far side of the kitchen. She waved Meg toward the front of the inn. ''Get that for me, will you?'' she called.

Meg sighed and slipped her apron over her head. She knew a losing battle when she saw one. She ought to; she'd been fighting—and losing—battles with Maisie all her life. She didn't exactly hold Maisie's persistence against her. She couldn't. Though Maisie could be meddlesome, she was well-intentioned. There were only three things she put more energy into than Cupid's Hideaway: Doc Ross, the retired family practitioner she spent most of her free time with, and—now that Maisie's only daughter and son-in-law were retired and living in Florida—her two granddaughters. Laurel, Meg's older sister, was married now and expecting her first baby in a couple of months. She was deliriously happy with her husband Noah, and while Maisie glowed at the prospect of becoming a great-grandother and the satisfaction of having been instrumental in bringing Laurel and Noah together, not having a romantic project to keep her occupied made the old lady chafe.

It also left her with a lot of time on her hands—a lot of time to decide that Meg's love life wasn't what it should be.

''No news flash there,'' Meg mumbled to herself, and because she refused to think about her lack of a love life—just like she'd been refusing to think about it since Ben Lucarelli had cut her heart into little pieces as only an experienced sous chef could—she thought about the Crawfords. And thinking about the Crawfords made her think about the Love Me Tender room. And thinking about Love Me Tender naturally made the commercial she'd heard earlier that morning pop into her head.

Whenever Meg thought of a song, she couldn't resist. She couldn't keep the words inside.

''Love my Tenders. Love them lots. Shaped like little steaks.'' Meg walked into the lobby, singing the now-familiar-to-everyone-and-his-brother words with all the enthusiasm of the comical dog in the commercial. ''Love my Tenders. Eat them all. They're not fried, they're—''

When she saw that the guy standing at the desk—the guy who must be Gabriel Morrison—was staring at her as if she'd just strolled in stark naked, she jerked to a stop in front of the ten-foot tall Christmas tree near the front desk and stared right back at him.

And the thought that she wouldn't mind seeing him stark naked sent little sparks of electricity tingling along her spine.

Meg cringed at the realization, but even realizations and the cringes they brought along with them weren't enough to erase the impressions that flashed through her head.

Gabe Morrison was gorgeous enough to be a man-of-the-month: tall, broad-shouldered, hair the color of the chocolate pudding in her soon-to-be-famous (she hoped) pie and eyes that reminded her of brandy, the secret ingredient in her spinach-salad dressing.

He had the kind of face that couldn't fail to make a woman's heart flutter. Not as craggy as it was chiseled. Not weathered but tanned, and not a store-bought tan, either. He obviously spent a lot of time outdoors in the wind and the sun, and for the nano-second Meg needed to take it all in, she wondered if he might be a sailor. If the expensive luggage he held in each hand hadn't set her straight on that notion, the Porsche she saw through the front window did. Most sailors, even the wealthy ones who vacationed on the island, left their expensive sports cars at home.

Good-looking or not, there was no mistaking that Gabe Morrison was worn to a frazzle. His shoulders were slumped inside a green golf shirt with some expensive designer logo over the heart. There were dark shadows almost the same color as his faded jeans under his eyes, and a crease in the middle of his forehead that told her he frowned far too hard and too often. In spite of his expensive haircut, the left side of his hair stood up on end, as if he'd been tugging at it. His jaw was square and covered with a shadow of dark stubble. As he stared at her, it went a little slack.

For the second time in just a few minutes, Meg found herself on the defensive. It was a feeling she didn't like, one she'd never been prone to feeling back in the days before her life had been whipped out from under her like the tablecloth in the old magician-pulls-the-cloth-away-and-leaves-the-dishes-on-the-table trick. Feeling it only made her more defensive. So did the barely controlled animosity on Gabe's face.

"What?" Eyes narrowed, Meg closed the gap between them. "Something wrong with my singing?"

She knew the answer to her own question. Fact of the matter was, Meg Burton had a terrible singing voice. She's been banned from the high-school choir and asked (politely) not to participate in the caroling either at the island's real Christmas bash or at all the parties planned for this week. But though she might've been ready to hear a critique of her dubious talents from the people she'd known all her life, she'd be damned if she was going to put up with it from a perfect stranger. Even if *perfect* was the operative word.

She squared her shoulders and lifted her chin. "So, you're going to tell me my singing stinks, right? And then you're going to ask me for a room. And I'm going to remind you that you're only here because, from what I've heard, this is the last room left on the island. So if you want a place to stay tonight—one that *isn't* that sweet little car of yours parked in the no-parking zone in front of the inn—you may want to reconsider. Now, let's try again. What?" She paused just long enough to make sure he got the message. "Something wrong with my singing?"

"Your singing is fine." With a sigh that seemed to be torn from somewhere deep inside him, Gabe set down his luggage and stretched, working a kink out of his neck. Big points for him. Even though he was clearly trifling with the truth, he said it with nearly enough conviction to make Meg believe he was sincere. Nearly.

"It's not your voice," he said and he didn't even try to hide a shudder of revulsion. "It's that song. That commercial."

"Love Me Tenders! What a hoot!" Meg hurried around to the far side of the desk. When she'd been on the mainland the day before, she'd stopped for a quick bite to eat and had sweet-talked the teenager at the drive-through window into one of the Duke the Dogs usually reserved for their kid customers. She grabbed it now from where she'd tossed it under the front desk and flashed it at Gabe. "Isn't he adorable?"

It was the wrong thing to say. Gabe's face paled a little. A muscle at the base of his jaw jumped. He took one look at cute little Duke and his top lip curled.

"Duke the Dog is spoiled, temperamental and addicted to sugar in any form," he said from between clenched teeth. "Besides that, Duke isn't a duke at all. That's just a stage name. Duke's real name is Diana, and she's a bitch."

"Imagine that!" Meg leaned her elbows against the counter and propped her head in her hands. Okay, so the guy was gorgeous. He was also a stick-in-the-mud and she couldn't help herself. She just had to tease him. She held up her little stuffed Duke and turned him so the light of the pink bulbs on the Christmas tree sparkled against his gaudy jumpsuit. "He looks great in sequins."

"You think?"

"And he sings like an angel. No! Wait! Are you going to tell me—" She gave Gabe a wide-eyed look and wondered if he knew she was kidding. "Are you going to tell me that's not really Duke singing?"

He managed what was almost a smile. "It's not Duke…er, Diana…singing," he said. "Diana can't carry a tune."

"Then Diana and I, we have something in common."

"You're lots better-looking."

The compliment was so matter-of-fact and so unexpected, it almost made Meg blush. Rather than let him know it—and rather than let him know how easily he'd turned the head of a woman who, at least up until a few minutes before, had been pretty good at keeping her head on straight—she reached for the guest register and slid it across the desk toward him. He took the hint, or if he didn't, he didn't press the issue. At least not until he was done signing his name.

When he was, he pushed the book back over to Meg. Was it an accident that he held on to the register? That he didn't flinch when his hand stopped so close to hers?

Meg wasn't about to even consider it. Just because a good-looking guy happened to be (maybe) coming on to her didn't mean she had to melt like a pat of butter in a hot skillet. Just because he was (maybe) unattached didn't mean she was anything close to interested. Just because she (suddenly) couldn't catch her breath didn't mean anything. Not anything except that it was going to be a warm day and that the Ohio humidity was headed from sticky all the way to downright sultry.

Just because Gabe (definitely) let his gaze slip from her hair to her face and from her face to her neck and from her neck to her breasts and then back up again, didn't mean she had to feel self-conscious about the smear of flour on her cheek, or the freckles sprinkled across her nose like cinnamon, or her electric-blue, sleeveless sundress, the one cut just low enough to show a little more skin than any guest had a right to see.

When he got around to looking her in the eye again, she was ready for him. "Are you done now—" Although she'd watched him sign his name, she glanced down at the guest register anyway. It seemed like a better option than drowning in those brandy-colored eyes. "—Mr. Morrison?"

"You can call me Gabe." One corner of his mouth twitched into a smile. "And I can call you—"

"Meg." It was a better answer than *anytime*. Which, for some unaccountable reason, was what she was tempted to say. In fact, she was tempted to say a lot of things. Like how tired he looked and how stiff his muscles seemed and how—once long ago and far, far away—she'd been known as the best sore-muscle massager on the east coast.

Like it or not, thinking about Baltimore and massaging sore muscles made Meg think of Ben. Sore muscles, sore egos. And that brought up a whole lot of memories that had been and still were a sore point.

Rather than risk even the remote chance of adding more painful experiences to her history, she decided it was smarter to keep the conversation on safer subjects. "How do you know all that stuff, anyway?" she asked Gabe. "About Duke and Diana. Was it in the latest issue of *People* or something?"

"Actually..." For just a second, she saw the weight of the world lift from his shoulders. As if he was used to receiving compliments and the rewards that went along with them, he stood tall and flashed her a smile so devastating, she found herself catching her breath. Just as quickly, the expression dissolved and he was back to looking tired and worried. "*People?* Yeah, something like that."

Meg could take a hint as well as anyone. Some matters were best left alone. Especially when there was a chance that bringing them up might offend one of Maisie's guests.

"I'll show you up to your room. I'm Maisie's granddaughter and the chef around here. Greeting the guests isn't usually my job, but Maisie's a little busy." The lie came out as smoothly as peanut butter. It stuck in her throat just the way peanut butter always did. But then, she figured a little lie was better than the big ol' truth, especially when the truth was all about how Maisie just happened to get busy at the most inopportune times.

Like when a handsome, unattached guy was checking into the Hideaway all by his handsome, unattached self.

Like when Maisie's stick-her-head-in-the-sand granddaughter was insisting she was doing just fine on her own, thank you very much, and that she didn't need anyone or anything to make her make her happy or to fill that little hollow spot right where her heart used to be. The spot that had always seemed filled to overflowing when Ben was around.

Meg dashed the thought away and grabbed the brass key chain with the name of the room etched on it. She dangled it in front of Gabe. "You're lucky there was a cancellation. This room is usually the first one to get booked." When he didn't respond to her offer of help with his luggage, she walked around to the other side of the desk and stepped aside so he could start up the stairs ahead of her. It took her a second to realize he hadn't moved—and that Gabe looked as if someone had pulled the tablecloth magic trick on him, too.

''What did that say?'' He pointed at the key chain in her hand. ''That key chain, what—''

''There are four of them,'' Meg explained. She glanced back to the desk, where the keys hung on their little brass hooks when guests weren't using them. ''One for each room. There's Smooth Operator, our secret-agent room. And Almost Paradise. That's sort of a tropical theme, what Maisie likes to call her Garden of Eden room. And then there's Close to the Heart.'' She made a face because although that particular room was popular with guests, it wasn't her favorite. ''Red velvet, lace, plenty of cupids,'' she said, as if that would explain it all. ''And this one. An experience straight out of the King's life. Complete with blue suede shoes under the bed.'' She tossed the key chain up in the air. ''You're staying in—''

Before Meg could catch it, Gabe reached out and grabbed the key chain. Staring at it, his cheeks went dark and he made a funny, choking sound. ''Love Me Tender? You're kidding, right?''

Meg grinned. ''Last room on the island.''

''Right.'' His shoulders slumped, Gabe stepped around a display of brightly wrapped packages and started up the winding stairs that led to the second floor and the inn's guest rooms. ''Looks like I'm stuck.''

Stuck?

Stuck was one concept Meg didn't want to think about. Not when it came to Love Me Tender. Because when she thought about Love Me Tender and she thought about stuck, she just naturally thought about the Crawfords. And thinking about the Crawfords made her all too aware that she was studying every detail of the way Gabe's jeans were worn and smooth over his backside.

''Not a good idea,'' she reminded herself. She shook

away the notion as well as the sensations cascading through her. The ones that made her feel as if she'd just gone under a Lake Erie wave and was having trouble coming up for breath.

Truth be told, she knew she'd be better off keeping her gaze on anything but Gabriel Morrison's rear end.

Which only made her notice exactly where she was still looking.

Meg grumbled a warning to herself. If she wasn't careful, she'd get trapped by the siren-call of lust and the heady promise of romance.

And that meant she could get stuck, too. Just like she had back in Baltimore when she refused to believe that Ben could be so heartless as to pretend to love her just so he could get his hands on her cooking secrets. She'd been blind. She'd been stupid. And until she came to her senses, what she got in return for trusting him with her heart was a mess of a relationship she should have gotten unstuck from long before.

No way.

No how.

Meg let the words echo through her head, a mantra designed to keep her fantasies at bay.

Stuck, she promised herself, was something she'd never get again.

Chapter Two

"Stuck."

Gabe couldn't imagine why, but when he grumbled the word, Meg's face went a little pale and her steps faltered.

"What's that you said?" She stopped a couple of feet away and gave him the kind of look he usually reserved for folks on the subway who talked to the empty seats beside them.

"I said stuck." Gabe rattled the brass knob on the door next to a metal sculpture that took up a good portion of the hallway wall. He knew he had the right room.

As if to reassure himself, he glanced at the artwork. It wasn't what he expected to find in back-of-beyond Ohio. Quirky, well done, inspired—the sculpture was a one-quarter-size flamingo-pink Cadillac, complete with wide tail fins and enough chrome to make it gleam, even in the muted pink light of the hallway. In honor of the island holiday, a red sack filled with gift-wrapped packages had been tucked in the back seat.

"Love Me Tender." He read the words painted on the trunk of the car in gleaming black enamel. "It's the right room, isn't it? But the door..." Just to show he knew what he was talking about, he turned the handle again and bumped the door to the room with his shoulder. It didn't budge. ''It's—''

''Stuck. The door. The door to the room is stuck.'' Meg breathed a long sigh that did remarkable things to the gauzy, hand-embroidered sundress she was wearing.

The fact that he wondered why she looked so relieved didn't seem as important to Gabe as the fact that he'd actually noticed the way her breasts pressed against the gossamer fabric, the way her cheeks darkened to a color that nearly matched the glistening stones in her dangling earrings.

So he wasn't completely brain-dead after all. And if the sudden fire in his blood and the fierce tightening in his gut meant anything, the rest of him was working pretty well, too.

That was enough to cheer him. He might be a man on the edge—of his patience, of his sanity and of what had once been a fulfilling, enjoyable, not to mention lucrative career—but at least all his good sense hadn't deserted him. He still knew a beautiful woman when he saw one.

''The door of Love Me Tender always sticks.'' Good thing Meg didn't know what he was thinking. Otherwise, she might not have been so quick to hurry over to where Gabe was standing. And if she hadn't, he wouldn't have been able to breathe in the mingled scents of cinnamon and herbs that surrounded her.

''There's a trick, actually,'' she said. To get to the door, she squeezed between Gabe and his luggage. Almost close enough to touch. The air warmed and Gabe's insides felt a little like they had on the ferry that brought him to the island.

''I should've warned you.'' For a second, he wondered what she was talking about. Warned him? About the sensation swooping through his insides?

She smiled and pointed to the door before she gave a demonstration that had nothing to do with Gabe's insides. And everything to do with physics. With a triumphant little smile that made her nose crinkle and brought out a dimple in her left cheek, she turned the shiny brass doorknob at the same time as she lifted it.

The door opened without a hitch.

"Your room." Meg stood back and made a sweeping gesture toward the room and Gabe grabbed his suitcases and went inside.

"If there's anything we can get you..." he heard her say from the hallway.

If he hadn't been so stunned, he might have suggested an ice pack and a couple aspirin.

Gabe deposited his suitcases on the floor and glanced around Love Me Tender. What had he been thinking? That just being with a woman as vivacious and beautiful as Meg was enough to make him forget his troubles?

Well, he could forget about forgetting.

One look at Love Me Tender, one moment over the threshold, and Gabe felt...well...

"All shook up." He didn't think he groaned the words loud enough for her to hear until Meg stuck her head back in the room.

"All shook up? That's over here." She darted around both Gabe and his suitcases and stepped further into the room. Past the stained-glass window decorated with peacocks that took up most of one wall. Past a full-size, honest-to-gosh classic pink Cadillac parked in the center of the room, one that had no roof, a waterbed where the front and back seats had once been and a pair of blue suede shoes tucked near the steering wheel.

Past a baby grand piano that gleamed in the afternoon sunlight and a wall covered with framed gold records. Along the far wall was a genuine fifties soda fountain, complete with bar stools with bright-blue vinyl seats. Apparently in honor of the week's festivities, there was a miniature aluminum Christmas tree on the bar, complete with bubble lights. Above the fountain was a sign. Meg pointed to it.

"All shook up. Maisie's idea of a joke. Shook up. Milkshakes. Get it?"

"I got it." Gabe was also getting a little queasy. He ran a hand through his hair. "I don't suppose any of your other guests might want to—"

"Trade rooms?" So, she was the resident mind reader as well as the inn's chef. Meg crossed her arms and stepped back, leaning against one of the bar stools. "Not a chance," she told him. "Honeymooners in Close to the Heart and they look like they're there for the long haul. A middle-aged couple in Smooth Operator. Regulars. Maisie wouldn't have the heart to ask them to move. And from what I've heard, card-carrying nudists in Almost Paradise. Don't worry," she added when his mouth dropped open, "they promised to dress for breakfast."

"This..." Gabe did a slow turn around the room. "It's a musician's—"

"Dream?" Meg suggested.

He was going to say *nightmare.* He stopped himself just in time. After all, it wasn't Meg's fault that he was feeling the way he was feeling, and there was no use taking it out on her or her grandmother. That didn't stop a cold chill from seeping through him. He got as far as the piano and paused there. Before he even realized he was doing it, his hands were poised over the keys.

For one brief, shining moment, hope blossomed in his chest and some of the tension that had been tying his stomach in knots for the last couple of months eased. As effortlessly as breathing, he played a C Major chord. He smiled when the notes vibrated through him, like a second heartbeat. Lost in the magic of the moment, Gabe closed his eyes, ready to ride the wave of creativity as he had so many times before.

He couldn't think of even one more note.

"You play?" Meg's voice reminded him what he was doing. Or at least what he was trying to do.

As if the keys were on fire, he pulled his hands to his side.

"Nah." Gabe backed away from the Steinway. "Used to," he admitted. "But that was a long time ago. I've..." He coughed away the sudden tightness in his throat. "I've forgotten how."

"Too bad." Meg walked back to the door. Her footsteps against the green shag carpet were as light as her laughter. "We've got another piano down in the parlor. And I'm always up for a song." In front of the stained-glass window, she swung around. "You're not just saying you don't play because you've heard me sing, are you?"

Not when she looked delicious enough to kiss.

Gabe's reaction caught him off-guard and he braced himself and wondered what was wrong with him, anyway. There were more important things to think about than the Hideaway's sexy chef. More important, sure, he told himself. But not nearly as delectable.

He wondered if Meg had any idea how incredible she looked against the backdrop of stained-glass colors made molten by the afternoon sun. The blue of the peacock's feathers matched her summer dress perfectly and brought out blue flecks in eyes that were a shade between the spicy green of a habenero pepper and the cool color of a crisp salad. The yellow in the bird's beak and the plume at the top of its head touched her shoulders like liquid sunshine and kissed the freckles sprinkled liberally over her arms and neck. The undulating red border around the bird turned the sun's rays into fire that was every bit as bright but nowhere near as beautiful as her mahogany-colored hair.

Sing?

She could sing to him, all right. Anytime. Anywhere. Even if her voice did remind Gabe of a not-so-happy marriage between the sounds of a freight train at full throttle and a coop full of frightened chickens. Her singing voice might make his teeth ache and for sure it was as flat as a pancake, but the rest of her was curved very nicely.

Taking his time, Gabe glanced from the tips of her toenails with their candy-apple-red polish to the top of her head. He stopped in between for a quick mental inventory of the more interesting places, wondering in spite of himself what a woman who was bold enough to wear a brightly colored dress with her ruddy complexion and Titian hair wore underneath.

Like it or not, the idea heated Gabe clear through to his bones.

Meg could sing him to sleep after a night of wild lovemaking, he decided. She could sing him awake just so that he could scoop her into his arms and stop her singing with a kiss before they started the lovemaking all over again. She could sing through his bloodstream and she could sing through his dreams. She could sing to him like—

"Your phone."

Meg's voice startled him back to reality. He found her with an expectant look on her face and her eyes homing in on the right side pocket of his jeans, where he'd tucked his cell phone before he hopped out of the car. "Your phone. It's ringing."

Gabe shook off the momentary paralysis caused by his own wayward thoughts. That was what he got for dipping his toe in the deep waters of fantasy. Blindsided. If he wasn't careful, he'd get drawn in and towed under and—

"Your phone is still ringing."

"Oh. Yeah." He plucked the ringing phone out of his pocket and bobbled it from hand to hand. At least it didn't play Beethoven's Fifth like it used to. Gabe had changed it back to an old-fashioned, boring, nonmusical ring a couple of weeks before. But although it wasn't loud, the ringing was insistent.

"You're not going to answer it?"

Good question. He didn't even stop to consider it. He tossed the phone over on the bed and watched it shimmy on the water-filled mattress.

It kept right on ringing.

"That's it?" Like a rubbernecker at the scene of an especially gruesome accident, Meg was staring at the phone. "*That's* how you answer the phone?"

Gabe poked his hands into the pockets of his jeans. "That's how I answer the phone."

She slid him a sidelong look. "Woman?" she asked.

Maybe it was his imagination. Or maybe it was just wishful thinking. He could've sworn that waiting for his answer, she tensed a little.

"Worse." He marched over to the 55 Cadillac, picked up the phone and shoved it under the pillows in their pink satin cases. It was still ringing, but at least now the noise was muffled. "Secretary."

Imagination again. It had to be. Meg looked... relieved.

She glanced toward the bed. ''Determined little devil. Must be some secretary.''

''Oh, she is. The best there is on the Left Coast. Way smarter than me. More organized than the dictionary. Has the scheduling talents of those folks at NASA who can make a camera do a fly-by of some planet a million miles away.''

''She is a paragon.'' Meg nodded. ''Can she leap tall buildings in a single bound?''

''Never seen her do it, but I wouldn't be surprised. Latoya is also—'' It wasn't until the phone abruptly stopped ringing that Gabe realized his thumbs were tight around his fists. He flexed his fingers. Forced the muscles in his neck and shoulders to relax. Unclenched his teeth.

When an entire minute went by and the ringing didn't start again, he let out a long breath. ''She is also persistent.''

Meg swung her gaze from the bed to Gabe. ''Which would make an ordinary person wonder about what Latoya's being so persistent about.''

Maybe because he'd dodged another Latoya bullet, Gabe felt unaccountably pleased with himself. Or maybe it was the shimmer in Meg's eyes, the impossible blue of her dress, the surprising way his blood buzzed when she flicked her tongue over her lips. Whatever the reason, he stepped just a little closer and lowered his voice. ''In most cases it would,'' he said. ''But you haven't known me long enough to find out that I'm far from ordinary.''

''Wrong, Mr. Morrison.'' As if the statement didn't make her very happy, Meg's bottom lip puckered and her eyebrows dipped over her eyes. She shook her head and though she moved as gracefully as a dancer, Gabe couldn't help noticing that when she spun around and headed into the hallway, it looked more like a retreat than a well-timed exit. ''I realized that,'' she told him, closing the door behind her, ''the moment I saw you.''

For what seemed a very long time, Gabe stood staring at the closed door, feeling as if the world had tipped on its axis. Crazy reaction. But then, he suspected there was a lot about Meg that would cause the kind of peculiar humming he felt in his bloodstream.

It took a couple of minutes for his thoughts to settle and a couple more after that before his heart rate throttled back to a beat that was even close to normal.

Cupid's Hideaway might be—as the lady at the local hotel where he'd first stopped for a room had informed him—the most romantic spot east of the Mississippi. But romance and the racing heartbeat that went along with it weren't on his agenda.

He twitched away the idea and hauled his suitcase on to the couch. He unzipped it and flipped it open, looking for a change of clothes.

Better to leave the romance to the honeymooners and the nudists, he told himself. All he wanted was a place to lie low. For as long as he could get away with it.

Sooner or later, he'd have to fess up and admit the truth. To Latoya. To Dennis. To the Tasty Time Burger folks.

Even to himself.

Did he really think hiding out on an island in the middle of Lake Erie would buy him some time?

''Damn straight,'' he grumbled.

He grabbed a handful of clothing and walked over to the dresser across the room to put it away, stopping to glare at the reflection frowning back at him from the mirror.

''Gabriel Morrison,'' he mumbled, addressing the worried-looking man in the mirror. ''World's greatest jingle writer. The guy who's got more awards piled up in his office than even Latoya knows what to do with. Aren't you the guy who's never at a loss for clever words? The one who can write music in his sleep? The clown who unleashed the Love Me Tenders commercial and Duke the Dog on an unsuspecting and gullible public? Good going, Morrison."

He yanked open the top dresser drawer, tossed his clothes inside and went back for another handful.

"A meeting in New York in two weeks and just like always, you've promised them the world, haven't you?" he muttered when he was in front of the mirror again. "Only this time, things are different."

The hard reality of the situation nagged at him while he paced between the kitschy fifties soda fountain and the pink Cadillac.

Things were different, all right. Because whenever Gabe had promised the world before, he'd always delivered it on a silver platter.

And this time?

This time, Gabriel Morrison, the Mozart of the advertising industry, the man whose name was synonymous with catchy tunes and clever lyrics and ad campaigns that never failed to raise clients' notoriety as well as their profits...

This time, Gabriel Morrison had a major case of jingle-writer's block.

"DELICIOUS!"

Meg didn't have to turn around from the stove. She knew when her grandmother walked into the kitchen from the dining room where she'd just poured the morning orange juice, she was definitely not talking about the ham-and-cheese omelets Meg was making. There was a little nuance in Maisie's voice, a little skip in her step that Meg recognized as having nothing to do with food—and everything to do with romance.

"Nice to know your guests are enjoying themselves so much." Meg was an expert at both cooking and ignoring Maisie's less-than-subtle hints, and she put both talents to use. She flipped the omelets, added a sprinkling of dill and firmly refused to get hooked by the bait Maisie was dangling in front of her. "The honeymooners are happy?"

"Nonsense!" Out of the corner of her eye, Meg saw her grandmother wave away the very thought. "Of course the Kilbanes are happy. Honeymooners are always happy. Since they've checked in, they've gone through two bottles of champagne, three boxes of scented candles and two pairs of those bubble-gum-flavored edible undies we have on special in the Love Shack. They're as happy as clams. I wasn't talking about Brian and Jenny Kilbane, and you know it."

"The nudists?" Meg slid the omelets onto china plates and passed the plates to Maisie. "Or the spy wannabes?"

Maisie nodded her approval of the omelets, but even so, she didn't look very happy. "You know exactly what I'm talking about," she said, frowning at Meg.

"I do." Meg reached for the pan of hash-brown potatoes that was sitting on the stove. She scooped a pile of perfectly browned potatoes onto each of the festive plates—decorated with fir trees and snowflakes—that Maisie used only twice each year, in December and for Christmas in July. "I know you're talking about Gabe Morrison." Finished with the potatoes, she set down the pan, wiped her hands on her white apron and gave her grandmother her full attention. With any luck, Maisie would catch on to the fact that she wasn't kidding.

Then again, if luck had anything to do with the way things were going, Meg wouldn't have spent the entire time since she'd checked Gabe into the inn thinking all the things about him that Maisie thought she should be thinking.

All the things Meg knew she *shouldn't* have been thinking.

Meg's spirits plummeted. *Delicious* was the least of her problems. When it came to their newest guest, there was also charming to consider—in those few and far between moments when he seemed to forget himself enough to allow his natural sense of humor to come through. Then there was gorgeous, available and successful. Not to mention tempting.

Meg drew in a long breath to steady her suddenly racing heartbeat. "I'm not interested," she told Maisie. And herself. "So whether Gabe is delicious or not doesn't change anything..." She looked the breakfast dishes over one final time. "I need something," she grumbled.

"Of course you do." Maisie's expression brightened. "It's what I've said all along. You need something. A little companionship. Is that such a bad thing? Or how about a full-fledged, all-out, over-the-top fling?" Maisie laughed the same throaty laugh Meg had heard from her grandmother's private rooms on the nights Doc Ross visited. "If you ask me, sweetie, an *amour* would do you a world of good. Help you forget that chef of yours, the one who had oatmeal where his brains were supposed to be and nothing but ice cubes inside his chest. You know, that what's-his-name."

"Ben." Still staring at the hash browns and omelets, Meg supplied the name automatically. It took her a second to realize that saying it didn't hurt. At least, not as much as it used to, anyway. "Ben," she said again, testing out the theory and discovering that for the first time in the fourteen months she'd been back on the island and out of the magnetic pull of Ben Lucarelli's overblown personality and his overrated talent, the very memory of him didn't skewer her like a shish kebab.

"And I wasn't talking about Ben." She looked at the door that led into the dining room where Maisie's guests were waiting for breakfast. "Or about anyone else, for that matter. I was talking about breakfast." She studied the plates, and the answer hit her. "Strawberries," she mumbled and she hurried over to the refrigerator on the other side of the room. She found seven of the plumpest, reddest strawberries she'd picked just two days before over on the mainland and, in a flash, had them washed, sliced, sprinkled with confectioner's sugar and arranged on each plate.

"Much better," She said with satisfaction. "The muffins are already on the table?"

"I did that first thing," Maisie assured her. "And everyone's enjoying them." Her expression fell. "Everyone but poor Gabe."

Meg already had four of the plates in her hands. She stepped back to let Maisie leave the kitchen with the other three, but not before she rolled her eyes, just so her grandmother would know what she thought of her little stab at theatrics. "And I'm supposed to care, right? I'm supposed to ask why he's not enjoying the muffins. Or am I supposed to be worried about why you're calling him 'poor Gabe'?"

"Good heavens, dear." Maisie clicked her tongue and went into the inn's dining room. Although she didn't have the nerve to pretend she was embarrassed, she at least had the decency to blush a shade darker than her hot-pink pantsuit. "You are so suspicious! You can't possibly think I'm so meddlesome that..."

Her comment trailed away, and Meg supposed it was just as well. She didn't need her grandmother to elaborate. Not about Gabe.

In the hours since she'd met him, Meg's own imagination had done enough elaborating for the both of them.

That brought her up short, and right before she bumped the swinging door with her hip and entered the dining room, Meg paused to catch her breath. The last thing she needed were her own fantasies sneaking up to destroy her self-control. Not when she was about to walk into the dining room and come face to face with the man who'd inspired those fantasies. All night long.

Meg twitched the thought away as inconsequential, inconsistent with what she wanted out of her life and her career, and just plain old insane. She gave the door an authoritative smack and got down to business—which would've been considerably easier if it wasn't for the scene that greeted her in the dining room.

Maisie was fluttering around the table pouring coffee and chatting up a storm, just as she did every morning when they had guests. The Kilbanes were holding hands and staring into each other's eyes. The nudists and the spies…

Meg glanced around the table. Because she wasn't usually involved in the day-to-day operation of the inn outside the kitchen, she wasn't sure which guests were the nudists and which were the James Bond fans. She did, however, know exactly which guest Maisie was referring to when she'd mentioned *delicious*.

Delicious was a word that didn't adequately describe how Gabe looked early in the morning.

He was wearing khakis and an inky shirt that brought out the highlights in his dark hair, and though he was sitting with his back to the windows with their view of the lake, she could tell he'd shaved since she'd last seen him. Yesterday's sprinkling of dark stubble was gone, replaced by a smooth sweep of jaw that was squarer—and more stubborn—than she remembered.

The impression did nothing to dampen the little thread of awareness that wound through Meg. Her mind on everything but the dishes she was placing on the table in front of their guests, she went through the motions, calling on a lifetime of experience in the restaurant industry and fourteen months' worth of experience in the I'm-thinking-about-him-but-I'm-not-going-to-let-anyone-know-it department. She succeeded at both. By the time she got around to sliding his dish in front of Gabe, the other guests were murmuring their admiration of her presentation, nodding their approval of her menu selection and digging in.

Gabe, on the other hand, was staring into his coffee cup which, Meg noticed, was empty.

''Coffee?'' When Maisie picked that exact moment to zoom by, Meg plucked the silver coffee pot off the tray she was carrying. She stepped back and waited for Gabe to answer and when he didn't, she gave it another try.

''Coffee?'' she asked again.

As if he'd been touched with a cattle prod, he snapped to attention and for the first time, Meg saw that while everyone else had been munching her island-famous blueberry muffins and making small talk, Gabe had been lost in his own world. He'd brought a legal pad down to the dining room and it was covered with doodles.

''Buildings.'' She tipped her head and examined the pictures that covered the entire top page of the pad. Though she was no expert when it came to art of any kind, she knew good work when she saw it. And Gabe's drawings were definitely good.

There was a sketch of the Chrysler building in New York on one corner of the pad. Another toward the bottom of the page reminded her of the glass pyramid at the Louvre. In between was a building she didn't recognize, one with broad lines and a bold silhouette.

"You're pretty talented," she told him.

"No. I'm not." Gabe frowned at the drawings before he ripped off the page and scrunched it into a ball. He glanced around as if he didn't know what to do with it and Meg held out her hand. "I'm just doodling," he told her, dropping the ball of paper into her hands. "Passing the time. Doodling."

"Whatever you say." Meg stuck the paper in the pocket of her apron and held out the coffeepot, trying again. Gabe finally took the hint. He held up his cup for her to fill and she had another chance to look at him. This close, she saw that there were still dark smudges under Gabe's eyes. He was just as on-edge as when he'd arrived at the Hideaway. Just as tired-looking.

As if she'd seen it, too, Maisie stepped in. "I do hope you slept well, Mr. Morrison." She offered him one of her patented smiles and an expectant look that told him whether he liked it or not, she was about to draw him into the conversation. "The Kilbanes here..." She tipped her head toward the honeymooning couple. "They were just saying that the bed in Close to the Heart is the most comfortable they've ever been in. For sleeping or for..." Maisie's gentle laughter rippled around the room. "Well, they are on their honeymoon, after all!"

The other guests nodded and smiled, and one of the other men (either the nudist or the spy) raised his orange-juice glass and proposed a toast. Gabe didn't say a thing. He drank some of his coffee and held the cup out for Meg to top off. When she was done, she backed away from the table and returned to the kitchen. Better to hide out with the dirty dishes and the greasy pans than to stand here and listen to Maisie's barefaced attempts at drawing Gabe out of his shell and into a heart-to-heart.

Once the door was safely closed behind her, she breathed a sigh of relief.

The reprieve didn't last long.

"I think it's going very well." Maisie breezed into the kitchen with the empty orange-juice pitcher, a smile on her face and a purr of satisfaction in her voice. "He's fitting right in, don't you think?"

"I think," Meg told her, being careful to keep her voice down, "that he's sullen and in a world of his own. Can't you see that, Grandma? The man obviously has problems, and I don't think your attempts to introducing hearts and flowers into his life will help. He's worried."

"He needs someone to help him not worry."

"He's crabby."

"Who wouldn't be if they were all alone?"

"He's not interested."

"Did I say anything about him being interested?" Maisie's silvery eyebrows rose nearly as far as the sweep of fluffy white hair that touched her forehead. "Really, Meg, I think you're way ahead of me here. You're having ideas I haven't even thought of. Do you want him to be interested?"

"I'm—" Meg grumbled her displeasure. Of Maisie's shameless tactics. Of her own inexplicable reaction to Gabe. "It doesn't matter whether I want him to be or not," she admitted. "He's obviously not."

Maisie leaned against the countertop, head cocked, eyes sparkling. "How do you know?" she asked.

"How do I—" Too restless to stand still, Meg tugged her apron over her head and threw it on the countertop. "Did you take a good look at him?" She pointed toward the closed door and the dining room beyond. "How can the man be interested in anything? He's preoccupied. He's troubled."

"Pish-tush." Maisie tossed her head. "I haven't met a man yet who's too preoccupied to notice a woman noticing him. And if I haven't told you this before, Meg, I've met plenty of men in my life." Warming to the idea, she went over to the coffee maker to refill the silver pot they passed around the table. "Maybe he just doesn't realize how interested he really is," she said with a mischievous smile. "Or at least how interested he could be, if he had half a chance."

"Oh, come on, Grandma!" Meg laughed, which was mighty peculiar considering she wasn't feeling the least bit happy with the way things were going. "Are you telling me that if I threw myself at the man—"

"Would I ever suggest a thing like that?" Maisie's cheeks went noticeably pale. "It's so...so low-class, this whole notion of women coming onto men as if that was the only way to attract their attention. You know me better than that! What you need to do is be more subtle. More discreet. Take my word for it, that will attract a man's attention surer than if you walked through the dining room stark-naked. Well...maybe if you walked through the dining room stark naked..."

"Oh, no! I'm not going for the Lady Godiva routine." Because she knew a losing cause when she saw one, Meg gave up the fight. She took the coffeepot out of Maisie's hands and turned toward the dining room.

"Bet you it's true."

The challenge was delivered in the sweetest tones, but it was a challenge nonetheless.

Meg turned and faced her grandmother head-on. ‘‘You mean about attracting his attention? Bet it’s not,’’ she said.

Maisie’s lips twitched with a barely controlled smile. ‘‘Bet if you flirted with him, he’d react. Big-time.’’

Meg clenched her teeth. ‘‘Bet he wouldn’t.’’

‘‘You brave enough to find out?’’

Whether it meant jumping into the lake from the highest rock on the shore, swimming the farthest, running the fastest or outrunning a storm in the family sailboat, Meg couldn’t stand to have her courage questioned. It was one of the reasons she’d gotten into so much trouble as a teenager. One of the reasons she’d had her eyes on a life on the mainland and her heart firmly set on Ben Lucarelli, even when everyone who’d ever met the man insisted he wasn’t right for her.

It was the one and only reason it had taken her so long to break up with Ben. Even when she finally found out that he wasn’t as interested in Meg the person as he was in Meg the chef, the woman who could make him—and his chi-chi Baltimore restaurant—a five-star hit.

Meg had never backed down from a challenge in her life.

And Maisie knew it.

‘‘All right. You want proof. I’ll give you proof.’’ Meg raised her chin in the kind of I’m-not-budging-an-inch-on-this-look she’d learned at Maisie’s knee. She put down the coffeepot long enough to pull the elastic band out of her hair and combed through her ponytail with her fingers. When she was done, she shook her curls loose and grabbed the silver pot again. ‘‘I’m going in there and I'm going to flirt with Gabe Morrison. And it's going to get me nowhere. Guaranteed."

"We'll see." Maisie nodded. "And if I lose—"

"You will," Meg assured her.

"If I lose and he's not attracted to you…well, I'll cook dinner for you one night. How about that? And if I win…"

"You won't."

"If I win…" She winked at Meg and, reaching for her, turned her toward the door. "If I win, you win, too. Now go get him," she said, and nudged her out of the kitchen.

"Fine. Good." Meg paused just outside the dining-room door, fighting the sudden urge to run.

She might have done it, too, if behind her, she didn't hear the kitchen door open just enough to allow Maisie to peek out. "Remember, be subtle. Bet he'll fall head over heels," Maisie whispered.

"Bet he won't," Meg insisted, and because she knew she'd talked herself into something she couldn't talk herself out of, she figured she had no choice but to get it over with.

Her shoulders squared, her jaw steady, her insides jumping like a fish at the wrong end of a hook, she marched back into the dining room to face Gabe Morrison.

And her own nagging insecurities.

Chapter Three

Gabe was drawing buildings.

Again.

Shaking himself back to reality, he studied the drawing that had somehow taken shape on the legal pad in front of him while he was lost in thought.

A facade that combined classical elements and postmodernist pizzazz. A frieze on the entablature. One that completely broke the rules when it came to horizontal bands of relief sculpture, dispensing with them altogether and replacing them instead with a loose pattern of lines that was less traditional carving and more like the empty staffs in an even emptier line of—

"Music."

Gabe grumbled the word and glanced down at the drawing that was staring back up at him.

Kind of like the other guests around the breakfast table were staring at him.

He felt their eyes before he saw them, and because he knew that doing anything else would only make him seem crazier and more conspicuous, he forced himself to look up. Six pairs of eyes were trained on him, six expressions both cautious and curious. Six people were gawking at him as if he'd been talking to himself.

Which he had been.

Gabe made a sound that might have been a mumbled excuse. Or a growl of discontent. In keeping with the peaceful atmosphere of the Hideaway and the feelings of love that were as conspicuous as the swarm of chubby cupids that decorated the Christmas tree in the far corner, his fellow guests apparently decided it was an apology.

The fresh-faced, starry-eyed honeymooners across the lace tablecloth grinned in unison. The other two couples smiled and nodded and finished their meals. Watching them eat, Gabe noticed for the first time that there was food on the plate in front of him. And he hadn't touched it.

"That's right. You would like music." The newly-wed groom was done eating. He stood and because he was holding her hand, his bride popped out of her chair right along with him. "You're staying in Love Me Tender. The music room. We haven't seen it, but we hear it's really cool."

"We could switch. Rooms, I mean." Gabe sounded a little too desperate, even to himself. He knew it. He didn't like it. He couldn't stop. The other rooms at the Hideaway might be heavy on the lace and light on the guy-all-alone-so-what's-he-doing-in-a-place-like-this factor, but they wouldn't remind him of the music he couldn't compose or the lyrics that refused to form in his head. No matter how hard he tried.

At least they weren't Love Me Tender.

This was his chance, and it might be his only one. He raised his eyebrows. "I don't have much to pack.

I could be out in less than ten minutes. If you'd like to check out Love Me Tender for the rest of your stay—''

''No way!'' The groom might be a quicker eater than his blushing bride, but it was clear from the start who was going to make the decisions in the family. ''Pink Cadillacs and Elvis pictures?'' She barked out a laugh. ''No—thank—you. Not exactly my idea of romantic!''

''That's not what the Crawfords thought!'' Chuckling, one of the other couples got up from the table. They were apparently regulars at the Hideaway and knew something Gabe didn't know. He didn't care, either, not if it meant he might get them to bite at his juicy offer.

He turned to them. ''If you think Love Me Tender is romantic—''

Before he could even finish, both the man and the woman were shaking their heads. ''Happy where we are,'' the man told him. He looped an arm around his wife's shoulders and gave her a squeeze before they walked out of the room. '''Smooth Operator' is our idea of romance, and besides, James Bond never visited Graceland.''

Gabe couldn't argue with that. He turned his attention to the only couple left.

''Not us.'' The man held up one hand, instantly rejecting the plan. ''We love 'Almost Paradise.' The plants, the waterfall, even the jungle noises piped in through the sound system. That's romance as far as we're concerned. Besides, I hear the bar stools in Love Me Tender have vinyl seats and frankly, vinyl and nudists…'' Even fully clothed, he squirmed in his chair. As if the suggestion was too much to take, both he and his wife got up and scurried out of the dining room as quickly as they could.

''Great.'' Gabe mumbled the word. Even though he was feeling anything but. ''Strike three. Me and Elvis. At least I don't have to worry about the romance.''

''What's the matter, Mr. Morrison? You don't like romance?''

Gabe hadn't noticed that Meg had come back into the room. A warm rush of awareness flooded the space between his heart and his stomach when her voice snuck up from somewhere behind him. Funny, although he'd been more than aware of Meg the day before, when she'd showed him to the fiasco that passed for his room, he'd missed the husky note in her voice. Ready to answer her—except that he wasn't quite sure what he was going to say—he spun around in his chair.

And stopped cold.

He remembered plenty about Meg, all right. But he'd forgotten that she was so beautiful.

When she'd come into the room earlier to pour the coffee, he'd been too preoccupied with the empty legal pad that dared him to try and fill its pages with clever jingle material. Or-not-so clever jingle material. Or anything at all except the doodles that were the only things that managed to ooze from his pen. He hadn't paid attention to the mossy green dress that floated around Meg's ankles and made her eyes look smokier—and far more sultry—than they had in yesterday's afternoon sunlight. He hadn't seen that today she was wearing her hair down, and that it brushed her shoulders in a riot of red tones that brought out the heightened color in her cheeks and made a startling backdrop for the turquoise earrings that peeked out from the tumble of her curls.

He certainly hadn't noticed her standing the way she was standing now, the silver coffeepot in one hand, the other propped on her waist, and her hip cocked just the slightest bit. Because if he *had* noticed…

Gabe braced himself against the heat that built inside him.

If he'd noticed, he didn't think he would've been able to sit still. He didn't think he would've been able to pay attention to…

To whatever it was he'd been paying attention to.

The reminder was all Gabe needed. As fast as the heat built inside him, it froze into a block the size of the iceberg that had finished off the *Titanic.*

He glanced down at the legal pad sitting next to his untouched plate of food. For some reason he couldn't explain and didn't want to understand, he flipped the page on which he'd been doodling. So Meg couldn't see it.

"I'm sorry. Did you say something?" Gabe had to give himself points. He'd recovered enough to sound perfectly normal. After all, the last thing he needed to feel on top of hopeless and discouraged was silly. "Something about romance?"

"Me?" Meg tried for a smile that she hoped looked a whole lot more seductive than it felt. It might have been easier if she wasn't feeling so foolish. And if she didn't know that Maisie had the kitchen door cracked a smidgen so she could watch the show. Her grandmother's challenge still ringing in her ears, she refused to give up. Foolish or not, audience or not, she had a mission to accomplish. And right now, that mission was all about making Gabe pay attention to her.

Her steps slow and fluid, she moved across the room straight toward him. ''Why on earth would I say anything about romance?'' she asked.

''No reason. I guess.'' He shrugged, ignoring the sway of her hips. And the hint of suggestion in her voice. He ignored it all. The cupids on the Christmas tree. The pink poinsettias that were everywhere. The picture above the fireplace that showed a sepia-toned couple in Victorian dress, the man in a top hat and tails and the smiling woman in nothing but a corset, a pair of fancy pantaloons and an elaborate red bow that had been taped to her rear in honor of the holiday.

It only proved her theory. If he didn't notice the atmosphere in the romantic center of the universe, there was no way she'd ever get him to notice her.

A funny little sensation clutched at Meg's insides and made her squirm. And that disproved her theory. The one about how much she didn't care what Gabe thought of her.

Meg shrugged off the thread of doubt that wound its way around her self-confidence and choked off its air supply. If she could make the effort to be friendly, the least Gabe could do was be polite in return. Then again, maybe he'd pay more attention to her if she was a blank piece of yellow legal-pad paper.

She followed his gaze down to the empty pad and the full plate of food beside it.

''You're a vegetarian.''

''What?'' As if he'd forgotten she was there, Gabe flinched. ''Vegetarian? No.'' He frowned at the ham-and-cheese omelet and the pile of hash brown potatoes that was looking less appetizing by the minute. ''I'm just not...'' He pushed the plate away and grabbing the pen that sat next to it, tapped out a fitful beat against the tablecloth. ''I'm not hungry.''

''I could fry up some eggs or throw together some pancake batter, if you'd prefer that. There's yogurt, too, if you're more interested in healthy things. And fruit and—''

''No. Thanks.'' The comment was heartfelt and the smile Gabe gave her along with it so genuine, it nearly took her breath away.

Meg steadied herself, one hand against the table. She had walked in here thinking of flirting and fully expecting that no matter how hard she tried, Gabe would never respond. She'd figured that she'd try out a few of the come-and-get-it moves she hadn't had the inclination or the opportunity to use in the last fourteen months, and that in spite of her best efforts, she would leave untouched—physically and emotionally. She was convinced she would win the bet and prove to her grandmother and, more importantly, to herself, that her mind was made up as far as romance was concerned, and that Maisie could stop with the matchmaking because it was just not going to work.

She hadn't counted on him upping the ante with a smile.

Because she didn't know what else to do, Meg held out the silver pot. ''More coffee?'' she asked, and this time, the breathiness of her voice was less her own doing than the fault of a heartbeat that refused to slow down.

''Sure.'' Gabe held out his cup and she refilled it for

him. While he drank it, she considered all the benefits of retreat.

She would have done it, too, if not for the quiet cough she heard from somewhere in the direction of the kitchen.

As tempted as she was to call off the whole bet, Meg was sure that if she gave up, she'd never hear the end of it. Not from Maisie. Not from her own ego, which had the tendency to remind her more often than she liked that she was piling up a list of failures.

She'd failed at life on the mainland. She'd failed to make a go of it in the big-city, trendy and very pricy restaurant she'd always dreamed would be the pot of gold at the end of her own personal rainbow. And even though she was self-aware enough to understand that most of what had happened between them was clearly Ben's fault, she knew for a fact that she'd failed there, too. She should have pegged him as a loser long before he dumped her heart into his Cuisinart and took it for a slice-and-dice spin.

She wasn't about to fail again.

She returned smile for smile and dropped into the chair next to Gabe's. "That is the idea, you know. The romance, I mean." She leaned closer. "Is it working?"

It wasn't.

The words reverberated in Gabe's head like the echoes of amplifiers at a rock concert.

The cupids weren't working. The fussy, pink decor wasn't working. Even the semi-suggestive picture over the fireplace wasn't working. Nothing could possibly make him think about romance. Not when his head was filled with the knowledge of how empty his imagination was. And his stomach went cold every time he thought about the Tasty Time Burger people and the knock-'em-dead ad campaign he had promised to deliver to them in just two weeks.

Nothing. Until Meg showed up looking like a vision straight out of a dream. Not until she leaned closer and the perfume of strawberries tickled his nose.

"It's not supposed to be working," he admitted. "I've got other things to think about. Other problems..." He tapped his pen on the legal pad. "And then you come in here and you've got me thinking about things I wasn't supposed to be thinking about." The whole situation was absurd, yet Gabe didn't feel like laughing. "Then again, how could anybody *not* think about romance in this place?"

"The Hideaway always has this effect on people," she told him, and from her tone, he wasn't sure if that was good news or not. "Young or old, it doesn't matter. I think there's something weird going on. You know, maybe Maisie built the house over a Native American burial ground. Or it's a regular stop on the UFO express lane to the universe. Or it might be hypnotism."

Gabe wasn't buying Meg's rationalization but he sure liked listening to her explain. He liked the way a little *V* of concentration crinkled the spot between her eyebrows when she was deep in conversation and how she worked her bottom lip with her teeth while she was collecting her thoughts. He liked the way she made him feel and the way thinking about the sway in her walk and the purr of seduction in her voice made him think maybe there were more important things in the world than empty legal pads.

He liked the kick of awareness that buzzed through

every inch of his body and he really liked the fact that when he leaned a bit nearer, Meg didn't back off.

"I'm thinking it's more physical than anything else," Gabe said. "At least what I'm feeling is." He paused for a moment. "Tell me, is there anywhere on this island where a man can take a woman? You know, on a date?"

She tipped her head, thinking and her hair spilled over her arm like a silky curtain. "There's the bait and tackle shop," she said and when his expression soured, she controlled a smile and went right on. "Then there's the hotel over near the marina. They have a great buffet most nights and karaoke on Tuesdays but, of course, that's a few days off. Let's see...where else... There's big doings in town tonight. Because folks can't easily get to the island in December, we have our Christmas celebration in the summer. I hear there's Bingo at City Hall. And free rides on the carousel in the park. It's fun, but the ride only lasts a couple of minutes, and I don't know... She gave him the once-over, her look so thorough and so frank, it actually made Gabe squirm. "Something tells me you're the kind of guy who likes to take his time."

"Think so?" Gabe liked a woman who knew what she wanted. "Glad you noticed."

"I notice a lot of things."

"Like..."

"You have impeccable taste," she said immediately. "And you don't mind showing it. Especially with clothing. You like fast cars and you've got a hair-dresser I'll bet you've been seeing for years because he really knows how to handle your hair, even though it's thick and probably not easy to cut." She let her gaze flicker away for a moment before she settled it again on Gabe's eyes. ''You like to indulge yourself when it comes to life's little luxuries,'' she said. ''Or did the expensive pen come from Latoya?''

''She spoils me shamelessly.''

''That must mean you're a good boss.''

''I'm good at a lot of things.''

''I'll bet.''

''I could show you.'' There wasn't much room between them but somehow, Gabe managed to close the gap. Meg's hand rested on the lace tablecloth and he set his a fraction of an inch from hers. ''You pick the excitement. I'm game for anything. That is, if you're not busy here with lunches and dinners and—''

''There's a reason it's called a bed-and-breakfast.'' Meg laughed and the sound of it shivered up Gabe's spine. ''One meal a day. That's all we provide. You found that out last night, didn't you? I hear you sent out for pizza.''

''It wasn't nearly as good as your cooking.''

She called his bluff. ''And you'd know that how?''

''Don't have to know it. I can tell.'' Snared by the dreamy sparkle of her eyes and the heady scent of ripe strawberries, Gabe lowered his voice. ''I can guarantee that if you agree to spend the evening with me, we'll have a terrific time. We can—'' He slid his hand over hers.

As if he'd been zapped by a two-twenty electrical line, Gabe sat up straight in his chair and yanked his hand back.

''Dancing hamburgers,'' he said.

''What?'' Meg wasn't sure she was hearing him right, but then again, she wasn't exactly sure she was in her right mind, either. She'd come in here, determined that no matter what she did, Gabe *wouldn't* notice her. And then she'd caved. Totally and completely. She'd fallen under the spell of the smile that wouldn't quit. Gotten drunk on those intoxicating brandy eyes. And now he was talking about—

"Dancing hamburgers? Did you say dancing hamburgers?"

Gabe grabbed his legal pad and she saw him scrawl the words across the top page.

"Dancing hamburgers." She read the words he'd written in his clear, distinct hand. "That is what you said. Only why—"

"I don't know." Still clutching the pad of paper, he bounded out of his chair, his eyes bright with excitement, his expression teetering just this side of bliss. "I don't know why I said it. I don't know why I thought it. I haven't been able to think of anything. All these months, I've been trying and I haven't had even a glimmer of an idea. And then I was sitting here talking to you and it came to me in a flash."

"Dancing hamburgers." Meg's shoulders drooped. She wasn't sure if she should be alarmed by the high color in Gabe's cheeks and the excitement in his voice. Or disappointed that what had all the makings of an interesting encounter was suddenly over. When he spun around and headed for the door, disappointment won. Hands down.

"Where are you going?"

"Going?" Gabe's body might be at the door of the dining room, but it was clear his mind was a million miles away. He turned, but only long enough to mumble, "Love Me Tender," then he was gone. His voice trailed behind him when he hurried across the lobby and toward the winding stairs to the guest rooms. ''Now that the juices are flowing, there's no stopping them. I need more paper. And the piano. And...''

Meg had no idea how long she sat staring after him. The next thing she knew, Maisie was standing at her side.

Her grandmother smiled. ''I'd say that went very well.''

''You think?'' Meg got up from her chair and reached for the breakfast plates, stacking them carefully. ''I'd say you owe me dinner, and if I'm picking the menu—''

''Dinner?'' Maisie laughed. ''No, no, dear. That was only if I lost. Only if he didn't notice you. And in case you missed it, he noticed, all right. Big-time.''

''Yeah, until the dancing hamburgers showed up.'' Meg made a face. Just when she was convinced that one evening with Gabriel Morrison was worth losing a bet for, she'd been rejected. Turned down. Overlooked. Ignored.

Ousted by dancing hamburgers.

''He did leave rather quickly.'' As if she couldn't believe it, Maisie studied the spot where a minute before, Gabe had been sitting. ''Was he upset?''

''Not as far as I can tell.'' Meg lifted a load of dishes into her arms and carried them to the kitchen. ''He seemed happy as could be.''

''That means...'' Maisie scurried ahead and held the kitchen door open.

''That means the experiment is over. Done.'' Meg set down the dishes and reached for her apron. Once she had it on and tied, she opened the dishwasher and started loading. ''Give up, Grandma. You're going to have to admit that this is one instance in which you did not know better than everyone else.''

''Perhaps you're right, dear.'' The lobby phone rang and, shaking her head, Maisie hurried out of the kitchen to answer it. ''Perhaps you're right, after all.''

''Of course I'm right.'' Meg finished with the dishes, added detergent, then slammed the dishwasher door closed. ''I was right all along,'' she mumbled. ''I said he wasn't going to notice, and he didn't. Well, not for more than a few minutes. I said he wasn't going to fall for the Meg-as-a-seductress act and he didn't.'' She punched the buttons and when the dishwasher started its cycle, she crossed her arms over her chest and leaned back against the counter, absently rubbing at the spot on her hand where Gabe's fingers had brushed hers. The spot where the skin still felt tingly. And hot.

''He's definitely not interested,'' she told herself. ''He's got a lot of nerve.''

Chapter Four

''Mr. Morrison?''

Somehow, the voice penetrated the fog in Gabe's brain. Or maybe the voice calling his name wasn't real at all. Maybe it was just an illusion. Like the taunting will-o'-the-wisp of an idea that had made him believe his writer's-block days were over.

''Mr. Morrison?''

Hard to deny the voice was real when it was followed by a light rapping at the door of Love Me Tender.

Gabe shook himself out of the daze that had enveloped him. He was sitting on the piano bench, engaged in a stare-down with the piece of paper where earlier, he'd written those two tantalizing words. The words that had made him believe he was on the verge of a breakthrough.

''Dancing hamburgers,'' he grumbled, and the sigh that followed sent the paper fluttering to the floor. It joined more than a dozen others—all of them covered with nothing but doodles—that littered the room like over-sized yellow confetti.

Did he say tantalizing?

Apparently, even dancing hamburgers weren't tantalizing enough.

He hadn't written another word—hadn't had another idea—since.

"Mr. Morrison?"

When the door snapped open, Gabe spun around on the bench.

"Oh!" Her cheeks bright with embarrassment, Maisie stood where the elaborately patterned Oriental rug of the hallway met the green shag monstrosity that carpeted the room from wall to wall. "I'm sorry," she said, taking a step back. "When you didn't answer, I thought you'd gone out. I was just going to leave..." She gestured with the tiny box of expensive candy she held in one hand. "You know, as a welcoming gift."

"Thank you." The words came automatically, though how he managed even that, Gabe didn't know. Putting two coherent words together was becoming more and more far-fetched by the moment.

"Mr. Morrison, has there been some sort of..." Maisie's bright-blue gaze surveyed the wreckage, and though she was too good a hostess to come right out and ask what the hell was going on, it was more than obvious that she was a little concerned. She came further into the room. "Has there been an accident?" she asked. "Would you like me to call one of our housekeepers and—"

"No. No accident." Because Gabe couldn't stand the thought of Maisie's discomfort, he pulled himself off the piano bench and picked up the discarded pieces of paper. One by one, they joined the stack until it was complete, the paper he'd written on at the top.

"Dancing hamburgers, huh?" The look Maisie aimed at the top paper was as innocent as Easter bunnies. And as curious as any Gabe had ever seen. When she saw that he was watching her, she grinned. "Maybe you need a break. Ready for dinner?"

"Dinner?" Still clutching the papers, Gabe stretched, working the stiffness out of his back. At the same time, he glanced over at the stained-glass window. It was lit from behind by a blaze of sunlight. Just as it had been the afternoon he'd checked in.

"Is it that late?" He turned to Maisie. "I didn't know...."

"You must be starving." She held the box of candy out to him and when Gabe rejected it with a shake of his head, she set it down on a corner of the piano. Lightly, she ran her fingers over the keys. "You play?" she asked.

"I don't." As he had the day before, he offered the lie without hesitation. But where the day before he'd planned to keep his secret from Meg as he'd kept it for so many weeks from Dennis and Latoya and the Tasty Time Burger folks, something about Maisie's warmth made him feel he needed to get it off his chest. He dropped back onto the piano bench.

"Writer's block." It was painful, but admitting it made Gabe feel better. A little. "I do play. At least I did. I'm supposed to be composing the music for a new jingle. And writing the lyrics. The Tasty Time Burger chain is introducing a new product, a burger with pepper bacon and honey mustard. But..." He shrugged, as if that would explain everything. "Writer's block."

As if she'd known it all along, Maisie nodded. "You've tried deep breathing?"

She was so sincere, Gabe didn't have the heart to tell her he was long past the deep-breathing stage.

"Yoga? Self-help tapes?" Her silvery eyebrows rose. "Chocolate?"

"I've tried everything." Gabe's shoulders sagged beneath the weight of the admission. "I figured I was working too hard, so I tried exercising more. Then I figured I was exercising too much, so I tried staying at the office later than usual. I actually saw a shrink for the very first time in my life. Know what she told me?'' Even so many weeks later, he couldn't believe it, and he barked out a laugh that sounded as hollow as it felt. ''She told me I had issues.''

He ruffled through the stack of papers, glancing as he did at the drawings that had taken shape while his mind was busy trying to come up with something—anything—that would pass muster as a commercial jingle. And not as a high-rise office building.

''Maybe I do.'' Gabe tossed the papers down on the piano bench next to him and they fanned out, revealing his drawings. ''Maybe I do have issues.''

Maisie's eye traveled over the sketches. ''Building issues?''

''Not as ridiculous as it seems. My family is full of architects. It's what I was supposed to be doing with my life.''

''But instead of designing buildings you write advertising jingles.''

It wasn't a question, and he had to give Maisie credit. She didn't make it sound as crazy as most people did on those few-and-far-between occasions when he divulged the truth about his family and his past.

''I was all set to go with the program, to fall in line with what was expected of me.'' Gabe hauled himself off the piano bench and paced as far as the dazzling window and back. ''Degree in architecture from MIT. Just like my father and my grandfather and his father before him. They had my life planned out for me, down to the corner office with my name on the door. A few years' experience and I'd be a partner. A couple more after that, and I'd head the firm. And why not? Grandfather was ready to retire. Mom's health wasn't the best, and she and Dad talked about a permanent home in a climate that was a little warmer than Boston's. They knew the firm would be in good hands.''

He wondered what Maisie's reaction would be when he told her the ugly truth. ''Instead, six months before I was supposed to graduate, I broke the news to them. Announced that I was giving it all up. I was going to LA and I was going to be a jingle writer.''

''It's what you wanted.'' Maisie repeated the words Gabe had used himself so often in those days. She sounded as if she'd been there at the time, as if she'd heard every one of the arguments—most of them heated—between Gabe and his grandfather. Every one of the long, awkward silences between Gabe and his parents.

''It's what I wanted.'' He shook his head, remembering. ''It's still what I want,'' he told Maisie. ''It's just that...''

There was no use trying to explain. He didn't understand it himself. Instead of even attempting it, Gabe gathered the papers and took them over to the soda fountain. Next to it was a wastebasket shaped like a guitar and he dropped the pages into it and watched them hit bottom. Pretty much like his aspirations.

''You followed your heart.''

Maisie wasn't nearly as judgmental as most of the folks who knew about his family. Only a handful understood how he could have passed on a prestigious position with one of the oldest and most respected architectural firms in New England, a made-in-the-shade expense account and a gold-plated key to the executive washroom.

He turned to find her watching him, a small smile tickling the corners of her mouth. ''You followed your heart,'' she said, and he wondered why she looked so pleased. "You did what you wanted to do. Followed your bliss and found success." As if she could see his Porsche where it was parked around the back of the inn, she nodded toward the window. "You must be a fine jingle writer."

Gabe couldn't help himself; he had to laugh. "You bet I am! Or maybe I should say I was. Believe it or not, there are a whole lot of folks who say I'm the best there is. Of course, that was once upon a time when I still had some good ideas. Or bad ideas. Or any ideas." He shrugged, honestly baffled. "I figured I was onto something this morning but…well…"

"When you were with Meg?" she asked. "Is that when you felt you were headed in the right direction?"

He'd been talking about his ad campaign. That was what he *thought* he'd been talking about. Yet listening to Maisie, Gabe was convinced that ever so subtly, the subject had changed.

As he supposed that, if nothing else, it proved he still had an imagination.

He dashed away the memories that scampered through his head. The ones that were all about Meg and how she'd looked in the dining room earlier that day. And how natural it felt to sit next to her while he drank his morning coffee. And how, in spite of his problems and the deadline that was breathing down his neck with all the delicacy of a fire-belching dragon, she made him forget everything except the way he wanted to feel her body moving against his. He remembered touching her and how when he had, the synapses in his brain reconnected somehow, and the electricity that arced—man to woman and back again—had fired his inspiration and ignited his creativity.

"It was the right direction." Even he wasn't certain if he was talking about the dancing hamburgers. Or

Meg. It didn't seem to matter. "Looks like I got derailed."

Gabe sank down on the piano bench. "Maybe Grandfather was right. All those years ago. He never did take opposition well. Still doesn't, I'll bet. When I chose song-writing over architecture, he disinherited me."

"He thought you'd fold like a cheap umbrella." Maisie grinned, apparently quite pleased that Gabe hadn't. "Bet he was surprised."

"Not surprised. Just angry. His anger is what's fueled my career. What's kept me going. I wanted to prove I could be successful and I did prove it. Until now." Gabe banged his hands against the piano keys, playing a dissonant chord. "His parting words were all about how I'd never be able to make a living writing jingles. Sooner or later, he told me, the ideas would dry up and I'd be left out in the cold. Maybe he was right."

"Maybe." Maisie went over to the wastebasket and retrieved the one page Gabe had written on. She slapped it down on the soda fountain. "But maybe not. You throwing in the towel?"

Was he?

The question reverberated through Gabe like thunder. "I don't want to," he told her. "I didn't want to then, and I don't want to now. I don't want him to win."

"Good." She nodded, content with his answer. "Then you'd better get on with it."

"Not the easiest thing to do. I've tried, Maisie. More than tried. I've lived and breathed this ad campaign since the day I snagged the account. It's the biggest one we've ever had and a lot of people are depending on it to be successful. They're expecting the best."

''Then all you need to do is give it to them.'' It was as simple as that. At least to Maisie. As if the conversation was over and all the decisions were made, she brushed her hands together. ''That explains what you're doing here. Why fate led you to our door. You're here to be inspired. That's what Love Me Tender is all about.''

''Love Me Tender. Yeah.'' For a second or two, her rah-rah speech had almost worked. Gabe looked around the room. The gold records mocked him. The piano reminded him that there'd been times he couldn't walk past and not sit down to plunk out one new tune or another. Even the life-sized cardboard cut out of the King—complete with Santa hat—that stood next to the bathroom door seemed to be laughing at him. All the light-on-good-taste, heavy-on-Graceland atmosphere managed to do was to remind him of exactly what he wasn't.

Exactly what he'd never be.

Not if he failed with Tasty Time Burger.

''You know...'' Gabe sat up, warming to an idea. ''Maybe things would be different if I could just change rooms.''

''Don't be silly, dear. You couldn't do any better than Love Me Tender.'' She sashayed past, brushing her hand against the top of the piano. ''It's my favorite room here at Cupid's Hideaway, though I don't let any of the guests in the other rooms know that. They have their own tastes, of course, and who's to say that one person's taste is better than another's? But music—it really is the food of love. Didn't one of you poets say that? And what could be a better inspiration than love?''

Gabe wasn't about to argue. He wouldn't have known how, even if he'd wanted to.

"So, that's that." Her mind was made up—even though Gabe wasn't quite sure what decision they'd reached. "You don't need a new career. You love what you do. And you don't need a new room because this one's perfect for you. What you do need is a little dinner. A little dinner and a little distraction. I've got just the thing for you. The answer to both." She picked up the box of candy and flourished it.

"No. Really." Gabe raised one hand. "I'm not all that hungry and besides, candy isn't exactly what I want for dinner and—"

"No, no, dear." Maisie giggled, the sound of it as airy as a girl's. "I wasn't talking about the candy for *you.* I was talking about it for Meg. She's very picky when it comes to food. And this just happens to be her favorite peanut brittle made at the island candy shop."

Even after only twenty-four hours at the Hideaway, if there was one thing Gabe knew for sure, it was that Maisie was anything but understated. Her plan was almost as transparent as the corset on the lady in that picture above the dining-room fireplace.

"I thought the candy was for me!" He laughed. "Now you're telling me—"

"I'm telling you that as innkeeper, one of my duties is to keep my guests informed and entertained. There's big doings in DeRivera Park tonight. Christmas in July, you know, and lots happening. When Meg left here this afternoon, she said she'd be there."

Maisie held out the golden foil box with its elaborate green velvet bow. But Gabe wasn't convinced. Earlier that morning, he'd noticed the sign on Almost Paradise, the room next to his. It was a tree branch carved from wood and wound around it was a plump snake wearing a smile that was all about temptation.

Exactly the kind of smile Maisie had on her face.

"Are you telling me you want me to track down your granddaughter and tempt her with peanut brittle?"

"A little distraction will do you good," she assured him again. "And inspiration is where you find it." She shoved the box of candy into his hand and walked to the door. "Temptation, however, is a whole different kettle of fish." Right before she stepped out into the hallway, Maisie aimed one final, persuasive smile in his direction. "You don't really think you need the candy for that, do you?"

DERIVERA PARK was jam-packed with partyers who spilled onto the sidewalk and into the marina across the street. It was hot, crowded and the music being played by a teenaged band from a makeshift stage outside one of the more popular downtown bars was way too loud.

Meg was loving every minute of it.

Along with the rest of the crowd, she applauded when Dave Montgomery—complete with white beard, red hat, Hawaiian shirt and Bermuda shorts—announced that the Chamber of Commerce promised a night to remember and a surprise none of them would ever forget. When volunteers came around with cups of hot chocolate and trays of Christmas cookies, Meg took a few, including one of the sugar cookies she'd donated. Somebody was handing out single-serving pouches of Love Me Tenders, and she grabbed one of those, too. Meg didn't have a dog, but her sister Laurel did. There was no surer way of gaining Felix's undying devotion than with food.

Meg refused a dance with Doug from the bait and tackle shop on the grounds that she didn't want to be responsible for what her two left feet would do to him. She chatted with Al, the man who owned the fishing boat she'd captained one summer, and waved to a group of long-time summer visitors who called her over and begged her to cater an upcoming bash. She excused herself around Betty and Dorothy Depp, sisters who lived not far from the Hideaway and were never happy about the traffic it attracted, and when she saw Dylan O'Connell, the island's police chief, on the sidewalk just behind the temporary stage, she went over to see what he was up to.

Dylan and Meg had gone to high school together and for all of two weeks in junior year, had gone steady. Their fling had consisted of a little-hand holding and few stolen kisses under the gym bleachers during a basketball game, but when it was over, seventeen-year-old Meg had played the whole break-up scene for maximum drama. In retrospect, she knew it was the best thing that could have happened. To both of them. Instead of having to consider Dylan her ex-anything, Meg was lucky enough to have him for a best friend.

He nodded a hello to her as he looked around, expertly checking out the crowd, pegging the troublemakers and keeping his eye on them. "You going to behave yourself tonight?" he asked. He never could understand Meg's tendency to talk loud, move fast, and find the most trouble she could get into in the shortest amount of time.

"Cross my heart." She drew one finger over her heart. "Just here to have some fun. Honest, officer. And after the show..." She glanced over to where the too-loud band had finished its act and was packing up its equipment. "Well, I have to stick around to see what the big surprise is going to be. You got an inside track on that?"

"Maybe." Dylan rocked back on his heels. "Maybe not."

"So that means maybe you'll tell me?"

"Maybe not." A group of kids in Santa hats who didn't seem old enough even to be *thinking* about going into a bar stopped at the door and Dylan warned them off with a frown. He watched them long enough to make sure they didn't double back and try again and when he was satisfied, he turned to Meg again. "I hear you may be headed for plenty of trouble."

"Really?" It was news to her, but Meg didn't really mind. She was dressed in her best jeans and a new neon-orange top. She was all set to kick back, and a little harmless trouble might be exactly what she needed.

At least it might stop her from obsessing about Gabe Morrison.

The thought snuck up and bit her and she flinched.

Leave it to Dylan not to miss a thing. His eyebrows sneaked up toward the curl of sandy-colored hair that drooped over his forehead. "I hear you've got a new guest at the Hideaway and that he's got his eye on you." Dylan never smiled, but that didn't mean Meg couldn't tell when he was teasing her.

Too bad he wasn't funny.

She folded her arms over her neon-orange top. "What else did you hear?" she asked.

He pursed his lips, thinking. "That he drives a very expensive car with California plates, that he hasn't said exactly how long he's planning on staying, that he ordered a pizza for dinner last night, though why, I don't know. The best cook this side of the Chicago works down in the Hideaway kitchen—and you always keep something extra in the fridge for guests."

She sent him a sour look. "You've been talking to Maisie."

"All part of my job." A silver-haired man walked

by with a bottle of beer and after a gentle but firm reminder about open-container laws, Dylan got back to the subject. ‘‘I can tell you some other stuff about your Gabriel Samuel Morrison, too. He’s a tad over six feet tall, weighs about one seventy-five. He has dark hair and eyes that are too brown to be called hazel and too tawny to be called brown. Which, should he ever be incarcerated—which he’s never been, in case you want to know—will mean that the arresting officer will have a heck of a time filling out all the paperwork. And getting it right.’’ He slid her a sly glance. ‘‘How am I doing?’’

He was doing a little too well. Dylan’s assessment pretty much went along with everything Meg remembered about Gabe. Except that he’d left out the hotter-than-blazes looks, the animal attraction and the raw energy that flowed off the man as smoothly as butter off a hot-out-of-the-oven croissant.

Not that she was about to let Dylan know any of it. If she did, he’d never let her hear the end of it.

Instead, she challenged him. ‘‘So you did what? Ran a wants-and-arrests on the man? You really are something! You think that’s fair?’’

‘‘You think I’m going to let my best buddy fall for some stranger when I haven’t checked him out completely?’’

‘‘I haven’t fallen for him.’’ Meg threw back her shoulders and lifted her chin. ‘‘And I don’t even have to ask where you got the idea. I swear, Maisie’s head is filled with nothing but romantic fantasies. She ought to write books.’’

‘‘Didn’t hear it from Maisie. Not all of it anyway. Didn’t have to. Want to hear what else I know about the guy?’’ He didn’t wait for her to answer. And that was probably a good thing. Meg couldn't afford to seem too interested.

"He's got one of those chiseled faces women are always so attracted to. You know, real California good looks. Small scar on his right forearm. He's walking around with a lost expression and he's carrying a box of candy."

"Oh, come on!" This was too much. Meg tucked her free sample of Love Me Tenders into her back pocket and poked Dylan on the badge that was pinned just above his heart. "You're taking this whole thing a little too far! Even you can't know that—"

"He's walking around with a lost expression on his face and he's carrying a box of candy." Dylan settled both hands on Meg's shoulders and turned her toward the crowd. Not twenty feet away, Gabe Morrison was edging through the partygoers. He was wearing a lost expression. He was carrying a box of candy.

And at the sight of him, Meg's heart skipped a beat.

"Go get him," Dylan whispered in her ear, and before she could tell him he was reading her all wrong, he disappeared into the crowd.

"There you are." When he saw her, a look of relief swept over Gabe's face. He sidestepped his way between a baby stroller and a trash can. "I never thought I'd find you in this crowd. What's happening here, anyway?"

"It's the last night of the Christmas in July celebration and this is always the biggest party." Meg hated it when her tongue got as tied up as New York traffic in rush hour. She hated it when her palms felt damp and her knees turned to the consistency of aspic, and each and every breath she took made her ribs feel like they were going to snap.

Almost as much as she hated remembering how, in

spite of her efforts at seduction—half-hearted as they were—Gabe had chosen dancing hamburgers over her.

Nothing like a little reality check to a get a girl back on track.

"Glad you could join us." She gave Gabe the kind of sleek smile he seemed to have noticed that morning. Until the dancing hamburgers showed up.

Maybe he didn't think about dancing hamburgers when he was outdoors. Or when it was evening. Maybe there was something about the party atmosphere or the perfect evening or the bright orange top and close-fitting jeans that made him see there was more to life than food products tripping the light fantastic.

This time, Gabe smiled back. "Maisie told me you were here and..." He held out the box of candy. The elaborate green velvet bow was rumpled and one corner of the gold box was crushed. No wonder, considering that Gabe must've been hanging onto the box of candy for dear life in the crowd.

As tempted as she was—by what she suspected was peanut brittle and by the smile Gabe offered her with it—Meg wasn't about to let him off so easily. "My favorite," she purred. Right before she pinned Gabe with an unwavering stare. "Something tells me Maisie does your shopping."

"No. I—" Gabe's smile wilted around the edges, but she had to give him big points. Even though he admitted his guilt, he didn't back down. "Busted." His face lit with a grin that warmed Meg clear down to her toes. "How did you know it was Maisie?"

Meg rolled her eyes. "It's always Maisie. She can't keep her cute little nose out of anyone's business. Especially when she smells romance in the air."

"Does she?"

For a second, she thought he was talking about

Maisie's annoying tendency to run everyone's life and she was all set to detail the high points—and the lows—of Maisie's career as the island's unofficial matchmaker.

Until she figured out that wasn't what Gabe was talking about at all.

Meg's breath caught behind a hiccup of excitement. "Does she? You mean, does she smell romance?"

Gabe stepped a little closer and lowered his voice. "Do you?"

Meg smelled peanut brittle and the fresh, limey scent of Gabe's aftershave. She smelled the hot dogs being sold out of a cart a few feet down the sidewalk and she smelled beer and cotton candy and popcorn. She ignored most of it, concentrating instead on the citrus scent and the reflection in Gabe's eyes of the Christmas lights strung around the park.

"I *was* smelling romance..." She dangled the challenge, wondering how he'd respond. "Until I smelled hamburgers."

"Dancing hamburgers. Yeah." Gabe backed off and took the peanut brittle with him. One corner of his mouth screwed up and his shoulders tensed. "You see," he said, "I've got this account to worry about. And this reputation."

"I'll bet."

"Not what I meant." In spite of the strain that showed on his face, he grinned. "I meant work," he said. "A reputation at work. There are a whole bunch of people counting on me to do a good job. A better-than-good job. They're counting on me to be brilliant and maybe I'm being big-headed and just plain delusional but I've always been brilliant before."

"So you don't want to let them down."

"You got it." As if even that little bit of understanding helped lift the weight from his shoulders, Gabe sighed. ''So while the whole romance-is-in-the-air thing is certainly intriguing, you'll have to forgive me if I seem a little distracted. It's not that I haven't noticed...'' He skimmed a look from Meg's face to the tips of her sneakers and back up again. ''I've noticed, all right. I've really noticed.''

Which meant Meg had lost her bet with Maisie.

And Meg hated to lose.

Which meant she should've been mad as a hornet.

But that didn't explain why she was suddenly feeling as if her blood had been replaced with expensive and very fizzy mineral water.

There was no use pretending she didn't know exactly what he was talking about. Though Meg liked to play hard, playing hard to get had never been her thing. A family trooped by behind her and she decided to give them plenty of room. She stepped a little closer to Gabe.

''I like being noticed,'' she told him. ''But then again, maybe you already figured that out. Bright colors. Bright hair. Bright fingernail polish.'' She wiggled her fingers and her red nails caught the light of the neon beer sign in the window behind them. ''I'm not exactly what you'd call subtle. The poor folks around here have been noticing me since I was old enough to insist on primary colors and socks that didn't match.''

''Heck, I'd notice you in sackcloth and ashes.'' Gabe flashed her another one of those grins that tickled along her skin, as light as a feather and as tempting as a lover's touch. ''Black clothes, gray clothes, no clothes...'' He sucked in the same kind of unsteady breath that Meg did. ''But I'm getting way ahead of myself. I haven't even tried the sure-fire temptation of candy. Maisie would be disappointed. Something tells me she believes there's a right order to everything. Even a seduction."

"Especially a seduction." Meg had no idea how she made herself sound so matter-of-fact. Not when she was feeling as if she'd melt into the sidewalk, nothing left of her but her sneakers as a warning to other women who might consider getting way too close to a man who was way too hot to handle. "Maisie's old-fashioned."

A smile lifted a corner of Gabe's mouth. "You're not."

It wasn't a question. It didn't need an answer. Meg decided to give him one anyway.

"I'm definitely not," she admitted. "Old-fashioned, that is. But just so you don't get the wrong idea..." She glanced down at the candy. "It's going to take a whole lot more than a box of peanut brittle you didn't pay for and a couple of slick lines to get me into bed."

"Glad to hear it." He *looked* glad, too, and just a little relieved. "That means I can take my time. Do this right. In spite of the very bad reputation men have for wanting things to be as quick and as easy as possible, I've got to tell you..." He leaned in close, the box of candy all that kept his body from touching hers. "There are some of us who prefer things nice and slow."

"And you're one of them?"

"I am most definitely one of them."

Box of peanut brittle or not, Meg couldn't help herself. She angled nearer, lost in the shimmer of his words and the glimmer in his eyes and the little rumble in his voice that told her that although he might very well be handing her a line, it was one she wouldn't mind grabbing and holding onto for the ride of her life.

"I'm really not interested," she said, because she

couldn't stand the thought of lying to him about something so important. "I mean, I'm interested...in you..." She gave him the kind of careful once-over he'd given her only a couple minutes before, stymied in her attempt by the box of candy that made it impossible to check him out any farther than his belt buckle. "But relationships and I..." She crinkled her nose. "We don't exactly get along."

"Maybe you just haven't had a relationship with the right guy."

"Maybe I thought I did."

"Ouch!" Gabe made a face and backed off. "I've got competition, huh?" He looked at the crowd. "The cop?"

"Dylan?" Meg laughed. "He's a friend. That's all."

"Then who?" Gabe glanced around at the sea of partyers. "Not the guy in the flannel shirt over there? The one talking to his dog?"

"Harry?" Meg shook her head. "Believe it or not, Harry happens to be one of the most successful businessmen on the island. That's his dog, Charlie, with him. He's married. Harry, not Charlie. And he's wild about his wife. Besides, he's not my type. And for that matter, neither is Charlie."

"Then what about that guy?" Gabe pointed to a man Meg didn't recognize. Thank goodness. He was dressed in a blue polyester leisure suit and he had a dog with him, too, a boxer who seemed unhappy about wearing a sort of black, fuzzy contraption on his head like a—

"Ducktail wig." Gabe's voice intruded on Meg's thoughts.

"That dog is wearing a wig. What a riot! I heard there was some kind of pet competition tonight, but I didn't pay much attention." Laughing, Meg looked around. Now that it was getting closer to the time the show was scheduled to start, there were a lot of people gathering around the stage. And a lot of them had dogs.

Dogs dressed in flashy, sequined outfits.

Dogs wearing black, fifties-style, rock-and-roll wigs.

Dogs that all looked just like—

"Duke?"

Gabe's voice was hollow. His eyes were glassy.

Meg followed his gaze over to where a man and a woman were coming their way. They were walking an especially ugly and very well-dressed bulldog.

"Duke?" Meg couldn't believe her eyes. "Duke the Dog? Here in Put-in-Bay?" The rest of the crowd couldn't easily see the celebrity in their midst, and before anyone else got in on the action, Meg hurried forward.

"Is this really Duke the Dog?" she asked the dog's two handlers, and when they nodded, she couldn't control herself. Thrilled to pieces, Meg stooped down and scratched Duke under his—or was it her?—chin.

The man holding Duke's sequined leash was in his upper twenties, tall, reed-thin, wearing black from head to toe. His counterpart was a whole head shorter, had hair bleached to a color that reminded Meg of whipping cream and a ring in her nose. It was clear from the start that they weren't paying any attention to Meg. Or to the celebrity who rolled his eyes and grunted, happy as a pig in mud when Meg reached a finger beneath his black wig and scratched him behind the ears.

They were staring over Meg's shoulder.

Right at Gabe.

"Is that Gabe Morrison?" The man handed the leash to the woman and stalked over to where Gabe was standing with his mouth open as if he'd just been pulled to the bottom by a Lake Erie undertow.

"It can't be." When the man stepped nearer, Gabe stepped back. "You can't be—"

"On a promotional tour!" Leaving Duke with Meg, the woman also ran toward Gabe. She stood on tiptoe and smacked a kiss against his cheek. "Out here in the back of beyond, pressing the flesh and thrilling the crowds. What a kick to see you, Morrison! And I'll bet someone else will be happy to see you, too." She stooped down and clapped her hands and though Duke actually looked up, he didn't move a muscle.

"Here, Dukey!" The woman reached into the pocket of her black jacket, pulled out a metal box of breath mints and shook it.

That got the dog's attention.

Dutifully, he trotted over, and, after he'd snarfed the mint, Duke sat down at Gabe's feet.

"See who's here, honey," the woman said, her hand on Gabe's arm. "It's Uncle Gabe!"

His top lip curled, Gabe looked down at the dog.

His top lip curled, Duke looked up at Gabe.

And though she couldn't tell which of them made the first move, Meg was sure of one thing.

One of them growled.

Chapter Five

''You know Duke the Dog? I can't believe you know Duke the Dog. I can't believe you didn't tell me you know Duke the Dog.''

If Gabe had been feeling a little more charitable and less like he'd been slammed in the solar plexus by a fighter with a fist of lead, he might've been more inclined to listen to Meg's excited chatter. Instead, he gave her a look that would have frozen a lesser person on the spot.

He should've known it wouldn't faze Meg.

''How do you know Duke? I mean…Duke the Dog!'' She sighed and clutched her hands to her heart. ''He's my hero. That handsome face. That dreamy voice. That—''

''Overbite?'' The way Gabe snarled the word made Meg laugh and the fact that she didn't appreciate the gravity of the situation only made him snarl more. Even her luminous smile couldn't improve the situation, and he turned away from her and toward the stage where Ingrid (Duke's personal publicist) and Travis (Duke's personal handler) introduced the Love Me Tenders tour show and Duke the Dog look-alike contest to a good portion of the residents of South Bass Island, a whole lot of tourists and what seemed like every remote crew from every TV station in three states and parts of Canada.

From where they were positioned at the front of the crowd and to the side of the stage, Gabe had a perfect vantage point. He saw the kids waving their stuffed Dukes in the air, and the adults who were laughing and gesturing and standing on tiptoe just so they could see the country's newest, hottest and (if the polls were to be believed) most recognizable advertising icon.

From there, his gaze slid to center stage where Duke was looking fat, dumb and happy. With the emphasis on fat and dumb.

Gabe shook his head. "That is the ugliest, the most contrary, the most ornery—"

"You don't really mean that."

Of course he did. Gabe just hadn't realized he'd said it out loud. "I mean it," he told Meg, because now that he'd committed himself, there was no use pretending otherwise.

"She's such a prima donna."

"He." The old lady standing next to Gabe blanched as if he'd just insulted one of her grandchildren. "Duke is a he," the woman told him.

As much as he was tempted, Gabe didn't correct her. It wouldn't do any good and besides, with the mood the crowd was in, any challenge to the Duke legend would probably have caused a riot.

"*He* is the ugliest, the most contrary, the most ornery—"

"Oh, lighten up!" Meg grinned at him, her eyes bright with excitement and the reflected glow of the Christmas lights. "He's adorable. That's more than I can say for some people."

She hadn't come right out and pointed a finger at him, but Gabe suddenly felt as though it was important to defend himself. He crossed his arms over his chest and narrowed his eyes, watching as the contestants trooped across the stage with their owners. The line up consisted of the boxer he'd seen earlier with the man in the blue leisure suit, a Pekingese that didn't look a thing like Duke but had one heck of a sequined costume, a basset hound with its ears tucked up under a Duke the Dog baseball cap and its tail poked through a one-serving size pouch of Love Me Tenders, and a bulldog whose owner apparently harbored some sick and not-so-secret crush on Duke. That dog was practically a Duke clone, from the outfit to the dribble of drool on its chin.

"I'm way more adorable," Gabe grumbled, and when Meg chuckled, he slanted her a look. "All right, so maybe *way more* is overstating the case. But there's no denying the more adorable part. More adorable than that flea-bitten diva."

"He didn't seem to think much of you, either."

"Duke has lousy taste."

"He's cute as a button. Can you get me his autograph?"

Gabe's smile was meringue-stiff. "Big news, he's illiterate."

"His singing makes up for it." Meg shivered. "Makes me tingly all over."

"Really?" Watching her orange shirt pull across her breasts when she moved did things to his insides and made his outsides feel pretty darned swell, too. For the first time since Duke the Dog had showed up, Gabe's spirits rose. He lowered his voice. "If it's Duke's singing that turns you on, then you really should know the truth. Duke's voice is—"

"Gabe Morrison!"

The sound of his own name echoing through the

park over the sound system stopped Gabe cold. His heart pounded a couple of painful times, then stopped completely. His mouth went dry. His stomach flipped. Almost too afraid to look, he glanced at the stage to see Ingrid scanning the crowd for him. When she spotted him, she called to him to come on down. The crowd took up the cheer.

"Gabe-ree-el! Gabe-ree-el!"

Meg was just as surprised as Gabe. For different reasons. Thrilled at what was happening, she grinned. "This is getting better and better. Now they want you on stage," she said and even before she bothered to notice Gabe's body language (which was definitely sending a clear signal), his facial expression (which was no less than thunderous), and the big, unmistakable *no* on his lips, she waded through the crowd, urging everyone to clear a path for Gabe.

By then, it was too late to do anything except fall in line, get with the program and get the whole thing over with. Hanging onto his temper and what was left of his self-respect, Gabe pounded up to the stage, exchanged glares with Duke and turned a frown of massive proportions on Ingrid.

She was young, overpaid and from New York. She didn't much care.

"Ladies and gentlemen..." Ingrid looped an arm around Gabe's waist and tugged him toward the microphone with so much vigor, he dropped the box of peanut brittle. "Ladies and gentlemen, this is Gabe Morrison, and though you may not recognize his name, I know you recognize his commercials. Gabe is famous in advertising circles. He's the one who discovered Duke the Dog and wrote the lyrics to Duke's famous song, *and...*" She held on to the word until the tension in the crowd stretched tight and was ready to snap.

''Gabe is the voice of Duke in the Love Me Tenders commercial and I think with just a little encouragement, he'd be more than happy to sing the song for us!''

The crowd went nuts. A couple months earlier, Gabe would have enjoyed every minute of it. Now he was tempted to step up to the microphone and tell them they were wasting their time.

So he was the boy genius who came up with the over-the-top concept of an ugly dog crooning a torch song.

So he was the one who sold the idea to the Love Me Tenders folks and made them feel if it was their honor to pay him a fortune for it.

So he was the one who wrote the lyrics and the melody, he was the one who did the voice-over for the dog and who was pretty much single-handedly responsible for making Love Me Tenders the most-purchased dog food in the country.

So he was the one who'd made Duke a household name, a cultural icon, a star.

So what?

It didn't mean a thing. Not unless he could do it all again with another product, another icon, another star. Not unless he could think of something for the Tasty Time Burger folks and think of it soon.

It was on the tip of his tongue to tell them the truth. That advertising was about as enduring as clouds. That fame meant nothing the day after you were famous. That his grandfather was right.

He would have done it, too, if Meg hadn't been standing in the front of the crowd. Her head was tipped up so that she could see the stage and in the blaze of the intense TV spots and the glow of the holiday lights strung in the windows of nearby restaurants and bars, her face was radiant, her cheeks stained with color and her hair looked as if it had been washed with light. Her eyes sparkled with excitement and her hands were clutched together, her index fingers tapping her chin to the same, fidgety beat that suddenly made Gabe's heart thump against his ribs.

Though he doubted there were too many guys who would've been able to resist the pull of her gaze or the temptation of those moist, inviting lips, Gabe knew he could have done it. After all, he had other things to worry about. Like his career and the futures of the people back in LA whose fates—and paychecks—depended on his creativity.

He would've done it, too. If Meg hadn't zapped him with a smile.

Mesmerized by the sparkle in her eyes that told him she wasn't just impressed, she was downright bowled over by everything that was happening, Gabe stepped up to the microphone.

"Love my Tenders."

There were hisses for silence all around the park as Gabe softly started in on the jingle, his eyes on Meg, his concentration so complete, it took him a second to realize that the only sounds in the park were the faraway rumble of laughter from a bar and the gentle swish of the lake against the shore.

"Love them lots."

He sang the words slowly, packing all the emotional punch he had the day he'd recorded his voice-over for the commercial.

"Shaped like little steaks."

Warming to the look in Meg's eyes far more than he was warming to the jingle or to the ridiculous notion that when millions of people heard his voice, they associated it with the Hound from Hell, he crooned his heart out.

''Love my Tenders. Eat them all. They're not fried, they're baked.''

The last note of the song hung in the air for one second. Two. Finally, the mood was broken when an older-than-middle-aged lady in lime-green shorts and an *I Love Santa* T-shirt heaved a sigh that echoed through the park. The crowd laughed. Then they applauded. Then they cheered. The Pekingese yipped. The boxer barked. Duke growled.

And none of it mattered. Because Meg was still smiling at him.

His bloodstream caught fire and Gabe backed away from the microphone. He would have cut and run right for Meg if not for the fact that Ingrid grabbed his hand and hung on like a limpet to a rock.

''You've got to help us judge.'' Ingrid scanned the line-up of contestants. ''Pick a winner, Gabe.''

''Winner?'' Gabe couldn't believe his bad luck. There was a plastic trashcan filled with Love Me Tenders samples nearby and he scooped up an armful and tossed them into the crowd. ''When dogs eat Love Me Tenders,'' he yelled, ''every one of them's a winner!''

It was enough to get the crowd pumped up but not enough to satisfy the owners who had subjected their pets to the clothes and the wigs. Gabe left the judging to Ingrid, and, while the crowd was still cheering and grabbing for samples, he made his exit.

''That was so cool!'' Meg was waiting for him at the foot of the risers that led to the stage. Okay, it was a little pushy of her. It might even have made her look like a groupie.

She couldn't care less.

The rest of the crowd milled around them, but Meg

refused to give an inch. This was too exciting and after all, technically, Gabe was her date. He'd come to the party in the park to find her. Earlier in the day, he'd mentioned dinner and sharing a few laughs. And he'd presented her with a box of candy.

Sort of.

Meg glanced over to the place where Gabe had dropped the box when he went up on stage. She'd been so busy paying attention to everything that was going on—so entranced by Gabe's singing and the tiny prickles of electricity his voice sent tingling into places that had been pretty much electricity-free since the day she'd finally realized what a conniving creep Ben was—she hadn't noticed that the box of peanut brittle had been stolen. There was no sign it had ever been there except for a bit of green ribbon lying near the microphone and a scrap of gold cardboard near the steps.

She decided right then and there that the whole experience was worth the loss of a box of peanut brittle. Even her favorite peanut brittle. Gabe ignored the outstretched hands and the excited squeals of his fans. He walked right up to Meg.

"That was the best!" She smiled up at him and when he smiled back, the sounds of the cheering and the laughter around her faded, the lights dimmed, the temperature kicked up a couple of degrees. "You could have told me sooner that you were a friend of Duke."

"Then I'd never know if you were interested in my sparkling personality or just my valuable connections." His smile never wavered but something told Meg he wasn't kidding. Not completely. At least not about being interested in him. And now that they had that awkward part of their relationship out of the way, all she had to do was find out if the feeling was mutual.

She hooked her fingers into the belt loops on her jeans and rolled back on her heels. He'd been staring at her neon-orange top ever since she'd seen him making his way through the crowd clutching the gold box. He might as well get his fill.

"It *is* tempting to dump you for the dog," she said, looking at the stage just long enough to see the Duke clone walk off with the grand prize. "But I'm thinking you might be a better conversationalist."

"I'm better at a whole bunch of other things." His gaze slid up from the orange shirt to her lips and from her lips to her eyes. His voice settled into something a little more intimate than it was friendly. His eyes glittered. His smile inched up a notch.

So did the heat inside Meg.

"Maybe we should start with the conversation." It wasn't what she wanted to start with. She wanted to start with hot kisses and hotter caresses. With whispered sweet nothings and soft laughter in the dark and the kind of temptation that made her crazy for more. She wanted to skip the preliminaries altogether and get right to the tearing off his clothes and jumping his bones part.

She figured conversation was more appropriate. At least while they were the center of attention. In the center of DeRivera Park.

"You mentioned something about dinner and—"

"And about checking out the festivities. Yeah. I remember." He looked around. Now that the contest was over, Duke had been hustled backstage. The owner of the voice that had convinced people everywhere to buy Love Me Tenders for their dogs was making it clear that he wasn't interested in anyone—or anything—except the lady in the bright orange top, so the crowd was starting to thin. "We pretty much took care of checking out the festivities. I don't know about you, but I'd say this was enough excitement for one night."

"You think?"

It was a little forward, even for Meg who didn't often mince words, never beat around the bush and hardly ever sat on the fence. Still, she'd been known to play it cool when it came to relationships. At least until she knew the lay of the land.

Of course, that didn't explain why the words just sort of fell out of her mouth. Or why, waiting to hear how Gabe might react to them, her stomach flipped and her heart pounded.

Just as she expected, Gabe got the message. Loud and clear. Meg could tell because his breath caught and the barest of smiles touched one corner of his mouth. The heat of it melted the tension inside her.

"I think..." He reached out to take her arm, but before he could, a horde of chattering little kids ran past and he had to back away or risk being flattened. Their arrival and quick departure broke the spell. When they were gone, Gabe said, "You want to start with dinner?"

She didn't. But it would have to do. For the moment. "I'm starving!" Meg told him, partly because it was true and partly because it was smarter—and safer—to talk about food than it was to give her imagination free rein and let it take her places it wasn't wise for her to go. "I thought you'd never ask." Meg turned, automatically leading him toward the bar she knew had the best fish fry in town. It wasn't until they were behind the makeshift stage that another thought occurred to her. "Can we say goodnight to Duke first?"

"Can we—" There was no mistaking that Gabe considered it just about the worst idea he'd ever heard. But there was something about a man who saw the promise of the night spread out in front of him, something about Meg's hint that there was even more to come that intrigued him enough to indulge her. The orange top might have had something to do with it, too.

He surrendered with a good-natured shrug. "All right." They stopped near where Ingrid and Travis were letting folks pat Duke and have their pictures taken with him. When Ingrid caught sight of them, she hurried over.

"You're a good sport, Morrison. Thanks for helping us out." Ingrid was short, pale and very thin. Next to her drab black clothing, the red shirt Gabe was wearing looked as vivid as a glass of pricey shiraz. His hair looked darker. His shoulders broader. The blue jeans that hugged his muscular thighs and that nice, tight butt of his looked as if they'd been painted on by an artist whose sole purpose was to bring every woman's most wicked fantasy to life.

And Meg's imagination was getting out of line and way too poetic for her own good.

She slapped it back in place—again—and after the old lady ahead of her slipped Duke a red-and-white-striped mint, she knelt down to scratch the dog under the chin.

"It must be ESP or something," she heard Ingrid tell Gabe. "I mean, tripping over you like this. Not three days ago, I tried calling you at your office. Just to tell you I think you're the biggest genius since Leonardo freakin'-da Vinci. I mean, this Duke phenomenon is *big*. We've done twelve cities in the last two weeks and this crowd tonight? This is nothing! You should've seen how many people turned up in Detroit. They love Duke. Everyone loves him."

"Her." Travis dropped the leash and went over to join Ingrid. "You'll offend her sensibilities, darling," he said, giving Ingrid an anemic peck on the cheek. "We can't risk damaging her self-esteem by calling her sexuality into question."

"Whatever!" Ingrid rolled eyes the color of the pale-blue china Maisie used for high teas and bridal showers. "The point is, Duke is a hit. A superstar! Twelve cities in fourteen days and my brain is mush and I want a day off so bad I can taste it. I don't remember Latoya saying anything about you being in—" She scanned the crowd and the TV crews just putting away their equipment, and it was clear even to Meg that they must have looked just like the crowds and the TV crews in every single one of those twelve other cities. Ingrid brushed it all off with a laugh. "Wait until I call Latoya and tell her I just happened to bump into you on some nothing island in the middle of nowhere!"

"Call her?"

There was so much honest-to-gosh horror in Gabe's voice, Meg couldn't help but be curious. Anxious to find out what was going on, she grabbed Duke's leash and led the dog to where Gabe was standing, his gaze pivoting from Ingrid to Travis and back to Ingrid again, his cheeks suddenly pale, his expression teetering between *please tell me you're kidding* and *you wouldn't dare.*.

"Latoya?" Gabe choked on the name. "You wouldn't really call Latoya, would you? I mean, *why* would you? Why would she care?"

"Why wouldn't she?" Even Ingrid picked up on the undercurrent of panic in Gabe's words. Interested and not averse to letting him know it, she gave him a penetrating look. "What are you up to, Morrison? You're not hiding from Latoya, are you? You're not..." She stared at Meg and instantly read more into the situation than she should have. "Latoya said you were supposed to be on your way to New York for business. Business, Gabe?" There was a smile on her face and a little trill of laughter in her voice. "Or monkey business?"

"Business. My business." Gabe's frown reminded Meg of the one he'd aimed at the Steinway when she led him up to Love Me Tender. It was enough to make Ingrid instantly back off. "Latoya doesn't need to know and you're not going to call her. Tell me you're not."

Ingrid and Travis exchanged looks.

Duke gobbled up what was left of a hot dog wrapper that had been thrown on the ground.

Meg kept out of it, watching the scene unfold. There was no mistaking the fact that Gabe was anxious to avoid Latoya. Meg knew it, and although Ingrid and Travis had no idea he'd been dodging phone calls back at the Hideaway, it was clear from their self-satisfied expressions that they now knew it, too. The only question in Meg's mind was why it was so important in the first place. The only one in Ingrid and Travis's was obviously how far Gabe was willing to go to keep his whereabouts a secret.

It didn't take long to find out.

"You said you wanted a day off." Gabe plunged into the discussion the way Meg imagined he tackled a business negotiation. "When's your next appearance with Duke?"

"Not until Wednesday," Travis answered automatically. "We do Cleveland on Wednesday, then Pittsburgh and Wheeling and—"

"Then you really could have three days off." Gabe dangled the offer in front of Ingrid and Travis, then pulled his wallet out of his back pocket. "You two like roller coasters, don't you?" He pulled out a fifty-dollar bill. ''I remember that from the time you visited us in LA and Dennis took you over to Disneyland.'' He drew out another fifty. ''You two like roller coasters and we're are just a few short watery miles away from—''

''Cedar Point!'' Like a true believer sighting the Holy Grail, Travis whirled toward the lake, as if he was imagining the delights that awaited just a few miles across the water.

Ingrid's nose twitched. ''You mean the amusement park?'' She breathed the words on the end of a trembling sigh. ''The amusement park with all the roller coasters that are supposed to be—''

''Best in the country.'' Gabe plucked out another fifty. ''That's what I'm told. There's a young couple staying up at the Hideaway where I have a room. I heard them talking at breakfast this morning. They say it's a terrific place and it's not very far away. You'd only have to hop back on the ferry...'' He pulled two more fifties out of his wallet. ''Why take just one day off when you could take three? Three days of rest, relaxation and roller coasters.''

''Deal.'' When Travis grabbed for the money, Gabe held it just out of reach.

''It's only a deal if you don't call Latoya,'' he reminded them.

''Done.'' Ingrid moved faster than Travis. She snatched the money out of Gabe's hand and started for the hotel. ''I hear the ferries run late this time of year,'' she said, her arm already looped through Travis's. ''If we hurry, we can collect our luggage and catch the next one. We could get be on the mainland tonight and ready to roll bright and early in the morning.'' She tossed a look over her shoulder toward Gabe, Meg and Duke. ''We'll call you when we get there.''

''Call me?'' Gabe scooped up the dog's leash and

followed with Duke in tow. ''You don't have to call me. You're not calling anyone, remember? All you're supposed to do is have fun and—''

''You don't think we can take the dog, do you?''

Meg wasn't especially surprised by the announcement, but it was clear from the way his cheeks went ashen and his eyes wide that Gabe was.

''What do you mean?'' he asked. ''What do you mean you can't take the dog? What do you expect me to—''

''What do you expect *us* to do with her?'' Ingrid laughed. ''I mean, if we're riding the roller coasters, who'd watch out for Diana? She just can't sit on a park bench and wait for us, you know.''

''Oh, no!'' Gabe held the leash out to them. ''You can't leave him…er…her with me. You can't just go away for three days and—''

''We could just call Latoya.''

It was a low blow but Meg couldn't really blame Ingrid and Travis. They were the ones who'd been lured into this little trap by Gabe and all those fifties. They were the ones who'd been promised three days of roller-coaster riding and time away from the crowds of adoring Duke fans. They knew it. And so did Gabe.

Rather than remind him, they smiled in unison, turned and marched over to the hotel.

They left Gabe holding the leash. And the dog on the end of it.

Meg slipped a finger beneath the ducktail wig and scratched the dog behind the ears. ''Looks like you're going to get a little time to bond.''

Gabe was not impressed. He scowled down at the dog and a noise rumbled from deep in his throat.

Not to be outdone, Duke stared up at Gabe and let go with a booming burp.

At close range, Meg caught a distinct whiff of peanut brittle.

Chapter Six

"I thought sugar was bad for dogs."

"It is. For dogs." Gabe glanced down at the bulldog waddling along on the other end of the leash. Minus the ducktail wig and the dazzling jumpsuit, Duke was nothing but plain ol' Diana. And uglier than ever. "In case you haven't noticed, Diana is not technically a dog. She's a cantankerous prima donna. Sweets can't hurt her. Nothing can. Not even contempt."

"Good thing." Meg stopped in the middle of the sidewalk and crouched down to rub Diana's ears. "She's a beautiful dog. Aren't you?" She nuzzled her nose against the bulldog's while she scratched the patch of brown-and-white fur where the top of Diana's chubby tail met her even chubbier body. It was a move that never failed to win Diana's undying devotion. The wagging that started in Diana's tail scooted along her broad back and over her chunky shoulders. Pretty soon, the entire dog was one big wiggle.

Much as he hated to identify with Diana, Gabe couldn't help thinking he'd react the same way if Meg looked at him like that.

He dashed the thought away just in time to see Meg glance up from the canine love-fest. By now, they were a couple of blocks from downtown. The twinkling

Christmas lights, sparkling trees and wreaths that decorated the shops and restaurants were nothing more than a memory. Meg's eyes shimmered even without the lights. "Cheer up," she told him. "You look like you're mad enough to bite through bricks. It's not so bad. You only have to watch her for three days, and she's an adorable dog."

"So adorable no one would let us into any of the restaurants with her."

"Health regulations." Meg pulled herself to her feet and brushed off the seat of her jeans. "They can't make exceptions. Even for superstars." She bent down and patted Diana on the head. "They wanted to. Every single owner of every single place we stopped. You saw how excited they all were. Every one of them wanted to let Diana in. They knew they couldn't. If they did, they'd have to let all those other dogs in, too, and no one would want to eat at a restaurant—"

"Yeah, yeah. I know." Gabe gave the leash a little giddyup snap and Diana started her snail's pace toddle down the sidewalk again. "No one would eat in a restaurant that was full of dogs. Can't say I blame them. But I'm hungry. And it's late. And by the time I get back to the Hideaway with this flea-bitten femme fatale, Maisie's sure to be in bed and you said yourself there isn't much to be had in the kitchen in the way of dinner and—"

"I've got a solution to that problem." Without warning, Meg crossed the road and headed off down an intersecting street lined with small, neat houses. Though he had no idea where she was going, Gabe was more than willing to follow.

He'd already taken a step into the street when he felt a tug on his arm. Leave it to Diana to chose that moment to get interested in a clump of ragged, knee-high weeds that grew along a stone wall in front of a nearby house, where an inflatable snowman shared space on the front lawn with two pink plastic flamingos.

"Why should we settle for a greasy fish fry?" Meg twirled around and called to him from across the street. "We'll have gourmet food instead."

"Gourmet? Out here in the middle of nowhere?" Gabe tugged at the leash. Diana planted all four feet and refused to budge an inch. He yanked the leash again. She turned her head and curled her top lip.

Gabe snarled back.

Seeing that they were getting nowhere, Meg slapped her thigh and whistled. Diana's head came up and as if it was her idea from the first, she took off after Meg at a trot. Gabe jogged along.

"What did you have in mind?" he asked when they finally caught up to Meg. "Pâté? Quail? Maybe a tasty little quiche?"

"How about some home-cooking?"

He'd been so focused on the ridiculous notion of playing baby-sitter to the canine version of Jabba the Hutt that he'd nearly forgotten who he was with. Not only was Meg the most gorgeous woman within miles, she also had a reputation for being a terrific chef. "Are you serious?"

"As a heart attack."

"You mean, you'd—"

"Take you home and feed you? Yeah. I've always had a soft spot for strays." Meg grinned and combed her fingers through her hair. Gabe decided right then and there that he was going to bury his face in that silky hair, that he was going to get drunk on the scent and the heat that rose off Meg's skin. That this might not be the time or the place, but he was going to do it anyway.

Because he couldn't stand to wait another minute.

He would've done it, too, if Diana hadn't chosen that moment to tug at the leash and nearly pull Gabe's arm out of its socket.

Grumbling, he yanked the dog away from the curb and the Christmas cookie that had been tossed there.

If Meg suspected how close he'd come to taking her in his arms, she didn't show it. She called to Diana and continued down the street. "I owe you," she told Gabe. "If you weren't at the park looking for me, you never would've been roped into this bonding experience with Diana. Something tells me you aren't very happy about it."

"It shows, huh?"

"A little." Farther up the street, Meg turned onto a slate walk bordered by flowers so lush they dipped over the walk and tickled Diana's nose. The dog stopped and sneezed once. Twice. By the time she was ready to get moving again, Meg had already climbed the steps to the front porch, where white wicker furniture vied for space with pots of flowers and an old dining room buffet that had been painted purple and red and was crammed with candles, candleholders and pots of herbs.

"You must want to avoid Latoya really bad." Meg tossed the comment at Gabe while they waited for Diana to pull her bulky shape from step to step. "I mean, you practically bribed Ingrid and Travis just so they wouldn't call her."

"Practically, nothing." At the top of the steps, Gabe waited for Diana to catch her breath and to check out the leg of the wicker rocker and just about the entire surface of the faded oriental rug at their feet. "It cost me a bundle, and I figure they got the better end of the deal."

When Diana stuck her nose into a pot of geraniums and snuffled, Meg laughed. "Oh, I don't know. You got Diana. That's definitely a plus. But you know, Gabe…" She pushed open a front door decorated with a pine wreath, a red bow and silver stars and moved back to let him walk inside ahead of her. "A girl's got to be curious. I mean about why you're trying so hard to avoid Latoya."

So Maisie hadn't told her.

Since Maisie hardly seemed the type who'd keep secrets, that was a bit surprising. It wouldn't have been nearly as disconcerting if Gabe didn't realize it meant that, sooner or later, he'd have to fess up. About hiding out from Dennis and Latoya. About the corner office with the view of Boston. About how, after all these years of following his heart and the inspiration that had always been there when he needed it, he'd arrived at a dead end.

He wondered why the idea of confessing it all to Meg made him feel so lousy.

He looked down to see that Diana was licking his shoe.

Gabe nudged the dog aside and entered the house, and as soon as he did, Meg sidled by him and flicked on a light. The room burst with color as startling as the ones Meg usually wore. Red walls. Yellow furniture. A rainbow of glass balls hanging in the front window and in the windows on either side of the fireplace.

"Home, sweet home." She gestured toward the room, her expression softening with warmth and obvious pride. "It's not much but—well, I figured that for as long as I stayed, I might as well make myself comfortable."

The second the words were out of her mouth, Meg regretted them. She hadn't meant to slip up and tell him that she had no intention of making the island her long-term home. She cringed, and hoping Gabe didn't notice—and that he wasn't nosy enough to ask what she was talking about if he did—she covered by hurrying toward the kitchen at the back of the house.

"Sit down," she called to him while she rummaged through her cupboards for a placemat, a bowl and a plate. She tucked the plate and the placemat under one arm, filled the bowl with water and holding it in both hands, carefully made her way back to the living room. She set the bowl on the coffee table, near where Gabe had plunked down on the couch, laid out the placemat on the hearth in front of the fireplace and called Diana over.

"Here you go, sweetie!" Meg set the water in front of the dog. "You must be very thirsty."

Diana was.

She lapped up the water with so much gusto, it splashed everywhere. Meg laughed as it spattered against the hardwood floor, the brightly patterned rug beneath the coffee table and the stack of magazines she hadn't gotten around to reading.

Gabe flicked a drop of water off his cheek. "Just goes to show that I have no business being in charge of a dog. I never thought of water."

"And food." Meg reached around to her back pocket and pulled out the sample of Love Me Tenders she'd been given at the park. "The poor darling must be starved."

"Unless she's full of peanut brittle."

"Even if she's full of peanut brittle. Hey, I like it as much as the next guy. Or girl." She patted Diana's head. "Especially when I'm upset and craving the kind of comfort only junk food can give. But even I have a taste for a good steak once in a while." Meg tore into the dog-food bag with her teeth, ripped it the rest of the way and dumped the little T-bone-shaped pieces onto the china plate.

Gabe's eyes went wide with horror. "You're not letting this mangy mutt use your good dishes, are you?" he asked.

"The dishes are old," she told him. "Besides, Diana is a star and deserves to be treated like one." She stooped and set the plate next to the water dish.

Diana took one look at the Love Me Tenders and her ears went back, her tail tucked under.

"She doesn't like them." Not sure she was seeing right, Meg knelt on the floor beside the dog. She showed Diana the dish of food, just in case she'd missed it. The dog's top lip curled and Meg could have sworn she rolled her eyes. "She doesn't like it." Meg set the plate on the floor and sat back, looking at Gabe in wonder. "She doesn't like Love Me Tenders."

He didn't seem the least bit surprised. Gabe shook his head, no happier now than he'd been when Diana first made her appearance at DeRivera Park. "It's not exactly something the fine folks at the Love Me Tenders company want everyone to know." He turned to Meg and there was just enough of a glimmer in his eyes to let her know he was kidding. Sort of. "I'm going to have to swear you to secrecy."

She crossed a finger over her heart. "Done. Only if Diana won't eat Love Me Tenders, what will she eat?"

Gabe frowned at the dog and his eyes narrowed. Just like Diana's did when she looked at him. "Peanut butter," he grumbled. "Popcorn. Corn chips, but only if they've been left out for a day to get stale. Beef jerky, the Cajun spice kind. Pork rinds, marshmallows, breath mints. Which, in case you haven't noticed, don't do a thing for her. Her mouth smells like the bottom of a Dumpster.''

''Of course it does with a diet like that!'' Meg rubbed the dog's head. ''I can't believe anyone would be so cruel to her.''

''It's called spoiling. They're spoiling her because she's a brat. Unfortunately, she's a high-priced brat. She started making commercials when she was a puppy and she's been working steadily ever since. No one wants to take the chance of offending her because when she's not happy, she refuses to perform.''

''Well, I'm going to get her some real food.'' Meg got to her feet and went back into the kitchen and Diana trotted along beside her. ''I've got some veal,'' she told the dog. ''And there's a grilled chicken breast left over from last night. There might even be some blue cheese.'' The dog plunked down and wagged her tail and Meg got to work. She already had the leftover chicken breast out and was slicing it when Gabe stuck his head in the room.

''Seems to me I heard something about dinner, too.''

He looked so at home leaning against the natural woodwork that framed the doorway between the kitchen and the dining room that Meg had to remind herself he was just a visitor. And practically a stranger. So why did her stomach flip and her heart turn over when he gave her a drop-dead smile?

She managed to smile back and hoped the slowness of her response didn't give away everything she was thinking. ''First things first,'' she told him. ''And the first thing we need to do is take care of the guest of honor.''

''Guest of honor.'' His smile was lost behind the thunderous expression that crossed his face. ''I'm a guest, too. I'm—''

It was so ridiculous, Meg had to laugh. "You're as spoiled as Diana," she told him. "Maybe that explains why you expect me to forget I asked why you're avoiding Latoya—and that you dodged the question."

Gabe plucked a piece of chicken off the cutting board and popped it into his mouth. "I never dodge," he insisted.

But that didn't explain why he was dodging again.

Meg studied him carefully. Whether at the Hideaway, in the park or in the close confines of her own kitchen, Gabe was as gorgeous as any man she'd ever met and as tempting as only a very few had ever been. But gorgeous or not, tempting or not, she noticed there was a certain wariness in his expression. It screamed self-protection. So did the fact that he'd crossed his arms over his chest.

It would take a stronger woman than Meg not to be curious. And when it came to curiosity, she'd never been strong.

"You haven't even told her where you are, have you? She knows you're somewhere between your LA office and wherever you're going, but that's all she knows." Meg scraped the chicken onto a plate and called Diana over. When she set the plate on the floor, the dog took one look at the perfectly grilled chicken and one noseful of the delicious aroma. With her front teeth, she picked up a piece of chicken. She rolled it around in her mouth, tasting it, snorting her opinion, she dropped it on the kitchen floor and waddled back into the living room.

So much for gourmet food.

Meg glanced at the untouched chicken and then at Gabe. "Latoya doesn't even know you're on the island, does she?"

"An island *you're* anxious to get off."

Meg had always believed that turnabout was fair play.

Except when someone turned the tables on her.

She picked up the plate of chicken and walked to the stove with it. She got out her wok, splashed some peanut oil into it and turned on the stove. There were mushrooms in the refrigerator and she sliced them and dumped them in, added some red pepper and sprinkled in some ginger.

And it wasn't until she did that she realized she was dodging, too.

''I never wanted to spend my entire life here,'' she said, and since it was no secret, she didn't mind sharing the information with Gabe. From the day she was four and had found out there was a whole other world on the far side of the water that surrounded South Bass Island, she'd never been shy about wanting to explore it. ''Spent most of my life telling everyone who'd listen—and a whole lot of folks who didn't—that someday, I was going to the mainland. I believed the sky was the limit. The day after I graduated from high school, I made good on the promise.''

''But you came back.''

It was so obvious, it didn't really deserve a reply.

She gave him one anyway.

''Tried my hand at life on the mainland.'' She tipped the chicken into the wok, as well as a half cup of the soy sauce and sherry concoction she mixed up ahead of time and kept in the refrigerator for when she made stir-fry. She heated it all through. ''Discovered I wasn't very good at it.''

''But you're planning on trying again.''

Meg looked at him over her shoulder. ''I've never had a problem admitting my mistakes, Gabe. Maybe because I've made so many that by now, saying *I'm sorry* is pretty much second nature. That doesn't help a lot. I swore upside down and inside out that I never wanted to see this place again. And now here I am and sometime while I wasn't looking, it somehow turned into home.''

That part was a secret she'd never meant to divulge—not to Gabe, not to anyone else—and why she'd done it was as much a mystery as why it seemed so important for Gabe to know.

''And you're telling me *I* sound spoiled?''

Not exactly the response she was expecting. When she went to get the dishes out of the cupboard, she saw him shaking his head in wonder.

''Let me get this straight,'' he said. ''You hated the island. The isolation. The boredom. Am I right?''

''You are.'' Meg piled chicken and vegetables onto the plates.

''You told everyone you hated it. Not surprising. You're not exactly the kind of woman who keeps a lot hidden.''

She wasn't sure if it was a compliment or an insult, and until she figured it out, Meg decided not to say a word.

''So you left. And then you came back. And now you've found out that instead of being the Black Hole of Calcutta the way you remembered it, this really isn't such a bad place. But just to prove a point, you're planning to leave anyway. Seems like that's going overboard, don't you think? You like it here, Meg. Why not just admit it? You like the people and the pace and if everything Maisie's told me is true, you like running the kitchen at the Hideaway and doing some catering on the side. And whatever you were running away from on the mainland can't find you out here in the middle of nowhere. You like that, too.''

This time he'd gone too far and just so he'd know it, Meg shoved one plate at Gabe, grabbed the bottle of soy sauce, two forks and two of the paper napkins she kept in the basket near the sink and went outside to the picnic table in the backyard.

Gabe watched the screen door slam behind Meg and decided right then and there that he was the biggest bonehead who'd ever walked the face of the earth.

"Everything was going so well." But that wasn't precisely true.

Everything was not going well. Not tonight. There was the Diana part of the equation. There was getting up in front of a thousand people and singing the ridiculous Love Me Tenders commercial. There was the part about Meg finding out he was supposed to be the *wunderkind* of advertising and, oh yes, the fact that she'd glommed onto how he was hiding out from Latoya.

"But other than that, things were going well," he mumbled. He didn't need to remind himself that he was the one who'd ruined it all.

Just like he didn't need to remind himself that it was all Meg's fault.

Gabe followed her outside to a pint-sized backyard hemmed in by a low stone wall. Right outside the back door was a redbrick patio surrounded by flowerpots, bird feeders and oil torches that Meg was lighting one by one. He set his plate down across from where she'd left hers, swung onto the bench that was pulled up next to the table, and propped his chin in his hands.

If it wasn't for Meg's smile and that damned orange top that had him staring at her like a starving man getting his first gander at an all-you-can-eat Las Vegas buffet, he wouldn't even have thought of broaching the subject of why she'd left the island and more importantly, why she'd come back.

But there was that smile. And that orange top. And because of it all, he wasn't satisfied with the kind of small talk he would've settled for with another woman.

He knew he never would be.

He wanted to get to know Meg. To really get to know her. He wanted to find out what made her tick and what she thought of cloning and baseball and world peace. He wanted to know what her favorite foods were and if she disliked hot tubs as much as he did, and he wanted to understand how she could be so stubborn that she'd leave a place she loved just to prove a point.

Most importantly, he wanted to know what had brought her back to the island. Because then he'd know the secrets of Meg's heart.

And Meg's heart was something he wanted to know intimately.

He decided now was as good a time to start as any.

He waited until she was finished with the torches, and when she sat down across from him, he saw how stiffly she held her shoulders. Although he'd sensed that the confession back in the kitchen had cost her, he hadn't realized how much.

Gabe picked up his fork and dangled it over his plate. ''You don't mind admitting you make mistakes, but you hate to lose. A fair assumption?''

''Damned straight.'' It was clear she was expecting something a little more heart-to-heart and just as clear that she was grateful Gabe had decided to take the high road, instead. ''I hate getting beat.'' She stabbed a piece of chicken with her fork. ''And coming back here and having everyone welcome me with open arms...

well, I'm a little too headstrong and independent to want to play the prodigal daughter.''

''So one of these days, you're going to take off again.''

Fork halfway to her mouth, she froze, and Gabe understood that the spark in her eyes had nothing to do with the torches that flamed all around them. ''I'm not running away,'' she told him.

''And I'm not saying you would be. I'm just saying...'' Gabe jabbed a piece of red pepper and a chunk of chicken. ''I'm just saying—'' The forkful of food was almost into his mouth before another thought struck. He dropped his fork and it clattered against the china plate. ''Is this the same chicken you gave Diana?''

Meg clicked her tongue. It's a perfectly good piece of chicken and there's no reason we should waste it and— Oh, my gosh!'' Even the orange glow of the torches couldn't hide how pale Meg's face had gone. She set down her fork and stared at the plate of food in front of her, her expression so filled with horror, Gabe couldn't help feeling sorry for her.

''I can't believe I did that.'' Meg's eyes were wide and her mouth fell open. ''I was so wrapped up in our conversation, and all the chopping and cooking, it's all so automatic and...I can't believe I really took the chicken I cut up for Diana and—'' As quickly as the color drained from her face, it rushed back up her neck and stained her cheeks and she burst into laughter.

''Wonderful!'' She jumped up from the bench. ''I offer you a gourmet meal and then I give you the dog's food. Great. That's a sure way to get a reputation as the finest cook on the island.''

It probably wasn't, but right about then, Gabe didn't care. Not about the chicken. Not about Diana who, at the sound of his fork hitting his plate, lumbered to the back door in hopes of finding some scrap of something dogs had no business eating.

It was hard to care about anything, even when Meg snatched the plates off the table and took them into the kitchen. Anything but her laughter that brightened the night and her smile, the one that outshone the moon peeking through the branches of the backyard cherry tree. That, and the smile that warmed Gabe clear through to the soles of his sneakers.

So, he was trying to get to know Meg's heart, huh?

Even after she was gone, the question dangled over Gabe's head, along with the subtle scent of raspberries that perfumed the air.

''Be careful what you wish for,'' he muttered to himself.

Because, though he'd been trying to learn the secrets of Meg's heart, it seemed that in the process, he'd uncovered a few of his own.

''DELICIOUS!'' Gabe brushed crumbs off his hands and sat back on the two-person swing at the far end of the brick patio. The movement sent the swing swaying and he glanced over at Meg who was sitting at his side, just out of reach. ''Who said you're not the Emeril of the island? That's the best meal I've had in ages.''

''Peanut butter and jelly doesn't exactly qualify as a meal.'' Meg waited until the swing slowed, then grabbed Gabe's plate and set it down with her own on the ground. ''Better than starving, I suppose. And better than sharing dinner with Diana.''

''Speaking of which...'' Gabe looked at the back door. For a second, he wondered what the dog was up to. Just as quickly, he decided he really didn't care. The night was warm and the blanket of stars above them was dulled only by the bright sliver of moon. Crickets chirped in the flowerbed, frogs croaked somewhere nearby, and he hadn't been kidding when he'd said dinner was delicious. Maybe it had something to do with Meg's kitchen magic or the kind of night that made a man too imaginative for his own good, but the peanut butter and jelly sandwich rivaled any meal he'd ever had.

And, besides all that, he was within arm's length of the most desirable woman he'd run into in as long as he could remember. Suddenly Gabe was willing to admit that the night had turned a corner and was headed in the right direction.

"Not how our date was supposed to work out."

No way Meg could've been reading his mind. Because he was thinking that the evening was just about perfect. Except that he hadn't kissed her yet.

And he was planning on taking care of that real soon.

"Oh, I don't know." Gabe slid his arm across the back of the swing. "Considering that you tried to poison me with dog food—"

"I didn't." She laughed.

"And that I've got to explain to Maisie how I left by myself and I'm bringing a dog back to the Hideaway with me..."

"I don't think she'll go for that." Meg shook her head. "You could leave Diana here for the night."

If he hadn't been planning on kissing her before, that one offer alone would've made him change his mind. "You're sure?" he asked, because it was the polite thing to do. Even if he was praying she wouldn't change *her* mind. "I wouldn't want to inconvenience you."

"Diana's too adorable to be an inconvenience. And I can take her with me when I go to the Hideaway to do breakfast in the morning—so you won't be without her for too long.''

He slid closer. ''Looks like I need to find a way to thank you.''

''Looks like you do.'' She turned just enough to tell him she knew exactly what he was planning.

''Any ideas?''

''A couple.'' Meg leaned toward him. ''How about you?''

''Oh, yeah.'' Gabe released the words on the end of a sigh that was half contentment, half ready-to-jump-out-of-his-skin. ''I'm thinking we could start with a kiss.''

''And?''

''And take it from there. You got any objections to seeing where it all might lead?''

''My only objection is that you're making me wait so long.''

''Then we'd better get going.'' He twined his fingers through hers.

He was expecting to feel a tingle of excitement when his hand touched Meg's. He was even counting on it.

What he wasn't expecting was an out-of-the-blue bolt that shot through him with the punch of lightning.

That, and the snatch of song lyric that suddenly filled his head.

''Tasty Time Burger, what a treat. Tasty Time Burger can't be beat!''

''Huh?'' Her head already tipped, her lips already parted, Meg froze in place. She was all set to get lost in the dreamy look in Gabe's eyes, and suddenly, the dreamy look was gone.

As if he'd poked a pair of scissors into an electrical outlet, he sat up straight. His eyes glinted. A smile split his face. A smile that had nothing to do with the promise of kisses and where they might lead.

"Tasty Time Burger, what a treat. Tasty Time Burger can't be beat." He repeated the strange words he'd mumbled when he took Meg's hand. They didn't make any more sense than the first time he'd said them.

"Did you hear that?" Gabe scrambled off the swing. "Did you hear what I said? I said Tasty Time Burger, what a—"

"I heard you, all right." Trying to stop the swing from swaying, Meg braced one foot against the ground. It worked for the swing. It didn't do much for the sudden swooping inside her stomach. Stunned, she watched him hurry toward the door.

"I'll see you tomorrow," he called to her and when he opened the back door, Diana rumbled outside. He stepped over the dog and into the kitchen. "We'll talk. Tomorrow. I promise. Right now, I've got to get back to the Hideaway and..."

She heard the front door close and the sounds of Gabe's footsteps as they faded away.

"Looks like it's you and me," she told the dog. Absently rubbing her hand where her skin still tingled, she stared at the spot where, only moments before, Gabe had been sitting and ready to kiss her. "I don't know about you," she told Diana, "but I'm thinking junk food is definitely in order."

Diana barked her approval of the plan and side by side, they went into the house in search of corn chips and marshmallows.

Chapter Seven

The first time Gabe opted for dancing hamburgers over Meg, she'd been nothing if not confused.

This time, she was just plain mad, and not even the bag of corn chips, the roll of breath mints or the ice cream sundae she'd shared with Diana the night before had helped.

She punched her fist into the football-shaped lump of bread dough on the marble-topped table in the Hideaway kitchen.

"Tasty Time Burgers, what a treat!" Meg grumbled the words while she kneaded the dough, lifted it, slapped it down and started all over again. "That's the last time I'll—"

"Oh, raisin bread!" Maisie pushed open the kitchen door and stopped in her tracks. It was too early for any of their guests to be up and Maisie was still in her pink chenille bathrobe and the pink fuzzy slippers Meg had bought her for her birthday. Breathing in the aroma of cinnamon, she walked into the kitchen smiling. "You hardly ever make raisin bread. What a treat!"

"Like—" Meg slapped the dough on the table "—Tasty Time Burgers?"

"Tasty Time Burgers?" Maisie tilted her head, studying Meg's *thunderous* expression and the way she was manhandling the dough. Even this early in the morning, Maisie was wearing lipstick and she pursed her bright pink lips. "Something tells me we need coffee."

"Not to stay awake." Meg caught herself with her fist clenched and her arm cocked, ready to give the dough another vigorous punch. If there was one thing she was proud of, it was the taste and texture of her breads, and she knew that overkneading and rough handling would result in a bread that was coarse and far below her usual high standards.

She punched the dough anyway.

"Been up all night," she told Maisie. She had greased a large bowl earlier and she set the dough in it and covered the bowl with a cloth. She carried it over to the warm, draft-free spot near the pantry and set it down on the countertop. "First I had a pity party. Then I couldn't sleep because I ate so many corn chips my stomach was in full rebellion. And even if I hadn't..."

She went back to the marble table and starting cleaning up, and though she'd never put much stock in the symbolism her English lit teachers had always insisted they found in novels, Meg couldn't fail to catch the significance. Clean it up, wash it up, put it away and forget about it.

If only she could do that to her relationship with Gabe.

Sighing, Meg turned and leaned against the table. "He's talking hamburgers again," she told Maisie.

"Hamburgers, huh?" Maisie waited while the coffeemaker finished dripping, then reached for two mugs and poured. She went to the refrigerator, got out a carton of cream and on her way back across the kitchen, grabbed a few packets of sugar out of the plastic container of fast-food extras Meg kept around just in case. Maisie didn't bother with the crystal cream pitcher or sugar bowl and that was significant in its own English lit sort of way. She raised her snowy eyebrows, the expression so innocent and so grandmotherly Meg knew she was in for the third degree.

"Is he doing this at…er…" Maisie's cheeks turned the color of the tea roses she'd bought on the mainland the day before to use on this morning's breakfast table. "What I mean to ask, of course, even though it's none of my business and I really shouldn't even be asking and…" She hauled in a deep breath. "Is he doing this at inopportune moments?"

Meg couldn't help herself. Sleep or no sleep, miserable or not, there was something about Maisie's attempt at decorum that made her laugh. "Inopportune moments? You mean like were we in the middle of some passionate scene straight out of a romance novel?" Meg didn't need to wait for Maisie to answer. Of course that was what Maisie meant. In one way or another, it was always what Maisie meant. "No," she said, her voice firm enough to let her grandmother know she wasn't kidding. "No passionate scenes." She caught herself sighing. "It never had a chance to get that far."

"Really?" It wasn't nearly as significant as it was embarrassing and exasperating yet for some reason Meg couldn't fathom, Maisie's eyes suddenly sparkled with interest.

"You're not surprised. About the hamburgers, I mean."

"Surprised?" Maisie ripped open three bags of sugar and added cream to her coffee. She stirred it, tapped the spoon against the rim of her mug and turned her attention back to Meg. "Not surprised," she said, blowing away the steam that drifted over the mug. "Not about the hamburgers, anyway. After all, Gabe is a busy man and quite prominent in his field, or so I'm told. He must spend an awful lot of time thinking about his work. But I am surprised he's thinking about it at such odd moments. Details?"

Bad enough that she'd been going over the details with Diana until the wee hours of the morning. Now Maisie wanted them, too? Meg set down her mug and got to work at the bread table, her movements quick, efficient and just twitchy enough to play into the whole symbolism thing. She forced herself to slow down and take it easy, using a plastic scraper to get the excess bits of dough off the marble. "There are no details," she told her grandmother. "No noteworthy details, anyway. We were at my house—"

"Were you?"

Meg didn't need to turn around to know that Maisie was giving that little detail far more emphasis than it deserved. "We had Diana with us. I mean Duke," she added just so Maisie would get the picture. "He... she—the dog is here on a promotional tour and Gabe is baby-sitting. We couldn't get into any of the restaurants in town because of the dog. I promised him dinner, we ate—"

"Something appropriate, I hope."

"Not if you're talking about oysters or a few pots of that aphrodisiac tea you sell in the Love Shack." Meg scraped all the little scraps of dough into one corner of the table, then scooped them into her hand and dumped them in the disposal. "We ate dinner," she said, getting her thoughts and her grandmother back on track. "And then we were sitting on the swing in the backyard and maybe I'm overimaginative but..." She paused near the sink, her mind drifting back to everything that had happened in the moonlit garden the night before.

Gabe with that delicious little half smile on his face and the reflected light of the torches glittering in his eyes.

Gabe leaning closer, telling her he wanted to thank her.

Gabe asking her if she had anything in particular in mind and knowing full well that the ideas rioting through her head and through her heart and through every inch of her body were exactly the ones that were playing through his.

Gabe, twining his fingers through hers.

And talking Tasty Time Burgers.

Meg's shoulders drooped. Just the way her expectations had the night before.

''I could have sworn he was going to kiss me,'' she said, her voice reflecting all the disappointment she'd felt then. And now. ''But he didn't.'' She leveled her grandmother the I-told-you-so look she'd learned from Maisie. ''He talked hamburgers instead.''

''Very interesting.'' Maisie went to the refrigerator for the pitcher of orange juice. She poured a glass, offered it to Meg and when Meg turned it down, drank it herself. Fortified, she faced her granddaughter again. ''So what are you going to do about it?'' she asked.

''Do?'' Meg glanced at the clock. She had another hour before she needed to serve breakfast. ''I'm going to fry some bacon,'' she said. ''I'm going to take out the butter so it will be room temperature when we serve it. I'm going to warm the muffins I made yesterday so we can offer them, and, for those of our guests who might not like muffins, I'm going to slice some bread, toast it and serve it with some of that raspberry jam I got over at the market and—''

''And that's not what I mean and you know it. What are you going to do, Meg? About Gabe?''

Though Maisie was over seventy, her hearing had never caused her trouble. Which made Meg wonder why her grandmother wasn't hearing her now. ''I'm going to make breakfast,'' Meg said. ''For your guests. And even though I don't think he's going to eat it because he'll be too busy drawing pictures of buildings or too busy mumbling about hamburgers, I'll even make breakfast for Gabe. Because it's my job. But I'm not going to hobnob, Grandma, if that's what you're thinking. I'm not going to sashay in there like some kind of floury seductress and try to get the man to notice me. He's made it pretty clear that's not going to happen. No matter what I do.''

''That's not precisely true, dear.'' Before Meg could budge, Maisie already had the bacon out and a frying pan on the stove. ''He did notice. You said so yourself. He was interested. He was all set to kiss you. And still…'' Maisie's voice drifted off. ''I don't suppose you'd like to take a tray of coffee up to his room?''

The expectant smile on Maisie's face disappeared when she turned her attention to Meg. ''No,'' Maisie mumbled, ''I didn't think so. Then we could find some other pretense to get you up there. We could pretend the phones aren't working. That we weren't able to make a wake-up call or—''

''No. No, no, no.'' Meg sidled around her grandmother, reached for the bacon and tossed it in the pan. ''Besides,'' she mumbled, reluctant to admit the truth, although she knew Maisie would give her no peace until she did. ''I've already been up to his room this morning.''

''You have?'' Maisie brightened like the lighthouse over near the Lime Kiln ferry dock. ''I ask for details and you leave that one out? It's fairly important, wouldn't you say?''

''No, I would not.'' While the bacon was sizzling, Meg got out the muffins and the butter. ''Nothing happened, Grandma. As a matter of fact, Gabe was sound asleep. He never even knew I was there.''

''Never knew—'' Maisie's snowy brows dipped over her eyes. ''Then why bother, dear? I mean, why even go up to Love Me Tender if you weren't going to—''

''I had a mission. I accomplished it.'' Though Meg knew her grandmother already had the table set with the Sunday china and silver, she went to the dining room, anyway. It was the only way she'd get a moment's rest from Maisie's endless questions and maybe—just maybe—the simple act of straightening the dishes, checking the linen and making sure the roses looked just right in the crystal vase at the center of the table would help keep her mind off other things. One thing in particular. One man.

Never one to be kept out of the loop, at least not for long, Maisie pushed open the swinging door and followed Meg. ''You left him up there?'' She sounded disappointed and unwilling to believe that any woman could walk away from the temptation of Gabe in bed. Almost as unwilling as Meg had been to do the walking away. ''All by himself?''

''All by himself? Did I say that?'' Because she deserved it for her attempts at matchmaking, Meg gave her grandmother a wide-eyed, innocent look. ''I never said he was all by himself. As a matter of fact, the last time I looked, he was in bed with a charming, popular, gorgeous female.''

GABE WASN'T THE TYPE who kidded himself. No more often than necessary, anyway.

He knew there was a difference between the dream he'd been having about Meg and the reality of the wet kisses he felt on his cheeks.

Too bad.

The dream was pretty good. Mighty sensual. Really graphic.

The dream was all about Meg, in—and out of—that orange top. Meg, in—and out of—those nice, snug jeans. Meg, out of—and in—the pink Cadillac bed. And Gabe, deep inside her with her body straining against his, their hearts beating a manic rhythm and every one of the fantasies he'd been having about her since the moment they met coming true in living color.

It definitely did not included dog kisses.

"Diana!" Gabe's eyes flew open and as he pushed the dog—and her way-too-slimy tongue—away. He sat up in bed. "What are you doing here, you mangy mutt? And how did you get in here in the first place?"

The answer seemed obvious and Gabe's hopes rose, and a certain sensitive portion of anatomy stood at attention, too. If Diana was in Love Me Tender, it meant Meg might be in Love Me Tender. And if Meg was here in the room, he just might have the opportunity to start making some of those dreams come true.

It only took one look around the room to prove that he was wrong; he was alone.

His hopes dashed, his expectations back firmly where they belonged and that certain, sensitive portion of his anatomy under control if not gratified, he scowled at the dog.

"You smell like corn chips," he told her. Any other female he knew would have had the decency to sneer back. All Diana did was drool.

Because he couldn't stand being in bed with any female who was drooling (unless it was Meg and she was drooling over him), Gabe pushed back the blankets and reached for his boxers. He pulled them on, scraped a hand over his face and looked around at the shambles that had once been Love Me Tender.

Sheets of paper on the piano.

Sheets of paper on the floor.

Sheets of paper were scattered across the trunk of the Cadillac. There was a trail that went from the couch and to the soda fountain.

All of them empty.

Before he could get too depressed, he reminded himself that it wasn't true. He went over to the piano and found the one piece of paper he'd written on as soon as he'd run in from Meg's.

''Tasty Time Burgers what a treat. Tasty Time Burgers can't be beat.''

At the sound of his voice, Diana tipped her head. She looked decidedly unimpressed.

''OK, so it's not Shakespeare.'' With a sigh, Gabe slapped the paper back on the piano. ''But it's a start. And hey, with the right music, the right special effects... It's not half bad.''

Even if it didn't do anything to alleviate the worried look on Diana's face, it should have cheered Gabe up. It actually might have if it wasn't for all those other pieces of empty paper. And the memory that after he'd come up with those two lines, his mind had gone completely blank.

Before he had a chance to dwell on that for too long, Diana barked. A clear sign that she was ready to get down from the bed and was not about to take *no* for an answer.

''All right.'' Gabe returned to the bed. One hand on

either side of her body, he lifted the dog off the mattress. She sagged like a bowl of jelly. She smelled like a teen-aged boy's gym locker. She weighed a ton.

When he set her on the floor, she thumped her appreciation and licked Gabe's ankle.

"Maybe you're thirsty, huh?" Gabe remembered how the dog dove into the bowl of water at Meg's. "I suppose we could find something to put some water in. What do you say?"

Diana didn't say anything. She did follow him over to the soda fountain, and when he found a small, shallow bowl and filled it for her, she showed her gratitude with a look that was almost a smile.

Gabe watched her drink and when the dish was dry, he filled it again. "So what do you think?" he asked the dog. "Looks like it's time to go downstairs and take our lumps. And I'm not talking sugar."

It was a lame attempt at humor. That probably explained why the dog didn't laugh.

"I owe her," he said, grabbing clean clothes out of the dresser drawer and heading for the shower. "I don't know what I'm going to say, but I do know I have some major explaining to do." He stopped next to the life-sized, cardboard cutout of the King. "It's now or never," he told the dog. "I'm going to be lonesome tonight and a permanent resident at the Heartbreak Hotel if I don't apologize."

Diana was apparently no connoisseur of music, but she knew the cold, hard facts when she heard them. She barked her agreement.

GOOD INTENTIONS WERE one thing. Following through on them was something else altogether.

Gabe searched high and low for Meg, both before and after breakfast. But even though plates of buttermilk pancakes, bacon and muffins were all on the table when he went down to the dining room, there was no sign of the chef. There was no sign of her when Gabe left with Diana for a quick walk at lunchtime, either, or when they went out again later in the day and returned with roast beef sandwiches from the little deli in town and thick chocolate milkshakes from the ice cream parlor they passed as they walked back to the Hideaway.

In fact, except for that one hairy little detail—Diana—there was no sign Meg had been at the Hideaway at all that day.

The dog nudged him with her nose and Gabe jerked back to reality. They were sitting on the wraparound porch that hugged the Hideaway, and while Gabe would have been content to stare at the slate-blue waters of Lake Erie and think about where he'd gone wrong and what he could possibly do to fix it, Diana was nothing if not single-minded. Panting, she stared at the milkshake. Panting even louder, she swung her beady little eyes to Gabe. When she'd finally hypnotized him and he reached for the spoon, she barked her approval.

"I don't know about you, but it looks to me like we're going nowhere at warp speed." He ladled a spoonful of milkshake into Diana's mouth. "Nowhere with Tasty Time Burger. Nowhere with Meg. Not exactly what I had in mind when I got onto that ferry. Maybe I should just—"

He was interrupted by the sound of a piano from inside the Hideaway.

Gabe turned toward the door. Hoping to avoid his fellow guests and maybe catch a glimpse of Meg coming into or going out of the kitchen door, he'd chosen this spot on the back porch with care. It sounded as though, in the meantime, a troop of guests had arrived in front. He heard laughter from the parlor and a piano rendition of "Anything Goes," played with a great deal of skill and no small amount of flamboyance.

"Party time," he told Diana. She'd apparently figured that out. Sensing that laughter and noise equaled an audience and that an audience equaled food and undivided attention, the dog took off running for the back door and would have clawed her way through the screen if Gabe hadn't opened it for her. As soon as he did, she waddled off in the direction of the voices.

"Just what every special occasion needs. A party crasher who eats too much, smells bad and sheds on the furniture." He took off after her, and when she barged into the parlor, he skidded to a stop at the door.

"Sorry." Gabe was talking to Maisie and the strapping man with the iron-gray hair who stood with her near the fireplace fawning over Diana and a chocolate lab. He was talking to the good-looking young man with a ready smile and a steady hand who was sitting on the piano bench and to the pregnant woman standing next to him—a woman who would've been the spitting image of Meg if she was taller, thinner and had redder hair.

He was talking to all of them.

And looking only at Meg.

He was talking about Diana.

And thinking about the night before.

Through it all, Meg sat perfectly still on the chintz love seat, her hands poised above a china pot and teacups. He had to admit she was nothing if not determined. After the momentary blip caused by Diana's—and Gabe's—entrance, she went right back to what she was doing. She poured the tea and when she was done, she called Diana and the other dog over, and slipped them each a piece of shortbread. She never once glanced in Gabe's direction.

"Perfect!" Maisie's smile was as bright as the sunshine outside the window, although what she was talking about was a mystery to Gabe. Perfect? There was nothing perfect about the firm set of Meg's chin, the rigid line of her shoulders. There was nothing perfect about the little voice inside his head, either. The one that reminded him that he'd chosen Tasty Time Burgers over Meg and now, he was getting his well-deserved comeuppance.

"This is perfect. Now we're all here." Maisie introduced Gabe to Doc Ross and to Meg's older sister, Laurel, and Laurel's husband Noah. Now that Christmas in July week was over, she explained, they'd all shown up to help get the decorations put away. "You'll stay and have tea, of course." She didn't give Gabe much of a chance to refuse the invitation. Before he could, Maisie had her arm through his.

"Mr. Morrison is the man who wrote the Love Me Tenders commercial."

"No kidding?" Laurel grinned. "Felix loves Love Me Tenders." The chocolate lab was nose-to-nose with Diana, having a conversation that pretty much consisted of woofs and grunts. She bent and called Diana over and though the dog didn't look happy about leaving her newfound friend, she also knew better than to miss an opportunity, for either adoration or food. Laurel laughed and scratched Diana's ears. "We never would've tried Love Me Tenders if not for Duke. He's adorable."

"He's a she." Meg popped off the love seat and marched to the door. Before she could get there, Maisie moved to block the doorway.

"Don't leave, dear. Mr. Morrison is going to play for us."

Gabe felt the blood drain from his face. His palms got damp. His mouth got dry. "I don't think so." Automatically, he backed away from the piano and when Noah slid off the bench to make room for him, Gabe backed up some more. "Another time, maybe. I'm kind of busy and—"

"We'd love to hear you play." Noah wrapped an arm around his wife's shoulders. "I mean, I play some. And I'm pretty good..." Although the conversation was about music, it was clear Noah and Laurel were communicating something else in the smile they exchanged. "But I'm a doctor, not a musician. It would be a real treat to hear a professional play."

"Play one of your own songs, Mr. Morrison," Laurel chimed in. "You've probably written hundreds of jingles. I bet we'd recognize some of them."

"Yeah, how about that Tasty Time Burger commercial you're working on?" There was no mistaking the chill in Meg's voice or the ice in the look she aimed in Gabe's direction. She was doing her best to give an iceberg impression, too. Cool and placid. But while the rest of them might have been fooled, Gabe knew better than to fall into the old appearances-are-deceiving trap. There were all kinds of things going on under the surface, and none of them were pretty.

"Oh no, not Tasty Time Burger." A force of nature in her own fluffy-old-lady way, Maisie laughed off Meg's suggestion and tugged Gabe toward the piano. "Gabe's just working on Tasty Time Burger and there's an old superstition, you know. A musician never previews the work he's composing. Not until he's absolutely ready."

There was no superstition. None Gabe knew of, anyway. But he'd have to remember that dodge in case he ever needed it again.

"I know. How about Love Me Tenders?" By the time Maisie suggested it, she was already elbowing Gabe onto the piano bench. Her hands on his shoulders, she persuaded him to sit. "Everyone's talking about it," she twittered. "About the lovely job you did at the party in the park last night. And such an exciting announcement! That you wrote the lyrics *and* the music. That you sing the song in the commercial."

Everyone applauded.

Everyone except Meg.

"Love Me Tenders. Sure." As if he was afraid they might jump up and bite, Gabe touched the keys gently. They responded the way they always did, or the way they used to, anyway. Effortlessly. And as naturally as taking his next breath.

Hope bubbled through him. He played one chord. Another.

Gabe exhaled a little sigh and grinned. "Okay." He sat back for just a second and pulled in a breath, preparing himself as he always did before he let the music take over and take him wherever it wanted to go. "Love Me Tenders," he said, although the tune needed no introduction. He played it through slowly and carefully and when each of the notes came out exactly as he'd written it, he sighed with relief and with satisfaction. He started into the jingle again.

This time, Gabe let himself go. It was hardly weighty music. He'd never fooled himself about that. But there was a certain sweetness to the tune, a certain tug-at-your-heart (and consumers' purse strings) enchantment to it, and he played it for all it was worth. The third time through, Laurel and Noah joined in.

"Love my Tenders. Love them lots."

Maisie and Doc Ross added their voices.

"Shaped like little steaks."

Not to be outdone, or maybe because she had a really mean streak, Meg helped with the big finish. Louder than the others. Stronger than the others. Her voice was as abrasive as cleanser. As unnerving as the squeal of tires peeling rubber against blacktop. As scary as the latest teen horror-scream flick.

"Love my Tenders. Eat them all. They're not fried, they're baked."

Gabe had never been a temperamental artist. He didn't believe in it, and he couldn't afford it. But even his artistic sensibilities couldn't stand up against the punishment of Meg's singing. He got to the end of the song and hit a wrong note.

As if the move was choreographed, everyone winced.

Gabe tried the last bar again.

He played it perfectly. Until the last note.

Then he hit a clunker.

Mortified, mystified and just plain annoyed, he tried a third time.

And hit a note so flat, it made everyone cringe.

"Oh, come on! I might not be able to sing but at least I can get a simple tune right." He already knew Meg was not the most patient of souls. Apparently, that impatience extended even to music. She leaned over Gabe's shoulder and plunked out the notes of the song one by one and when she got to the final note—the one Gabe hadn't been able to find for the life of him—she played it properly.

Everyone cheered. Except Gabe.

And that would have been the end of that if Meg's hand hadn't brushed his.

By now, the feeling was familiar.

As soon as Meg's hand touched his, Gabe felt the rush of heat. The tingle. The prickles of excitement and those first few tickles of inspiration.

Before he even knew what he was doing, his hands were on the keys again and he was playing. It wasn't much. Just a couple of opening bars, a catchy little bridge. Notes of a song he didn't recognize.

The song he knew was destined to have America humming along to his new Tasty Time Burger commercial.

When he was done, Gabe sat back, and awareness rushed through him. He'd finally figured out what was going on.

''No.'' He whispered the word and he didn't even care if the rest of them thought he was crazy. Maybe he was. He looked up at Meg who was completely oblivious. He looked down to where their hands were side-by-side on the keys.

''No,'' he muttered again. ''It can't be. It can't be true.''

The sick feeling in his stomach said otherwise and Gabe sat back, winded, shaken.

And completely flabbergasted.

Chapter Eight

"Love Nibbles, chocolate-flavored. Passion Plus, peppermint-scented. Wild Thing, vanilla. Tropical Nights, coconut. Eve's Temptation, green apple."

Leave to it Maisie to find flavored massage oils with the world's least subtle names.

Fighting to keep her mind on her work and off the thoughts that floated through her head as she checked inventory in the Love Shack, Meg marked off the appropriate items on the list she had attached to a clipboard. She moved on to the next row.

"Burning Love, apricot. Good Enough to Eat, tutti-frutti. Nuts About You, peanut butter. Paris Erotica, champagne. Oh!"

With a barely controlled screech, she gave up. She slapped the clipboard down on a nearby table covered with a lace cloth and a selection of scented candles with names like Seduction, Burning Love and Hot Stuff.

"This is the last thing I need," she muttered, but since she was alone in the Cupid's Hideaway gift shop, her protest went nowhere at all.

Unlike her fantasies, which were well on their way here, there and everywhere.

As long as *everywhere* was where Gabe happened to be.

No happier to admit the sorry fact than she was to realize there wasn't a thing she could do about it, Meg turned and went to the other side of the shop, far away from the gleaming blue-glass bottles of flavored massage oils and all the interesting possibilities they conjured.

Love Nibbles-coated Gabe. Wild Thing-scented Gabe. Those nice, muscular arms glossy with oil that smelled like Paris Erotica, tasted like champagne and made her just as crazy-drunk. Those long, lean legs glossy with the stuff and his hands, slick and hot, smoothing oil over her shoulders, across her breasts and—

This time, Meg didn't even try to control herself. She let out a shriek that was muffled by the wisps of lacy panties displayed on a rack to her right and the gauzy negligees hanging in the antique wardrobe on her left.

Spending the day in the Love Shack was, she decided, the equivalent of a chocoholic being sentenced to a long-term stay at a Godiva factory.

Temptation all over the place.

And no lack of ideas about how to turn that temptation into reality.

''Fat chance.'' With a sigh, Meg gave up even trying to make sense of the whole thing. Facts were facts and the fact was, ever since he'd stepped across the threshold of Cupid's Hideaway, Gabe Morrison had been her own personal equivalent of a solid-chocolate Easter bunny. Yummy. Mouth-watering. And oh, so tantalizing.

''Don't forget about bad for you, clogs up your arteries and stop your heart, makes you sick and miserable,'' she reminded herself.

Disgusted with herself and with the ideas that had been pounding through her head since the night Gabe had almost kissed her, Meg decided a change of venue was in order.

''No more massage oil,'' she told herself, and she checked the note Maisie had written on scented, flowery stationery before she'd left for a day of shopping on the mainland with Doc Ross.

''After the candles and the massage oil,'' the note said in Maisie's flowing, old-fashioned handwriting, ''don't forget the sex toys.''

Meg groaned and laid her head on the display case that also served the Love Shack as a counter. She stared down into the glass case.

And vibrators, glow-in-the-dark condoms and edible underwear stared back at her.

So did Diana.

''Diana?'' Meg stood up like a shot and peered over the display case. Diana plunked down on the floor, wagged her stumpy little tail and barked a greeting.

And if Diana was here…

Meg's heart thumped to a painful stop. Feeling as if she'd been caught shoplifting by the very person she'd lifted out of reality and dropped into a string of red-hot fantasies, she looked around the gift shop, not sure what she was going to say—or do—when she found Gabe looking back.

Luckily for her, Diana had wandered into the Love Shack without her baby-sitter.

''Good thing, too.'' Silly to think that even if Gabe happened to walk into the gift shop that sold anything and everything—but nothing in good taste—he could somehow read her mind.

Silly.

But she wasn't about to take any chances.

She hurried around to the front of the counter and shooed Diana toward the door. "The last thing I need at a time like this is company," she told the dog. "Especially when that company is—Gabe!" She screeched to a stop just a millimeter from running headlong into his chest. This morning, that chest was encased in a fire-engine-red golf shirt. Meg figured it was probably just a shade or two less flaming than her cheeks.

After what she'd been thinking about him, she should have been relieved when Gabe acted as if she wasn't there.

She was relieved, she told herself in no uncertain terms. Right before she reminded herself that she was relieved in a snubbed, insulted sort of way.

Stinging from the realization and hating to admit it bothered her so much, she stepped back to give Gabe—and herself—plenty of breathing room. Good thing, too. Otherwise he would have just about run over her in his attempt to catch up with Diana.

"There you are!" Gabe made straight for the dog. "I told you to stay close." He reached into his pocket and pulled out a bag of Cajun-spiced beef jerky. "You haven't finished your breakfast."

First it was dancing hamburgers.

Now it was beef jerky.

One look at the food and Diana forgot Meg was alive. Without standing up, the dog wiggled its plump little butt, shuffled its feet and turned. She gazed lovingly at Gabe. And at the strip of beef jerky he held in his hand.

"There you go." Gabe ripped off a piece of jerky and tossed it into Diana's mouth. When she barked for another bite, he obliged her, and it wasn't until she'd finished the entire strip that he brushed his hands together, tucked the empty package into the back pocket of his jeans and bothered to look Meg's way.

"Sorry." He wasn't a guy who did sheepish well. Which made Meg wonder why he looked as though he'd been called to the principal's office. After a quick smile aimed somewhere over Meg's left shoulder, he turned his attention back to Diana. "I told her not to come in here," he said. "I told her dogs probably aren't allowed to have the run of the place, but, well..." He glanced at the same spot again and curious, Meg looked over her shoulder.

Apparently, the map of the island hanging next to a sixteen-by-twenty reproduction of the sepia-toned picture from the dining room held more appeal than Meg did.

"No problem." Meg was talking about allowing Diana to make herself at home at the Hideaway, and just so Gabe wouldn't think she was talking about anything else—like his refusal to meet her eyes—she set him straight. "Now that the weekend's over, everyone else has checked out. Maisie said she didn't mind having Diana around. As long as she behaves herself."

"Oh, she will." When Gabe glanced down at the dog, he didn't sneer.

That only made Meg more curious.

"What's going on?" she asked, and maybe it was a figment of an imagination that had been in overdrive ever since she'd walked into the Love Shack, but she could have sworn he actually winced.

"Going on?" He smiled. "What do you mean, going on?"

"I mean you two. You. And Diana." Eager to put some distance between herself and the electricity that crackled anytime Gabe was near, Meg did a one-eighty.

She hurried around to the other side of the glass counter to track down the rest of the inventory sheets Maisie had promised to leave on top of the antique cigar box where she kept change. She retrieved the papers and tapped them into a neat pile against the display case. ''You two seem to be getting along pretty well.''

''We do? We're not.'' Gabe dismissed the idea with a twitch of his shoulders and a shake of his head that was so forceful, it caused a bit of inky hair to flop over his forehead. He brushed it back with one hand. ''She snores. She eats like a pig, and every time my phone rings—''

As if the scene had been planned, the cell phone in Gabe's pocket started ringing, and, on cue, Diana let loose with a high-pitched howl.

Gabe made a face. ''That's what she does,'' he said, yelling so he could be heard over both the phone and the dog. ''And she keeps it up. For as long as the phone rings.''

No question it was annoying. The howling and the ringing. Meg took a couple of steps back. ''Maybe you should just turn the phone off.''

''That doesn't work. It beep when there's a voice mail message and Latoya—''

''Leaves plenty of messages. Yeah. Then maybe you should just talk to her.''

Gabe plucked the phone out of his pocket and checked the caller ID. ''Not Latoya this time,'' he said and because Diana picked that exact moment to step up the volume of her song, he repeated himself. ''It's not Latoya. It's Dennis.''

As abruptly as it started, the ringing stopped.

So did the howling.

Both Meg and Gabe heaved sighs of relief.

"It wasn't Latoya," Gabe said, and even though he wasn't yelling any more, his voice sounded loud in the sudden silence. "It was Dennis. My business partner."

"You have a partner?" Meg turned the idea over in her head at the same time she reached for the postcards on the spinning rack set on the counter. The Hideaway wasn't a typical island tourist spot and the postcards it sold weren't typical, either. In addition to the ones that showed the marina, the monument commemorating a nearby lake battle from the War of 1812 and a shot of the downtown bars, most of the others were frilly and romantic. Hearts and flowers. Antique reproductions. A few that showed Victorian couples in what must have been—a hundred or so years ago—scandalous poses. They were way more tame than the covers on the paperbacks Maisie kept on the shelf in her office and Meg was way past the point where a little bit of skin and a hint of heavy breathing was going to do much for her libido. Still, she didn't need to take any chances.

She shuffled the Victorian scenes to the bottom of the pile and quickly counted the postcards; when she was done, she put them back where they belonged.

"This Dennis..." She marked the inventory sheet to show how many of each postcard the Love Shack had and how many had to be reordered. "He's trying to find you, too, huh?"

"It's not like I left them high and dry." Apparently, it was as straight an answer as Meg was likely to get. Gabe set his cell phone on the counter and, shoving his hands into his pockets, he did a turn around the shop. "I called them early this morning," he said, pacing to the door and back again. "Left a message on Dennis's voice mail. And just so you know, I left a message for Latoya, too. I let them know that I was alive and well.

You think they'd be happy. But no. They're still calling. Both of them.''

Meg propped her chin in her hands. ''Maybe they like to hear Diana sing.''

''Maybe if the world heard Diana's real singing voice, sales of Love Me Tenders would hit rock bottom.''

''So maybe Dennis and Latoya just want to hear *your* voice. To remind them that thanks to you, Love Me Tender sales are going through the roof.''

''Maybe not. And you see, that's what I wanted to talk to you about.'' Just as Gabe didn't do sheepish, he didn't do awkward, either. Probably never had. After all, why would any guy with looks, personality, a Porsche and a voice that made dog-food buyers swoon feel self-conscious? About anything.

None of that explained why he started pacing again. Or why, instead of looking at Meg, he kept his gaze firmly on the Oriental rug on the floor. ''It's this jingle I have to write,'' he said and for a guy who made more than just a good living writing jingles, he didn't sound very happy about the prospect of writing another one. ''It's for a fast-food place.''

''Tasty Time Burgers.'' The reminder was like a splash of ice water and Meg reined in her fantasies. She did a quick scan of the display case and refused to get sidetracked—even when she got to the glow-in-the-dark condoms. She marked the appropriate place on one of the inventory sheets. ''No big news there. You've been talking burgers since Day One.''

''I've been talking burgers, yes.'' Gabe paced to the armoire that took up nearly the entire far wall of the shop and from there, over to the door. The Hideaway (minus modernization and the anything-but-ordinary improvements Maisie had made to the place) had once been a private residence and at the time, what was destined to be the Love Shack was nothing more than an enclosed porch. It wasn't a big room and Gabe was mighty restless. He covered the length of the shop in five easy steps, pivoted and started back the other way.

"I've been talking Tasty Time Burgers and I've been thinking Tasty Time Burgers because I've got this jingle to write and it hasn't been coming easy. I mean, not as easily as it usually does."

"So you're preoccupied."

"Preoccupied." He nodded.

"And in a world of your own."

"Pretty much." Gabe stopped in front of the display case and for the first time since he'd walked into the Love Shack, he looked her in the eye and didn't drop his gaze. "Song writers can be—"

"Arrogant, rude, inconsiderate and insensitive? Yeah, I've noticed."

It must have had something to do with the practice-makes-perfect philosophy. This time, he did sheepish really well. And apologetic, too. One corner of Gabe's mouth pulled up into an expression that wasn't exactly a smile or a grimace. Instead it was a little of both. "Occupational hazard, I'm afraid." His gaze slid down from the top of Meg's head to the yellow T-shirt she was wearing with her jeans, and his expression softened even more. He propped his hands on the display case and leaned closer, letting his eyes drift down further. "Believe me," he said, glancing up at her face again, "it has everything to do with artistic temperament and nothing to do with not noticing you."

"Artistic temperament, huh?" It was the one excuse guaranteed to send her temper flaring and her memories plummeting back to everything that had happened in Baltimore. She stomped to the other side of the shop.

"I'm afraid the old artistic temperament cop-out doesn't hold much water with me. It's the same excuse Ben used."

As soon as the words were out of her mouth, she knew she'd made a mistake. She stopped and swallowed hard, waiting for the dozen or so questions she was bound to get from Gabe.

A couple of frenzied heartbeats later, when he hadn't said a thing, Meg got herself in gear again. She went over to the candle table, found the right inventory sheet and started counting.

"I could help."

It was on the tip of her tongue to tell him he couldn't. Not unless he was the one and only man she'd met in the last fourteen months who could help her forget that the last one-and-only man in her life had done a pretty thorough job of shredding her heart, destroying her dreams and making mincemeat out of her self-confidence.

If that was what he was talking about.

As if to prove it wasn't, Gabe came up behind her. "With the inventory, I mean. You're taking inventory, right? I've got nothing much else to do and Diana's going to want to nap before we take our walk at noon. I could help."

It wasn't a good idea. But that didn't explain why she turned around and gave him a careful look. "How good are you at counting?" she asked him.

"Gold-star student." A ready smile sparkled on his face. "Always did well at math."

"Fine." She stepped back to let him closer to the table where the candles were displayed. "Then start counting."

Gabe surveyed the candle display and picked up the pillar candles one by one. "One red Seduction. One black Burning Love. One orange Hot Stuff. One, two, three..." He counted under his breath. "Three little brass plates that probably go under the candles so they don't burn a hole in any of Maisie's furniture, and one, two, three..." He counted again. "Nine boxes of little votive candles, the kind that probably go in these one, two, three... Six different colors of small glass candle holders."

"You are quite a counter." Meg nodded and marked off the inventory sheet. "Now how about these?" The lace tablecloth hung all the way down to the floor and she flipped it back to reveal Maisie's extra stash of candles. Lots and lots of candles.

Gabe's smile withered and his shoulders drooped.

"What?" Meg plucked the candle sheet off the clipboard and waved it under his nose. "You're not tired of inventory already, are you?"

He gave in without too much of a fight and when he took the paper out of her hand and dropped to sit on the floor, Diana trotted over and sat next to him.

Her visitors taken care of—for now—Meg worked on the rest of Maisie's list.

Massage oil, check. Sex toys, check. Candles, check.

What wasn't so easy to check was the little stammer of panic that bubbled up inside her when she realized that Gabe had horned in on her inventory-taking—and made himself at home in a place where her fantasies were too near the surface for her own good.

Rather than tip him off by asking him to leave, she decided to get this over with as quickly as she could. He'd be busy with the candles for a while, and while he was, Meg would go through the rest of the inventory sheets. She started with the containers of aphrodisiac teas, and by the time she got to the boxes of heart-shaped cookies and the chocolates shaped like everything from rose buds to various portions of the anatomy, Meg decided she just might get the inventory finished with her pride and her peace of mind intact.

She should have known better.

"So..." Gabe stretched his arm, reaching for the boxes of candles all the way in the back. He dragged them out to the light and opened them one by one and although he kept right on working, there was no mistaking the curiosity that flashed through his voice. "Who's Ben?"

All set to grab a box of chocolate cupids, Meg froze in place. "Slick," she told him. "Wait until a girl's too busy to have her guard up and then zap her with a question you know she doesn't want to answer."

"It was good, wasn't it?" He grinned. "And now that you've stalled a second time—who's Ben?"

"Ben is history."

"I gathered that much." Gabe opened a box and counted the multi-wicked pillar candles inside. "Good history or bad history?"

"History." She finished with the chocolates and flipped to the next inventory page. Just what she needed, panties and garter belts.

Meg gave in with a mumbled curse. She went to the rack near where Gabe was sitting, but she didn't start counting. There was something a little too perverse about running her fingers over filmy undergarments when her thoughts were on Ben Lucarelli.

"I met him in culinary school," she said, surprised that the old story didn't clutch at her heart the way it used to, that it didn't make her stomach flip. But then, she hadn't gotten to the really good parts yet.

"Ben was a brilliant chef. At least that's what everyone thought."

"Everyone but you."

"Oh, no!" She wasn't proud to admit something she'd hidden from herself for so long. "I was as taken in by him as everyone else. More so. Ben was the center of attention wherever he went. When he arrived at the culinary school, he was a marginal student at best, but after just a little while, he really blossomed. It wasn't long before everyone worshipped him. They admired his technique. They were awestruck by his knowledge. They were bowled over by his presentation and the way he paired flavors and by his subtle use of color to convey taste and mood. They were impressed, all right. But I was the one who went to bed with him."

Gabe didn't look at all surprised. He did stop counting, though, and he sat back, one hand absently ruffling Diana's fur while he listened to Meg's story.

"We decided that after we graduated, we'd open a restaurant together. And not just any restaurant. We wanted upscale. Trendy. Pricy. I was prepared to play in the minor leagues for a while. You know, learn the ropes and make a name for myself. But although he agreed to it, that didn't keep Ben happy for long. He wasn't exactly the type who was willing to live outside the limelight. Artistic temperament, don't you know."

She knew the comment struck a chord when she saw Gabe look away.

"He took everything we had and never even told me. He invested it in a place in Baltimore."

"And it tanked."

"Oh, no." Meg tipped her head back, remembering those first heady months. "Earthly Delights was small, but we had plans to expand. It was definitely upscale. But back-to-nature, too. A blending of real honest-to-goodness healthy food with just enough panache to make the critics sit up and take notice. They loved us. So did our customers. For a few months there..."

Her voice drifted, along with her memories, and though she was over the misery that used to overwhelm her every time she thought about Ben, it was clear she hadn't gotten over what he'd done to Earthly Delights. Just thinking about the restaurant and everything it had meant to her turned Meg's stomach.

''It was like watching every ambition I ever had come true right in front of my eyes,'' she said. ''I always dreamed of a life far away from South Bass Island. I always dreamed of owning a restaurant just like Earthly Delights. And I knew I had Ben to thank for it. He was the one who'd pushed me into agreeing to open the restaurant. Even when I didn't want to be pushed. He was the driving force, the genius. That's what I thought.''

''But you found out differently.''

When Meg glanced at Gabe, he said. ''Hey, it doesn't take a psychic to figure out that something went wrong. Let me guess, he was skimming the profits. Or was it some nasty habit? Drugs, gambling? Or maybe booze from the bar?''

''How about the pastry chef?'' Meg had never been good at sarcasm. That was probably why the words stuck in her throat. She coughed away the tightness and turned away. Better to look at the wall display of how-to sex books than risk seeing anything even close to pity in Gabe's eyes.

She knew exactly when he stood and walked up behind her. It was early, but the day promised to be warm. It suddenly got even hotter.

''I know, it's not exactly a new story.'' Meg shrugged, as if that would help her shed the memories. ''Happens a thousand times a day. To a thousand different people. But the cute little blonde wasn't the worst of it.'' She finally looked at Gabe because she knew that if she couldn't face him, she'd never be able to face the truth about herself and about everything that had happened with Ben.

"He admitted that it wasn't the first time. It was the way he got through culinary school. Romancing local chefs, stealing their secrets. Not the first time, and it obviously wasn't going to be the last. Then he hit me with the real zinger. I was the most talented chef he'd ever met, he told me. I had the best ideas. The finest eye for detail. The kind of ability that separates the good chefs from the great ones. It was the only reason he had stayed with me."

"Huh?" Maybe a man who lived his life outside the pressure cooker of the hospitality business just didn't get it. Gabe looked confused.

"It wasn't *me,*" Meg explained, and as she did, she wished Gabe was a little quicker on the uptake. Bad enough to have to say it all once. Way worse to have to grind through the story again. "It was never me. It was what I brought to the table and I mean that literally. Ben stuck with me because he thought I was a rising star. We weren't famous because of him. Earthly Delights wasn't famous because of him. It was me all along. And he didn't want to let go of that. Even when it meant pretending to be in love with me."

"The guy must've been breathing too many garlic fumes." Gabe shook his head in wonder. "What kind of lunatic would risk losing something so precious?"

"It's a cut-throat business and restaurants fold all the time."

"That's not what I meant and you know it."

It wasn't. She could tell by the spark that kindled in his eyes. By the way his gaze dipped to her mouth and stayed there a bit longer than was polite. She could tell because she'd always been good at sensing what people wanted. And right then and there, she knew that Gabe wanted her more than he wanted his next breath.

"It's because of the Love Shack." It was a lame excuse but she had to at least try. "This place gives people crazy ideas."

"I know." A smile skimmed across his face. "I've got a crazy idea."

Meg had crazy ideas, too. Crazy ideas about Love Nibbles and Wild Thing and how much fun it would be to smooth it on, and how much more fun it would be to lick it off.

But all the flavored massage oil in the Love Shack didn't change a thing. And never would.

"Chocolate Easter bunny," she reminded herself. "Solid. Even the ears."

Before Gabe could ask what she was talking about, she stepped around him. There was no way she was going to count panties and garters while he was around, but there was only one sheet left on her clipboard. Like it or lump it, she didn't have much choice. It was panties or nightgowns, and because it would obviously be a retreat to do anything else, she walked over to where the lingerie was displayed.

The antique armoire was eight feet tall and almost as wide. It was Maisie's pride and joy and she kept the black walnut polished so that it gleamed. The door of the armoire was always open and inside, an assortment of sweet and not-so-sweet lingerie hung on little satin hangers. Meg started on the left, shoving the hangers as far to the right as she could, then sliding the hangers toward her and checking them over one by one.

The first item was a red baby-doll nightgown. Cut up to here. And down to there. Dutifully, Meg found it on the list, checked it off and slid it to the left.

Second item: white nightgown. Floor-length. And

except for the satin cabbage roses near the hem, one hundred percent see-through. There was a snag in the fabric near what there was of a left shoulder and Meg pulled the hanger out of the wardrobe and held it up to the light.

Snag or not, all she could see was Gabe looking back at her from the other side of the gauzy fabric.

"You don't want to hear my crazy idea?"

"I don't want to hear about dancing hamburgers."

"I could tell the hamburgers to sit down and shut up."

"You could, but they don't seem to listen well. Maybe you should just go back up to Love Me Tender and—"

"You coming with me?"

It was either the opportunity of a lifetime or the biggest mistake she'd ever make. The cold, hard reality was that she didn't know which. That helped Meg make up her mind. "I've got inventory to finish."

"And I told Maisie I'd help."

"So Maisie put you up to this?"

"Not exactly." Gabe stared up at the ceiling, suddenly as tense as he'd been when he'd walked into the Love Shack. "But I told her I was looking for you and she said you'd be working in here all day. I told her we needed to talk."

They didn't.

Not about anything.

Before she could tell him that, Gabe plucked the hanger out of Meg's hands and held out the white nightgown. "Nice," he said, nodding his approval. "Did you check it off the list?"

She hadn't. Meg told him she had, anyway, just so he wouldn't get any ideas about who was in charge.

She retrieved the nightgown and hung it back up,

then went on to the next item. Black. Lacy. Almost nonexistent. A pair of thong panties and a strapless bra that was barely more than a strip of lace.

"You'd look terrific in that."

Meg forced herself not to flush, even when Gabe's words wrapped around her, far hotter than the tiny bra and panty set would ever be. She scanned the list once, then had to look again because she was so shaken she missed it the first time. Still, she made sure her gaze was nice and steady before she allowed herself to glance up at Gabe. "Forgive me for stating the obvious, but I can't believe you'd notice."

"Oh, I'd notice, all right."

"Uh-huh." Honeyed words and a hot-as-hell look to go along with them, but she wasn't going to fool herself. Not again. "Just like you noticed the dancing hamburgers?"

"Aw, come on, Meg! You're never going to let me forget the dancing hamburgers, are you?"

She supposed it was a rhetorical question.

That didn't mean she was going to let him off the hook.

"I am not going to let you forget the dancing hamburgers." Meg hung the bra and panties where they belonged and reached for the next piece of clothing, a leather bustier that came with a pair of fishnet stockings.

"You'd look great in that, too," Gabe told her.

"And you're not listening to me." She plopped the hanger back in place before she'd even checked her list, and grabbed the next hanger without bothering to look. "I'm not going to forget the dancing hamburgers, Gabe," she said, making sure her voice was calm and her words were slow. Just in case he really was as dense as he was pretending to be. "I'm not going to forget them because you can't forget them. You're the one with Tasty Time Burgers on your mind."

"Not when you're holding that thing."

The wide-eyed, punch-drunk expression on his face warned Meg she should have looked before she leaped. Or before she took the hanger out of the wardrobe. She braced herself and peeked at the hanger in her right hand.

Black satin tap pants. Downright discreet considering the other items of clothing she'd taken out of the armoire.

Except for the two barely-there pasties. With sparkling tassels.

"Gee, maybe I should just walk around carrying this little number. What do you think?" Just to get his goat, she held the boxy tap pants up to her own body and because he was obviously on the verge of telling her it was the best idea he'd heard yet, she slammed the hanger back on the rod and banged the door of the wardrobe shut.

"Inventory is done," she told him, moving toward the door. "I'm done. I've had it with the teasing and the suggestions and the hot looks that go nowhere but hamburger heaven. We're finished, Gabe."

"You might be finished. I'm not." He stepped in front of her, blocking her way. "I came in here to do something and I haven't done it."

"So do it. Get it over with."

"Really?" He was surprised that she'd given in so easily but a man like Gabe didn't stay surprised for long. Before Meg could move out of reach, and long before she understood what she'd gotten herself into, he pulled her into his arms and brought his mouth down on hers.

Chapter Nine

Hamburgers.

As soon as the word flitted through his head, Gabe did his best to squelch it.

The kiss had nothing to do with hamburgers, he assured himself. It had nothing to do with the Love Shack, either. Nothing to do with the heady scents that filled the air from candles and massage oils that had names he couldn't even think about without getting all hot and bothered.

It had nothing to do with the little wisps of gauze and lace that passed for clothing and hung all around the room, like fantasies made real. Nothing to do with those silky black shorts Meg had held up in front of herself. The ones that looked like men's boxers except that they were paired with two tassels that, he suspected, served the purpose of some manufacturer somewhere who had a naughty mind and the capital to bring those wicked fantasies to life.

The manufacturer's plan worked like magic.

He pictured Meg in the outfit, those little black shorts skimming her hips and smooth over her behind. Those little tassels jiggling with every move she made, inviting him to run his fingers through the fine, silky cords and over all the luscious bare skin exposed around them.

Just as quickly, he pictured himself helping Meg out of the outfit, one little tassel at a time.

OK, so the kiss had something to do with the lace and the gauze and the tassels.

Gabe was man enough to admit that much to himself.

He was also smart enough to know that while the urge to kiss her might have had something do with the sensuality that was as heavy in the air of the Love Shack as the aroma of rose potpourri, it had more to do with Meg.

No, he corrected himself. It had everything to do with Meg.

Hamburgers.

It had nothing whatever to do with hamburgers.

Just to prove it—to himself and to his imagination—Gabe pulled Meg closer. Her breasts pressed against his chest, her nipples hard, and he responded instantly and fiercely, his body tightening until it screamed for release. Her mouth opened beneath the pressure of his and he deepened the kiss, and when she arched her back, inviting him to touch her, he was completely lost. He skimmed his hand over her yellow shirt, tugged it out of her jeans, and glided his fingers under it and across her skin.

Dancing hamburgers.

He fought to ignore the words that started up inside his head, nonstop and merciless as the hum of desire that made him feel as if his blood had been replaced with jet fuel.

Tasty Time burgers, what a treat.

He smothered the voice by burying his face in Meg's hair. He stifled the words by kissing her ear and her neck and that smooth little hollow at the base of her throat. He banished the image of hamburgers by fingering the lace that edged her bra.

Tasty Time burgers can't be beat.

The music he'd played on the piano in Maisie's parlor filled his head and before he even knew what he was doing, he was stroking Meg's breast in rhythm to the tune.

He dipped two fingers inside her bra and rolled her nipple between them and when Meg groaned—

Tasty Time burgers singing and dancing.

When Meg groaned—

Tasty Time burgers dressed in wedding clothes.

When Meg groaned—

A Tasty Time burger bride. A Tasty Time burger groom and—

Gabe told himself he was a fool for ruining a moment that was pure heaven, but he knew he had no choice. If he didn't stop touching her, he'd go stark, raving mad.

When he drew back, he made sure it looked more like a rest than a full-scale advance to the rear. He stepped out of reach, and something told him the slightly stunned expression on Meg's face pretty much matched his. For different reasons.

"You're a darn good chocolate Easter bunny." He didn't know what she was talking about, but he wasn't about to argue with it. Her smile lit up the Love Shack and heated Gabe through to his bones.

Which would've been darned nice. Except that even Meg's smile and all the heat it generated couldn't melt the ice that filled his veins once he realized that when he kissed her, all he could think about was his ad campaign.

"And just think..." They were standing close, but

Meg managed to shuffle closer. Her breasts nearly brushed his chest. Her thigh was a New York minute away from rubbing his.

Hoping it didn't look as awkward as it felt, he stepped back just enough to avoid making contact.

Meg didn't notice. She stroked one finger from the collar of Gabe's golf shirt over the crest embroidered above his heart, down across his stomach and back up again. "Not one word about hamburgers."

Tasty Time burgers in the biggest Ziegfeld-like production number ever seen on the small screen. A starry sky looking down on the hamburgers. A smiling moon. And that happy couple, the bride and groom. Two happy hamburgers and—

Gabe backed away from Meg's touch and all the surprising things it was doing inside his head. Which was nothing compared to the not-so-surprising things it was doing to the rest of him. "No hamburgers." He beamed her a smile that felt stiff around the edges. "Not one word."

He wondered what she'd say if she knew there were dozens.

Because he couldn't stand to think about it any more than he could stand to be within three feet of Meg and not snatch her into his arms and start kissing her again, Gabe glanced around, hoping for some way out of this mess. When he looked at Diana, some silent message passed between them. The dog let out a bark.

"Diana." Gabe hauled in breath after breath, fighting to still the pounding of his heart. As if she sensed that he needed to escape or he was going to explode, Diana barked again. "She has to go outside." He placed his hands on Meg's shoulders and gently backed her away.

Burgers descending a winding staircase and—

He dropped his hands as quickly as he could and withdrew an extra step as an added precaution. "You know what Maisie said." Somehow he managed a smile.

"Run of the Hideaway. As long as she behaves herself." Meg's voice was a perfect blend of anticipation and satisfaction. Her eyes glided over Gabe and there wasn't a doubt in his mind that she was imagining the same things he'd been imagining.

Minus the hamburgers, of course.

She tugged her shirt back into place. "Yeah. I remember. And much as I hate to play second fiddle to Diana, I'd hate it even more if Maisie came home and found a puddle on one of the Oriental rugs. Go ahead. Take Diana outside." She glanced toward the door, then gave him a look that was practically hot enough to make Gabe combust. "I'll be right here when you get back."

The next thing he knew, he was out in the lobby, fighting to catch his breath and wondering when and where he'd picked up the willpower that allowed him to walk away from Meg. Especially when her lips were swollen from his kisses. When her cheeks were nice and rosy and the heat of her skin was still burning through his. He was already on his way up the stairs for Diana's leash when he saw that he'd forgotten the dog.

"Diana!" He slapped his thigh, the way Meg always did, and called to her and when she came waddling out of the gift shop, he told her to sit, asked her to please stay, and hurried upstairs for her leash.

Remarkably, when he came downstairs again, she was waiting right where she was supposed to be.

Just like Gabe knew Meg would be as soon as he got back to the Love Shack.

The very idea should have cheered him. Heck, a couple of months earlier (before the Tasty Time Burger cloud darkened his doorway), it would've had him feeling high as a kite. Today, all he knew was that he had to get away—right now—and try to make some sense of everything that was happening.

He snapped Diana's leash on her collar. Apparently, she was under the impression that Meg was coming along. She automatically headed toward the Love Shack. Gabe tugged her in the opposite direction, and when they got to the back door, Diana gave him a look, one wrinkled brow raised. He closed the door quietly behind them and hurried out to the road.

"No use taking any chances," he told the dog.

Except that he already had.

"It's not like I didn't suspect it was going to happen," he muttered, and he didn't bother to add that while he'd *guessed* it might happen, he'd hoped it wouldn't. Hoped it for Meg's sake. And for his own.

While Diana snuffled through the flowers that grew along the border between Maisie's property and the lot next to it, Gabe went over the incident in the Love Shack. "I mean, it's why I went in there in the first place."

The dog curled her lip.

"To kiss her," he told his furry companion. "I went in there to kiss her. And don't look at me like I'm some kind of gigolo. It was...you know...an experiment. I had to find out. For sure."

And now he had.

And what he'd learned left him feeling as if he'd just been whacked upside the head with a two-by-four.

"I can't believe it." Gabe kicked at a loose stone in the middle of the road and sent it flying off into the high grass across the street. "I can't believe it's true, but...well, facts are facts, aren't they?'' Diana didn't answer. She caught the scent of something interesting and yanked at Gabe's arm; because he wasn't in the mood to argue, he let her take the lead. In a daze, he walked behind the dog, getting farther and farther from the Hideaway with each step.

And no farther at all from the disturbing thoughts that stomped through his brain in football cleats.

''It started that first morning,'' he mumbled, and he supposed anyone who came along and saw him talking would think he was talking to the dog. Instead of to himself. ''I touched her. There at the breakfast table.''

Diana stopped in her tracks and glanced back at him.

''It was all perfectly innocent.'' Gabe defended himself. ''Except that the moment I touched her—well, that's when I came up with the idea. For the dancing hamburgers. After all those weeks of not thinking anything at all. And I never made the connection. I just figured the writer's block was over and the ideas would start flowing again. Only they didn't.''

Diana sniffed the post of a mailbox and checked out the inside of an empty paper bag lying on the side of the road.

''Then it happened again,'' Gabe told her. ''That night you showed up. We were in her garden, and I touched Meg and—wham! Not that I wouldn't feel like that, anyway. I mean, Meg...''

Gabe threw back his head, his face to the late-morning sky. The sun was shining, but there were fat gray clouds gathering across the lake. Even the prospect of rain wasn't enough to dull the bright memories. His body warmed with the delicious sensations that had blindsided him when he kissed Meg. ''She's beautiful. She's fun. She's smart. She's a great cook.''

Diana barked her agreement.

"So ordinarily, I wouldn't think anything of it if I touched her and got all sorts of ideas. Only they weren't *those* sorts of ideas." The very thought was as amazing now as it was then, and he tried to resist it. "They were jingle ideas. And the other day when I was sitting at the piano? As soon our hands brushed, the notes popped into my head. All these months, my brain's been as dry as the Nevada desert. And then I touch Meg and..."

He'd seen where things were headed. After all, it was the reason he'd decided on the experiment in the Love Shack, the kiss that was going to prove that what he suspected was true. But the gravity of the situation hadn't hit him full force until right then and there. And when it did, it staggered Gabe.

He froze in the middle of the road and stared, seeing nothing except the inescapable truth.

"She's my muse." He whispered the words, too afraid that if he said them out loud, they'd sound as crazy to the world as they sounded to him. "Meg is my muse. She's the only one who can jump-start my creativity. The only one who can get the Tasty Time Burger juices flowing."

Diana might not have known much about inspiration, but she knew the word *burger.* Sensing lunch, she barked and turned in the direction of the town. In shock, Gabe stumbled along after her.

Now that the truth had been revealed, part of him should have been thrilled. He'd found the solution to his problem. The magic open-sesame key to the door that had been shut tight on his creativity all these months.

A little more Meg, a little more jingle.

Not a bad prospect, considering how one kiss had proved so much. That she was his muse, yes. It has also proved what he'd suspected all along: he wanted her more than he'd ever wanted any woman. And that meant that besides the very obvious advantages to be gained by kissing her, there was an added bonus. Every time he touched her, another area of his brain woke up and other piece of the Tasty Time Burger campaign plunked into place. In no time at all, he'd have the whole jingle written.

But another part of him knew it wasn't that easy.

And that knowledge made Gabe feel sick and uncomfortable. Because he wished Meg could be his friend, his confidante…his lover.

But now he knew for certain that she could never be any of those things.

The words settled inside Gabe like lead weights, sinking his spirits and threatening to drag what was left of his self-confidence as an artist all the way down to the bottom.

Because if Gabe needed to find inspiration outside himself, it meant his creativity had run dry. His career as a songwriter was at a dead end.

Just as his grandfather had always said it would be.

Facing the truth wasn't easy. Or pretty. But Gabe knew he didn't have any choice. Even though Diana didn't like it, he turned around and walked back to the Hideaway. There was only one thing he could do, and he had to do it fast.

Before he talked himself out of doing it at all.

MEG FINISHED THE INVENTORY. Or at least she thought she'd finished the inventory. It was hard to tell when she was so preoccupied trying to figure out what the hell had just happened.

One second, she was scared to death. The next second, she was astonished. She wasn't looking for a relationship. She didn't *want* a relationship. Now, whether she liked it or not, what seemed to be the chance of a lifetime had come at her out of nowhere. And the most surprising thing was that she was starting to enjoy every second of it.

After all these days of acting as if being around her was about as much fun as having a tooth pulled, Gabe had actually taken the big step. He'd kissed her. No, she amended the thought, he'd kissed her and not talked about hamburgers. Not the dancing variety. Not the plain old sit-on-a-plate-variety, either.

Like the bubbles in a champagne glass, her blood fizzed and sparkled—until the next second ticked by and she found her doubts coming back stronger than ever.

And the second after that?

The second after that, she decided she didn't care. Not about any of it. Hard to care about the confusion that racketed through her head when the rest of her was humming. Hard to care about being bewildered when being attracted and very interested was taking up so much of her time.

As for the hamburgers…

Meg tapped the inventory sheets into a neat pile and left them on the counter where Maisie would find them when she returned from the mainland.

She was pretty sure she'd heard the last of the hamburgers. The heat of Gabe's kiss had assured her of that.

More than a little satisfied with how the day was going, Meg did one more turn around the Love Shack, just to be sure she hadn't missed any of the items she was supposed to count. After Gabe left with Diana, she'd finished the candles and counted the panties and garter belts, the books and the scented soaps. She taken a quick trip into the kitchen to tally how much champagne they had and how much they needed to order, ducked into Maisie's office to check out a shipment of suggestive greeting cards that had just arrived and hadn't been put on the shelves yet, and made sure all the candles sitting in the middle of the floor were put away.

And Gabe still wasn't back.

Meg went out to the lobby and glanced at the antique grandfather clock that stood outside the parlor door. Gabe and Diana had been gone an awfully long time but then, she supposed that wasn't so unusual. Diana needed a lot of pampering and as reluctant as Gabe might be to provide it, he was smart enough to know that the dog needed plenty of exercise.

While they were still gone, Meg would just…

She looked around the lobby. Because Gabe was the only guest currently registered at the Hideaway, things were under control. Margaret, the grandmother of six who helped with the cleaning as a way to make some extra money, had already come and gone, so Meg knew the rooms were taken care of. The kitchen was spick-and-span. The lobby was spotless and ready for the two sets of guests scheduled to check in the next morning.

That didn't leave much for Meg to do. Especially when all she could think about was how anxious she was for Gabe to get back.

So they could start all over again. Right where they'd left off.

She found herself drifting back to the Love Shack.

''The scene of the crime,'' she purred, glancing at the place she'd stood when Gabe kissed her. From there, she looked at the armoire.

And she had an idea.

It hit from out of nowhere and while it wasn't exactly out of character, even she knew it was a little premature. She almost rejected it on the spot. But then she reconsidered. And that only made the idea sound better and better.

She opened the armoire and ran her hands through the gauzy fabrics and the frilly lace. ''Premature, huh?'' she asked herself. ''Maybe this is exactly what Gabe needs, a wake-up call.''

She went through the outfits one by one. The white nightgown was too formal for this time of day. The red baby-doll outfit was too over the top. The tap pants and tassels were intriguing, all right, but not for the first time. She wanted to seduce Gabe; she didn't want to make him wonder if he'd gotten involved with a crazy woman.

She settled on the black thong panties and the wisp of lace that was supposed to be a bra, and she already had the outfit off the hanger and her jeans unzipped when she heard a noise out in the lobby.

Gabe was back, and she cursed herself for not being fast enough and for not making up her mind sooner. She would've loved to see his face when he stripped off her T-shirt and found the barely-there bra underneath it.

Then again, there might be something to be gained from not wearing the bra and panties yet, and using them to tease him.

The idea caused a flicker of heat and smiling, Meg zipped her jeans. She sashayed into the lobby twirling the panties in one hand.

And stopped dead when she saw Gabe hurry past the front desk carrying his suitcases.

''You're leaving?''

OK, so it wasn't subtle. Neither was the fact that he was obviously trying to sneak out the back door.

At least he had the guts to stop and face her. Gabe set his suitcases down on the rug and although he didn't say anything, he didn't have to. Diana's leash was on the front desk, along with three bags of Cajun beef jerky, a bag of mini marshmallows and a note addressed to Maisie. Meg didn't have to read it to know it was all about how Diana should be taken care of until Ingrid and Travis returned.

"What's going on?" Funny, Meg's question sounded rational and calm. Exactly how she *wasn't* feeling. Before Gabe could notice the bra and panties and realize that she'd been planning to put them on, that she'd been arranging a private showing and that she'd been counting on everything that was going to happen afterward, she stuffed them in her back pocket. "What's going on here, Gabe? Are you—"

"Heard from the office." He might have had the nerve to lie to her, but fortunately he didn't have the audacity to smile when he did it. His expression was cast-iron, his shoulders were set. There was a shimmer of some emotion in his eyes that Meg couldn't read. "I have to get back. Now. I heard from Latoya and—"

Meg braced herself against the punch-in-the-stomach sensation. "Latoya communicates by ESP, huh?"

"ES—" As if they'd been attacked with a pair of sharp scissors, his words were abruptly cut off when Gabe recognized his mistake.

But that didn't stop Meg from pointing it out. "You left your cell phone in the Love Shack and it didn't ring. Not even once," she told him. "The Love Shack. Remember? That's where you left me. You said you were coming back."

"I did say it. I was. I meant to." He took a step toward her, but the scowl on her face warned him to keep his distance. The look on *his* face told her that while he was disappointed, he was also relieved, and that, more than anything else, hurt.

Meg swallowed the pain and waited for an explanation.

Gabe didn't have to be a mind-reader to know what she was thinking. He shrugged. "It's hard to explain," he said.

"Try."

"It isn't you."

"And that's supposed to make me feel better?" Meg barked out a laugh.

"It's supposed to tell you that it isn't about you. You're wonderful, Meg."

"So wonderful that you kiss me and then decide to cut and run. Unless one doesn't have anything to do with the other?"

"It doesn't." He was a lousy liar. "I told you, it's not you. You're perfect."

She gestured at his suitcases. "Well, you've certainly found a unique way to get your point across. Kiss a woman. Tell her you'd love to see her in satin and lace…"

"I would." Like a physical pain, a grimace crossed Gabe's face. "There's nothing I'd like more." His eyes warmed but there was still a shadow in them, the shadow of something she didn't understand and couldn't put into words. "It isn't you," he told her again. "It's me."

"Then maybe I should be the one who decides if you go or stay."

"No. You can't. You don't know—"

"I know there's something between us, Gabe. And don't tell me I'm imagining it. I know that when you kissed me, something was going on."

"It was going on, all right. And it was great." This

time he wasn't lying. She could tell from the smile that simmered with the memory. "It was the best, the most perfect kiss..." Gabe scraped a hand through his hair. "But I'm sorry. That doesn't change a thing. I have to leave. Right now. As much as I'd like to stay, I can't. As much as I wish I could take you in my arms again, and—"

"And you think I'd *let* you?" Meg was hearing it; she just didn't believe it. Just to show him what he was missing, she whipped the bra and panties out of her back pocket and tossed them down. They landed in the center of the Oriental rug, a ribbon of lace, a strip of barely-there satin.

The color drained from Gabe's face. "You weren't..."

"Oh, yes, I was." Maybe it was perverse, but Meg actually enjoyed seeing the disappointment that swept over his face. "I was planning on putting them on. And I was planning on letting you help me take them off. I was planning on a lot, buddy. But if you have the right to change your mind, then so do I."

"I'm sorry."

"Sure."

"I am. It's just that—"

"You know what? I don't want to hear it." She turned around and stomped back into the Love Shack.

At least with some solid walls between them, she didn't have to face Gabe and try to figure out where things had gone wrong. Especially when they'd looked as if they were going so right. And now they were going nowhere at all.

She went rigid when he walked into the gift shop behind her.

"My phone." Gabe edged his way over to the counter to retrieve his cell phone. It took a lot of self-control, but somehow, he managed to keep his distance. He found it impossible, though, to keep his eyes off her. She was beautiful, and all her beauty did was remind him that she was also completely off limits.

It meant he shouldn't have been staring at her fiery hair. It meant he shouldn't let his gaze glide over her curves, or think about how soft her skin was. It sure wasn't smart to remember that when he touched her, she responded to him just the way the piano keys used to, singing with every move. Because if he thought about all that, he wouldn't have the courage to leave.

The more he stared at her, the more he ached. And the more he ached, the more he knew for certain that she was the one and only woman who could make the ache go away.

Too bad she was also the one and only woman who reminded him of exactly what he *didn't* want to remember: that his creativity had dried up and gone. That he was a man who had depended on no one but himself all his life. And now he couldn't anymore.

"I'm just getting my phone..."

"Take it and get out." Meg's words sent an icy wave in Gabe's direction. "Get out of the gift shop. Get out of the Hideaway. Get off my island."

"I don't blame you for being upset."

"It's not your place to blame me or not blame me. This is my life and I was handling it very nicely, thank you, until you came along and decided to mess with my mind. So if you're done, you can leave now. And I can go back to my ordinary life."

"You'll never be ordinary." A smile blossomed inside Gabe but he knew better than to let it show. This wasn't the time to try for cheery. He wasn't feeling cheery and besides, he didn't think Meg would appreciate it. "You'll always be far from ordinary."

"Thanks." Meg didn't sound as though she meant it. She steered a path around Gabe and went into lobby, toward the kitchen. Even though she must've known Gabe was right behind her, she didn't bother to turn around.

"You'll take care of Diana?" It was the only thing he could think to say. The only thing that might keep Meg from disappearing into the kitchen. And out of his life.

She whirled around, her fists on her hips. "You can be pretty sure that we won't be nearly as heartless as you. We'd never let Diana believe we liked her and then—"

"I do like you."

"We'd never let her believe she was special and then—"

"You're the most special woman I've ever met."

"We'd never let her believe there could be any sort of relationship between us when—"

"There could have been. Honest." Gabe swallowed the sour taste in his mouth. "I can't explain right now, Meg. Mostly because I don't understand it myself. But I will someday. I promise. I'll come back and—"

"Don't bother." There was no doubt that she meant it. Meg's back was stiff, her shoulders rigid. When she looked at him, her eyes narrowed and there was a furrow of annoyance between her brows. "You're not welcome here. Not now. Not ever again."

Gabe wasn't surprised. It was what he deserved. What did surprise him was that getting banished from the Hideaway made him feel far worse than he'd felt the day his grandfather had told him he was no longer welcome at the family business or in the family home. He stuck a hand into his pocket, reaching for his car keys, and when he pulled it out again, he was holding a package of breath mints he'd bought for Diana.

"If you could just..." He held the mints out to Meg.

She stepped back and crossed her arms over her chest. "You want to give the dog mints, you give them to her. You should face her like a man when you say goodbye."

Gabe might not be quick on the uptake but the message was unmistakable. Just to prove to Meg that he had the guts to face Diana (even though he hadn't had the guts to do the same for Meg), he slapped his thigh and called the dog.

She didn't come.

"Diana!" Gabe tried again. He shook the little plastic box of breath mints and when the noise didn't bring her running, he picked up one of the plastic bags of beef jerky and ripped it open. "Diana, I've got jerky!" He held up a piece.

"Like that's going to help." Meg went into the dining room and from there, to the kitchen. She came back shaking her head. "No sign of her in there, either," she told him. "You're sure you brought her back?"

He didn't dignify that question with an answer. He jogged up the stairs, but since the doors to each of the Hideaway's four rooms were closed, he knew she wasn't up there. He came back downstairs again, just in time to see Meg walk out of the room on the far side of the lobby that was used for linen storage.

"No Diana." She shook her head. "She's not on the front porch, either. I already looked there."

"Well, she's not upstairs." Gabe glanced toward the far end of the inn and the door where he'd planned to make his escape. "You checked the back?" he asked Meg.

"Not yet." Their minds working as one, they moved

toward the door together. And stopped dead in their tracks when they saw that it was wide open.

Nobody needed to tell Gabe what it meant.

Diana was gone.

Chapter Ten

Meg did her best not to panic. She figured that was probably good. Gabe was panicking enough for both of them.

Not that he was about to let on. There wasn't even one tremor of emotion in his voice when he called Diana. There wasn't one tremble in his hands when he held up the bag of jerky and shook it, hoping to entice her with the smell and the sound. There wasn't one quiver in the set of his shoulders or in the steps he took when he did another turn around the lobby, and looked in the parlor and went into the linen room even though Meg had already looked there.

But Meg could tell.

She could tell because Gabe grabbed the bag of mini marshmallows off the front desk and hurried onto the back porch. He called the dog. He tried tempting her. He even promised corn chips. When none of that worked, she heard him yell to Diana (wherever she was) that if she didn't get her chubby little body back here as fast as she could, he was going to make sure she spent the rest of her career hawking ambulance-chasing attorneys and used-car dealerships.

That was when Meg knew he was desperate. That was when she knew he cared.

And that, she told herself in no uncertain terms, was the reason she offered to help.

Meg stepped onto the back porch and nearly squished a small mound of marshmallows Gabe had poured out of the bag and onto the floor.

"About the only thing you're going to accomplish with those marshmallows is attract every bee on the island," she told him. "I think we need a more scientific approach."

"We?" She wouldn't have caught a glimpse of the worry that darkened his eyes if he hadn't been too surprised to hide it when he spun around. He hid it as quickly as he could, but he didn't try to disguise his disbelief. "You'd help me? After I—"

She didn't want to hear it. She didn't even want to think about it. "I'm not helping you," she said, just so he didn't get any wrong ideas. Just so she didn't talk herself into believing they could get back to where they were in the Love Shack. "I'm helping Diana. I'd hate to see anything happen to her."

Gabe opened his mouth to say something, but Meg wasn't in any mood to stand around and listen. She stomped down the steps and the length of the slate sidewalk that divided the back lawn and led to the street. Beyond the street was a strip of beach and on the other side of that, the lake. Meg was all the way to the water's edge before she acknowledged that Gabe had followed.

"No sign of her down here, either." Meg didn't bother to look at him. She knew if she did, all she'd picture was Gabe hauling her into his arms and kissing her. That, and Gabe carrying his suitcases as he tried to sneak out. It was the last thing she needed because if she allowed it, the memories would topple what was left of her composure. She couldn't afford that. Not while Gabe was around to see it. And not while they had Diana to worry about.

She held a hand above her eyes to cut the glare of the sun off the lake. A fat cloud rolled across the sky, blocking the sun, and she had a clear view up and down the shore. The lake was calm and the beach was empty. Except for the rippling marks where the water washed against the shore and the scratch-like prints left behind by gulls, the sand at their feet was smooth. "If she was down here, we'd see paw prints."

"Or the dent her fat furry butt made in the sand."

When Meg rolled her eyes, Gabe let out a sigh. "All right, all right. I know. Cut the sarcasm and let's get down to finding the dog. Only I don't even know where to begin." He tried yelling again. The only response he got was a call from the gulls who soared overhead, then dipped down to the water for fish.

"This is great." It wasn't, of course, which was exactly why Gabe sounded so disgusted. "Ingrid and Travis are going to show up for that mangy hound and she's going to be nowhere in sight."

"Is she insured?"

Gabe snarled at her the way she'd seen him snarl at Diana.

Meg got the message. "Look, if we stand here arguing about it, we're going to get nowhere. I know you're worried about Diana but—"

"I am not worried about Diana." Gabe crossed his arms over his chest. "She's a nasty beast with bad breath and worse manners, and I wouldn't care what happened to her except that there are a whole lot of people who are going to be unhappy when they find out she took off for parts unknown. Including the insurance company, because yes, she is insured. For a whole lot of money. And they're not going to like it when they have to pay out because thanks to me, Diana ended up on some island road, flattened like a pancake."

"She's not going to get flattened." Meg was pretty sure of it but glanced at the road, just in case. "There aren't many cars on the island," she told him and reminded herself. "Most of the residents have golf carts and the tourists rent them, too. Golf carts don't move very fast."

"Neither does Diana. Leave it to her to be the first golf-cart fatality in island history."

"She's not going to be a fatality." It wasn't a pretty picture and Meg refused to consider it. She calmed herself with a deep breath. "Look," she told him, "I know you're concerned."

"Not." Gabe's mouth thinned. "I'm simply being responsible. That's all. I was put in charge of the rotten creature and now—"

"All right." Meg knew there was no use fighting. Not about this. Not when there were so many other things they could've been fighting about. Like the way he'd been prepared to walk out and leave her while she was humming with the anticipation of his return. And how he wasn't even going to say goodbye. Like the fact that though he claimed she was beautiful, that he said she was wonderful and perfect, he couldn't wait to get away from her.

She'd settle for responsible. Responsible was kinder than what she was tempted to call him.

"Well, Mr. Responsible, let's examine this logically. She can't have gone very far."

"Who would've thought she'd have the ambition to waddle anywhere except in the direction of food?" Gabe looked back toward the road and the rambling Victorian Hideaway. The inside Christmas decorations had been taken down and put away, but Maisie was still waiting for the college kid who was supposed to help with the outside work. The inn was draped with pine boughs and dotted with wreaths. Elaborate red bows festooned the doors, and the pine tree on the lawn was bright with bows and tiny mirrors and crystals that reflected the sunlight and broke it into hundreds of sparkling rainbows.

The festive scene was a stark contrast to the worry that gnawed at Meg's insides and darkened Gabe's expression. "Diana's as graceful as a Sherman tank. How could she make tracks that fast?"

"Maybe we're just searching in the wrong place." Meg hurried back across the beach. "We came this way. Maybe she went the other way. Maybe she's sitting at the front door right now, wagging her tail and barking to get—" Her foot slipped in the sand and her logical line of reasoning dissolved in a shriek of surprise when she went down. She would've hit the beach face-first if Gabe didn't grab her.

He lifted her, both arms around her waist and her back to his chest, and for an instant, Meg hung suspended over the sand. Her heartbeat raced and something told her it didn't have nearly as much to do with nearly falling as it did with the feel of Gabe's arms around her. Her breath caught, and it wasn't because she was afraid she'd get hurt or because she was embarrassed. She experienced the same feelings that had flooded her back in the Love Shack when he'd taken her in his arms. The tingle that tickled from her head all the way down to her toes. The sizzle that crawled along her skin. The heat that burned right through her and threatened to reduce her good intentions to ashes.

Now, just like it did then.

Before Meg had a chance to remind herself that it

wasn't a good idea (even if it was an intriguing one), Gabe set her on her feet. As if she were on fire, he let go of her and backed off. He didn't bother to ask if she was all right. Once he saw that she was, he marched across the road and over the lawn and toward the Hideaway.

Watching him go, Meg wondered if maybe she'd hit her head, after all. Major mental impairment might help explain her completely irrational obsession with Gabe. Why did just being with him turn her knees to jelly? Why did the way the sunlight glinted off his hair make her long to run her fingers through it? Why, when he touched her, did she feel as if she were well on her way to nuclear meltdown?

''Why can't you see the truth when it's staring you in the face? Yeah, major head injury might explain that.'' She walked over to the inn, and by the time she caught up with Gabe, he'd already been around to the front of the building.

''No sign of her.'' He shook his head, baffled. ''You suppose we could call that friend of yours, the cop?''

''Dylan?'' Meg didn't see why not. She just didn't want to be on the receiving end of a lecture when Dylan reminded her—as he was certain to do—that he had more important things to worry about than dogs. ''I'll tell you what. You call Dylan, I'll go get Maisie's golf cart. We'll cover more ground that way.''

Meg gave him the number and left Gabe to the task, then trotted over to the garage. Maisie owned a car, but there wasn't much point in using it on the island unless the weather was bad. Parking downtown was at a premium and besides, Maisie insisted a golf cart was better suited to the island's leisurely pace. It might also move just slowly enough make it easier to look for Diana.

Maisie and her golf cart were something of an institution on the island but of course, Gabe didn't know that. He was just putting his phone back in his pocket when Meg pulled up in the shocking-pink cart. He stopped and stared at the fringe that dangled around the roof, the pink velvet seats, the rhinestone-studded hubcaps and the grinning cupid painted on the side.

Meg motioned for him to get inside and Gabe sat gingerly on the plush seat. He did a double-take when he noticed the lace-covered steering wheel and the brass key chain that swung back and forth from the ignition—one that featured a naked man and a just-as-naked woman in an embrace that was nothing less than torrid.

"Don't say a word," Meg cautioned him and apparently, he took the warning to heart. He cleared his throat and when Meg put the cart into reverse and backed up, he looked over his shoulder, too.

"Dylan says he'll be happy to look around for Diana as soon as he leaves the day care, where he's giving a talk on safety. And he says you owe him one."

It was exactly what Meg had expected. "I'll bet. Dylan always thinks I owe him one. Some police chief, huh? Ask Dylan for a favor and he wants something in return. He loves my—"

"Your what?"

Meg hit the brakes with a little more force than she'd intended and they jerked to a stop. But when she glanced to her right, Gabe looked away. Too bad. She would've liked a chance to try and figure out what he was thinking. If she didn't know better, she would've thought his question showed a little too much interest.

But she did know better.

The realization settled down inside her and she moved the lever on the transmission into drive and hit the accelerator. She stopped at the first cross street. There wasn't any traffic and she nudged the cart out into the intersection and hit the road at a breakneck fifteen miles an hour.

They looped around to the front of the inn and quickly surveyed the porch and the lawn. They saw plenty of pine boughs, ribbons and twinkling lights. And no sign of Diana anywhere. "My cinnamon rolls," Meg said. "It's my cinnamon rolls Dylan loves. If he does me a favor and searches for Diana, he's going to want a batch of fresh-baked rolls in return. Thought you'd like to know." She tried to gauge Gabe's reaction.

"I didn't mean—"

"No. Of course not." She turned a corner as fast as she could, getting a certain amount of satisfaction from seeing Gabe scramble for a handhold. Ever since he'd come to the island, Meg had been feeling much the same way.

Grappling to get a hold on reality before she lost her sense of balance together.

She wasn't sure if it was a good feeling or a bad one.

She wasn't sure she wanted to find out.

About the only thing she *was* sure of was—

She noticed something on the side of the road and slammed on the brakes. "What was that you said?" she asked, turning in her seat to face Gabe. "Back there at the lake, what was that you said about how Diana didn't have any ambition to waddle anywhere..."

"Except in the direction of food." Gabe sounded as puzzled as he looked. Until he followed her gaze and saw what she was staring at. He sat up and, for the first time since he realized Diana had pulled a disappearing act, he actually smiled.

"I always told her too much fat would do her in," he said.

Meg studied the trail scattered along the side of the road.

A trail that consisted of one shredded potato chip bag, what was left of a candy cane (very little) and a Tasty Time Burger milkshake cup that had been torn open and licked clean.

It wasn't much, but it was more than they'd had before. Meg inched the golf cart forward. Something told her they were finally headed in the right direction.

THREE HOURS LATER, Gabe was much pretty convinced that they'd seen every inch of South Bass Island.

They hadn't caught one glimpse of even one hair on a certain dog's head.

He sat up in the pink velvet upholstered seat and stretched. Three hours, and all they'd accomplished was to find a trail that led from one side of the island to the other. A trail of food wrappers and crumbs. "I can't believe there's this much litter on one island."

"Tourists aren't always as careful as they should be." Meg shook her head, obviously not pleased. "Besides, not all of it's been litter. There was the stuff taken from that backyard picnic table and the food snatched from the garbage cans behind the open-air market and—"

"Yeah. I know. But I feel like Hansel and Gretel. Only there doesn't seem to be a witch at the other end of the breadcrumb trail." Gabe rubbed his hands over his face. Sometime while they'd been searching the island, the fat gray clouds that had been gathering on the horizon had arrived overhead. He heard a rumble of thunder from somewhere far out over the lake and glanced up at the fringed roof of the golf cart.

"This thing any good at keeping out water?"

Meg peered up at the clouds. "Depends how much water."

Though her words were light, there was a frown of worry between Meg's eyes and her shoulders drooped. She looked as tired as Gabe felt, and as frustrated. She looked…

When he caught himself staring, he turned on the cushy seat and told himself to keep scanning the landscape for Diana. Better to look for the dog than to look at Meg. Safer and less painful. Guilt-free.

Because when he looked at Meg, all he could think about was what had happened on the beach. How when he wrapped his arms around her to keep her from falling, another piece of the Tasty Time Burger commercial kerplunked into place in his brain.

He didn't need any more proof of everything Meg was.

And everything he wasn't.

He didn't need to feel any worse about the decision he'd made earlier in the day—to sneak out the back door and run away from Meg and everything she stood for and everything she meant. Because he felt plenty lousy already.

"She's gone. She swam to Canada." He couldn't tell Meg how he felt, so Gabe figured he might as well whine about Diana. "Let's face it. We'll never see her again."

"She didn't swim to Canada." Though she sounded confident, Gabe couldn't help noticing that Meg glanced at the lake. Word had it that on a clear day, island visitors could see clear across Lake Erie to Canada from the top of the 1812 War memorial in the center of town. But it wasn't a clear day. And Canada was too far away for a chubby dog to swim to, anyway.

They both knew it. It didn't keep a wave of concern from washing over Meg's face.

And damn it, the fact that she cared that much squeezed Gabe's heart so hard he couldn't breathe.

''So maybe she commandeered a boat and sailed to Canada.''

''Maybe she's still around her somewhere.'' Meg caught sight of an empty iced tea bottle and slowed down to scan the area for other evidence. There wasn't any, but another rumble of thunder vibrated through the air, and this one sounded closer than the last. ''Is she afraid of storms?''

''Afraid?''

''You know, does the noise bother her?'' Meg's thin-lipped expression told him she couldn't believe how insensitive he was. ''Some dogs are, you know. Some dogs are afraid of fireworks or of cars backfiring. Some dogs are afraid of thunder. If Diana's one of them—''

''I honestly don't know.'' Gabe defended himself instantly, then instantly felt more defensive for feeling he had to. ''I mean, it's not like we spent a lot of quality time together. We saw each other on the set when the commercial was filming. We decided that our dislike was mutual. That's as much as I know about Diana. Except that she's ugly as a mud fence and that she's spoiled and she won't come when we call her, which means she's stubborn, badly behaved and inconsiderate, too.''

''So she's spoiled and inconsiderate and ugly…'' Meg glanced at Gabe as she wheeled around a corner. ''But you're looking for her anyway.''

Gabe recognized a trap when he saw one. If he took the bait, he'd be caught, and dragged into a conversation about how he really had a warm and fuzzy side and how he shouldn't be afraid to show it.

No way! Warm and fuzzy talk was bound to lead to warm and fuzzy feelings. And he couldn't afford warm and fuzzy feelings. Not when he was alone with Meg. A little warm and fuzzy thinking was bound to lead to warm and fuzzy action. Which would lead straight to another flash of inspiration and another piece of the Tasty Time Burger puzzle.

He told himself that was completely unacceptable.

He could write his jingles himself, thank you very much. He didn't need help. Not from Meg. Not from anyone.

And he didn't need another reminder that with every passing day and every blank piece of paper that stared at him defiantly, the corner office in Boston looked better and better.

Because he refused to even think about it, Gabe crossed his arms over his chest and sat back. He watched the street in front of them get polka-dotted with the first few fat drops of rain. ''I'm out here searching for Diana because I'm responsible. Remember?''

''Yeah, I do.''

It was another snare. More subtle than the first but equally effective. This was a trap of the say-just-enough-and-then-look-enigmatic variety, and although Meg was very good at it and Gabe recognized it for what it was, he bit.

''You're going for sarcasm here, am I right? You're talking about the fact that I was leaving.''

Meg slowed the cart to a crawl. With the weather getting worse, there was little traffic on the roads and not much chance they'd be a hazard. ''Was I?'' she asked. ‘‘Seems to me you’re the one who brought it up.’’

‘‘I brought it up because you brought it up. You said I was responsible.’’

‘‘Sounds like a compliment to me.’’ They were inching along on a straight road and except for two cyclists who zipped by racing for cover, there was no other traffic. Still, Meg kept both hands on the steering wheel and her eyes on the road. ‘‘If you don’t think it’s a compliment to be called responsible, maybe there’s a reason. Maybe there’s something you’re feeling guilty about.’’

‘‘Aha!’’ Gabe waved a finger at her. ‘‘Got you there. You complimented me just to make me feel guilty.’’

‘‘Do you?’’

‘‘Do I what?’’

‘‘Feel guilty?’’ She stopped the cart completely and turned in her seat to face him. ‘‘Do you feel guilty about trying to sneak out without even saying goodbye?’’

‘‘I don’t have anything to feel guilty about.’’ It was a great argument. Except that it didn’t fool either of them. ‘‘It wasn’t like I was doing it to hurt you.’’

Meg was gracious enough not to mention just how patronizing that sounded. The wind whipped up and caught the cart from behind and she scooped her hair away from her face. ‘‘You don’t owe me anything, Gabe.’’ She looked at him levelly, the vivid color of her eyes muted in the fading light. ‘‘It’s not like I think that kiss was a pledge or anything.’’

‘‘I know.’’ Yet he wished the kiss had meant more. To him and to her. ‘‘It’s not like I thought you were going to pull out the shotgun and march me to the altar.’’

‘‘Then why?’’ Meg had no idea what he was going

to say. But she didn't back down. That, more than anything else, made Gabe decide he owed her the truth, or at least as much of it as he could manage to explain.

"It's all because of Boston," he said.

Whatever she'd expected, it obviously wasn't this. A skeptical smile fluttered across her face and was gone. "Boston? Come on, Gabe, you can do better than that. You're a writer, after all. And a pretty darned good one if what I hear is true." She hit the accelerator and the cart jerked forward. "You could at least come up with something dramatic. For instance, you don't like the way I taste."

"You taste like heaven."

"Or that our relationship could never go anywhere."

"You know that's not true."

She darted him a look. "Another woman?"

"No other woman," he said. "Unless you count Diana. And Latoya. And actually, Diana and Latoya are what this is all about. That and Boston."

The drumming of the rain against the roof started in earnest and Meg pressed down on the accelerator. It was a pretty clear sign that she wasn't buying any of what Gabe was saying.

That didn't keep him from continuing.

"I'm from Boston," he said, and when she didn't tell him that she was pretty sure none of it mattered, he figured he should go on. "I haven't been back there in years. My family disowned me."

This was enough of a surprise to grab her attention. A flicker of sympathy softened Meg's expression. It didn't last long. Like the lightning that snaked through the sky over the lake, anger flashed in her eyes. "What the hell is wrong with those people? *Disowned* you? How can anybody disown anybody? I mean, how could anybody—"

She didn't expect Gabe to laugh, and the fact that she didn't—and the fact that he did—helped put everything in perspective for him. ''I brought it on myself,'' he confessed and for the first time in years, he realized it was the absolute truth. ''They wanted me to join the family business. Architecture.''

''That explains the buildings.''

He nodded. ''Yes, that explains the buildings.''

''And you—''

''Wanted to write jingles. Which explains the disowning.''

''It certainly does not.'' Her comment was as fierce as the gust of wind that sent up a cloud of dust around them. Meg slowed the cart. She coughed and squeezed her eyes shut and when the blast died down, she picked up speed again, her eyes on the road and her lower lip caught in her teeth.

''It's crazy,'' she said, her voice brittle. ''No family would do that. Just because you didn't want to be part of some two-bit—''

''Largest and oldest family-owned firm in New England,'' Gabe said.

''Still...'' They'd arrived at the far end of the island, and the state park. Meg pulled the cart into the almost-empty parking lot. ''There aren't many campers this time of the week, but there are a few. Maybe somebody spotted Diana.''

''Maybe nobody in their right mind is out here.'' Gabe's words were carried away by the wind. He scanned the broad expanse of parking lot and the green grassy slope beyond it. On the other side of that was a wide beach. There wasn't a soul on it and it was no mystery why. The wind thrashed the lake into a frenzy of gray and green waves that crashed onto the beach with a noise like the thunder that growled through the sky.

"There are a couple of tents," Meg yelled, pointing toward the two campsites across the parking lot. "We're here anyway. We might as well ask."

Even though he wasn't sure it was a good idea, Gabe nodded his agreement. He was no expert when it came to weather. After all, he was from LA and in LA, they pretty much didn't have weather. But he knew a doozy of a storm when he saw one and this doozy was brewing all around them. Another bolt of lightning split the sky and the trees that ringed the parking lot bent toward the ground.

By the time they made it over to the campsite, the rain had escalated from steady drizzle to all-out shower. They talked to the people huddled in the first tent (who'd seen nothing of Diana) and found that the second tent was empty (no doubt because the people staying in it had more sense than to sit out a storm under a canopy of canvas). By that time, the shower was a certified downpour.

They paused outside the closed flap of the second tent. For the moment, they were safe and as dry as they were likely to be. There was a slight overhang on the tent and as long as its owners were away, it seemed a shame to let it go to waste.

"So what do you think?" Gabe looked across the parking lot. The cart appeared to be a long way off. "Want to make a run for it?"

"We're okay for now." Meg glanced up. The overhang didn't offer a lot of protection but it was better than nothing. She wiped a finger across her wet cheeks. "Do you regret it?" she asked.

"Not running for the cart? Nah." Though he knew he would've been far more comfortable in the cart, heading back to the Hideaway, Gabe didn't regret not running. Not running meant he had more time to stand and enjoy the way Meg looked with her drenched hair plastered to her head and her wet T-shirt stuck to her breasts like a second skin. It meant he could savor the way the humidity in the air brought out the scent of something fresh and herbal that she'd splashed on her skin.

Caught in the moment, he watched a single drop of rain drip from her hair and skim down her neck. From there, it slipped inside the neckline of her shirt. He told himself it wasn't a good idea, but Gabe couldn't help remembering that back at the Love Shack, he'd slipped his hand inside her shirt, too. He steadied himself against the sensations that crashed over him like the waves against the shore.

The warmth of Meg's skin. The size and shape of her breast in his hand. The feel of her nipple and how, when he'd touched her there, the murmur from deep in her throat told him she wanted more.

"I was talking about walking away."

Meg's words yanked him out of the fantasy that was heating him inside in spite of the rain and wind chilling him outside.

"Walking away from the corner office with the killer view, my family or—" He pulled in a breath to steady himself. "Walking away from you?"

"I was talking about your family."

"I wasn't." He turned to her, and when he did, the overhang protected only half of him. His right shoulder got drenched and the right leg of his jeans soaked through. "Do I regret walking away from my family? Never have. I always dreamed of being a songwriter and I wasn't going to let anything get in the way of that dream. I figured they'd come around someday, see that it was meant to be. Maybe someday…''

Maybe that someday was here and maybe his plans had been turned upside down. Maybe he was the one who was coming to an epiphany of sorts. One that showed him how silly jingle-writing had been from the get-go. And how right his grandfather had been all along.

Gabe banished the thought that had been hanging over his head ever since he'd kissed Meg, and because it was too painful to consider what had once been the bright prospect of his future, he concentrated on the kiss instead.

''Do I regret trying to walk out on you this morning? You bet I do.'' The truth of the statement twisted through his gut. ''You're a good friend, even to Diana the Terrible,'' he told her. ''You wouldn't be out here in this miserable weather searching for her if you weren't. You're kind and you're loyal, too. You'd never dream of doing what my family did to me. Not to anybody.''

She laughed. ''Now you're making me sound like man's best friend.''

''You are. You're a great friend.'' He didn't dare tell her that he wished she could be more. It wasn't fair. Not to him, and certainly not to Meg.

''A friend, huh?'' She paused long enough for him to know she was offering him the opportunity to tell her he wanted more than just friendship from her. When he didn't—when he couldn't—the expression in her eyes grew shuttered. She stepped into the rain. ''Come on,'' she said. ''I think it's time to get going.''

It didn't seem like the best idea. Heck, it didn't even seem like a good one. But since there was nothing left for them to say and nothing for Gabe to do but kiss her, he figured a thorough soaking was as agreeable an alternative as any.

He followed Meg into the rain and they ran for the cart.

They were almost all the way there when Gabe thought he heard a noise. He would have chalked the whole thing up to imagination if Meg hadn't stopped dead, too.

Gabe knew his ears weren't playing tricks on him. Just as Meg turned and headed the other way, Gabe spun around and headed for the beach.

Toward the sound of frantic barking.

Chapter Eleven

To the west of the beach lay nothing but water. Facing the water across thirty feet of sand was a slope that gradually rose to become a gentle hill protecting the campground on the other side from the worst of the lake weather. At its farthest end, the beach disappeared in a tumble of boulders and scrub, and on the other end, the path that led from the parking lot squeezed between the hill on the right and a massive boulder on the left. The boulder blocked at least some of the wind. But beyond it…

The rain beating on her face, Meg fought to catch her breath. She arrived at the entrance to the beach just a couple of steps behind Gabe and stopped when he did. They stared at the chaos just a few feet away. Huge waves pounded the shore, churning the water until it was a color that reminded her of slate and blended so perfectly with the gray clouds that it was hard to tell where the sky ended and the water began. The wind from the northwest hammered the trees on the hill opposite the water and tossed their branches. The rain kept up, so heavy and so fast, it was hard for Meg to keep her eyes open.

"Do you see her?" Because a roar of thunder cracked in the sky directly over them, Meg had to yell and even then, she wasn't sure if Gabe heard her. She waited until the vibration eased in the air and in her bones, before she tried again. "Do you see Diana?"

She couldn't hear his answer but then, she didn't have to. She saw the way his brows dropped and eyes narrowed. She knew he was worried.

"I swore I heard her." Gabe edged close enough to the beach to get drenched by the next wave that blasted through. He nearly lost his footing and braced himself, one hand on the boulder. "I know I heard a dog."

"I heard her, too." Meg inched nearer to the opening. She might have dared to move closer if Gabe didn't stiff-arm her to keep her back. Her gaze followed his over to where driftwood was getting tossed as far as the hill and at the way the sand reshaped itself every time a wave came and went. She could guess exactly what he was thinking: it was too dangerous to get any closer.

But that didn't mean she didn't want to. Or that she wouldn't have.

If only there was some sign of Diana. Somewhere.

"We can't try that way." Since he knew she couldn't hear him otherwise, Gabe bent his head nearer and yelled above the noise. "We could go around the other way." He pointed back toward the parking lot. "We could come around from behind. Up the other side of the hill. We might be able to see the whole length of the beach."

"We might." It was the best plan, but that didn't make it any easier. She pictured Diana out on the beach, alone and frightened.

However, that wasn't nearly as terrifying as picturing a wave coming by and scooping the dog into the water.

"But by then," she told Gabe, "it might be too late."

"Well, you're not going out there." A bolt of lightning split the sky and lit up the area and she saw him step to his left to block the entrance and keep Meg from heading on to the beach.

It was sweet, in an old-fashioned, completely anachronistic sort of way. And although it warmed Meg in some small part of her insides (the only part, she was convinced, that wasn't soaked completely through), it was also completely unnecessary. "Don't worry. I don't have a death wish. But don't think you're going out there, either." When it looked as if he actually might be considering it, she made a grab for him. But though she missed catching hold of Gabe's sleeve, her hand brushed the pocket where he'd stashed his phone. And that gave Meg an idea.

"Your phone." She pointed to his pocket. "Give me your phone."

He didn't have a clue what she was talking about but he got big points for not arguing. He handed her the phone and Meg dialed her sister.

"Laurel, I need you to call this number," she yelled, trying to be heard above the noise of the storm. "Yes, I'm outside," she said in response to her sister's question. "No, I'm not going to explain why. Not now, anyway. I'll tell you later. Or tomorrow. Or whenever. But I need you to do something for me. I need you to call a number. What number?" Meg looked at Gabe. "What number?" she asked, and he must have figured out what she was up to, because he nodded. When he supplied his cell phone number, she gave it to Laurel.

"Call it," she told her sister. "And I'm not going to answer, so keep calling, over and over."

Big points for Laurel, too. Although it must have sounded as bizarre to her sister as it would have to

Meg if she'd gotten the call, Laurel promised to follow instructions. A second later, Gabe's phone rang.

Once. Twice. Three times.

Eventually, Laurel must have gotten Gabe's voice mail message because after eight rings, there was a pause. Then the ringing started up again.

So did the sound of howling.

"You're a genius!" Gabe grinned and slapped Meg a high-five. "Now all we have to do is figure out where it's coming from."

They bent their heads, listening.

"The hill?" Meg pointed. "Somewhere over in that direction."

The ringing stopped and so did Diana's howling and they waited for both to begin again.

"It is the hill!" Gabe said when the howling started anew. He hurried back the way they'd come and Meg ran beside him. By now, the slope of the hill was slick with mud and with the leaves that had been ripped from trees. It took them longer than it should have to climb. When they finally got to the top, they were buffeted full-force by the wind.

Meg hung on to the nearest tree. Gabe hung on to the one next to it. Together, they listened.

"Over there!" Meg set off toward their right at as much of a run as she could manage in the mud. She slipped and went down and pulled herself up again before Gabe could offer her a hand. The phone stopped and started and somewhere in the tall brush up ahead, they heard Diana howl.

"Diana!" Gabe's voice was snatched away by the wind. "Diana! Come here, girl. Come here, Diana." There was a good-sized boulder just up ahead and he climbed over it. His sneakers were muddy and the boulder was wet and just as he got to the top, his feet went out from under him. He disappeared over the side of the rock.

Meg wasn't going to take the same chance. She squeezed between the boulder and a bush with little white flowers and very sharp thorns and found Gabe sitting on the other side in a puddle of mud. She was all set to offer him a hand up when she saw she didn't need to. Someone else had already come to his rescue.

Looking more than a little relieved to see familiar faces and way more bedraggled than any celebrity ever should, Diana waddled out from where she'd found shelter beneath an old, fallen tree. Her fur stuck up at funny angles. Her mouth was rimmed with all that was left of a Twinkie. She was drenched and coated with mud.

She barked a greeting, jumped into Gabe's lap and gave him a big, wet kiss.

"COME ON. COME ON IN." Meg flicked on her kitchen light and stepped back to allow Gabe into the house ahead of her.

He slid to a stop outside the door and looked down at his own mud-spattered clothes and at a filthy and especially aromatic Diana, whom he'd wrapped in the shirt he'd stripped off as soon as they got into the golf cart. "Your floor is clean. And we're filthy."

"It's just a floor." To prove to him that a little dirt didn't bother her nearly as much as the fact that they were all cold and shivering, Meg scuffed her sneakers against the floor. She left long streaks of mud behind and the water dripping off her clothes puddled around her feet. "There," she said. "Now it's not clean. It's a dirty floor. And it's not going to make any difference if you get it dirtier."

Maybe she was really good in the logical argument

department. Or maybe Gabe was just tired of being wet and miserable. He slipped off his sneakers, left them outside the door and stepped inside. He set Diana down. ''She needs a—''

''Towel.'' Meg already had one in her hand. It was a small-size kitchen towel and Diana was a jumbo-size girl, but for now, it would have to do. After Gabe had unwrapped the dog and lobbed his wet shirt into the sink, Meg tossed him the towel. He caught it midair and gave Diana a brisk rub. The dog made a noise from deep in her throat that was pure pleasure, and Meg swore she smiled.

Pretty much as she would if Gabe was rubbing her down like that.

She put a lid on the thought as fast as she could. Of course that didn't make it any easier to keep her imagination in check when Gabe ran a hand over his wet hair. Rainwater streaked over his bare chest and trickled down into the waistband of his jeans.

And before she could decide she was enjoying this just a little too much, Meg kicked off her shoes and hurried across the room to close the door between the kitchen and the dining room. It was one thing to have a muddy dog in the kitchen. It was another to allow her the run of the house.

She came back the other way, just in time to see Gabe shiver. ''You really need to get the rest of your clothes off,'' she told him.

No sooner were the words out of her mouth than Meg heated through as if she'd been zapped by the lightning that flickered outside the window.

Maybe the same lightning touched Gabe. He smiled. ''You'd better be careful, Meg. You never know when a guy might want to take you up on an offer like that.''

''Or maybe that's the whole idea.''

She wasn't sure exactly where the words came from. Just as she wasn't sure how on earth she had the nerve to say them. But Meg knew one thing. When it came to timing, she was something of an expert. She knew exactly how long to bake a soufflé and she was a wizard at whipping egg whites just enough to keep them from getting dry. Rather than risk ruining a moment that hummed with anticipation, or listening to Gabe offer some excuse about how nice it would be if only it wasn't for architecture and dancing hamburgers, she left the room in search of towels, dry clothes—and peace of mind.

Where were all the snappy comebacks when he needed them? For a couple of seconds Gabe's tongue was tied in the same tight knots that twisted through his gut until it ached. All he could do was stare at the spot where Meg had been dripping on the floor a heartbeat earlier.

''Guess I should've said something clever, huh?'' he asked Diana.

She barked.

''I'm not much good at clever these days.'' He threw the dog a sidelong look, half expecting her to agree with him, half hoping she'd give him a sign that told him it wasn't so. When she didn't do either, he surrendered with a sigh and rummaged through the cupboards. He found a bowl and though he'd seen enough water in the last few hours to last a lifetime, he filled the bowl and set it down on the floor for Diana.

''How's this one?'' Gabe asked. ''I could have said something like this.'' He cleared his throat, steadied his shoulders and switched to the kind of smooth and suave voice that was supposed to melt women into mush, but which always sounded lame to him. ''Well, little lady, if you want a guy to get naked with, maybe I'm just the man to oblige.''

Apparently, he wasn't the only one who thought it was lame. Diana snorted her opinion.

''All right, all right. Give me another chance.'' Thinking, he looked through the refrigerator and the pantry on the other side of the room. Meg's selection of fresh foods and leftovers was definitely more on the healthy side and less please-a-dog-with-a-sweet-tooth fare, but he managed to locate a can of mandarin oranges, the dregs of a bag of corn chips and a pint of ice cream that had yet to be touched. He opened the can and dumped the orange sections and their juice into a bowl.

''OK. I've got it. How about this?'' He sprinkled the corn chips on top of the oranges and went in search of a spoon. ''Maybe the whole idea is to get me to take off my clothes, huh? Well, that's all well and good, but you…'' He used the spoon to point to the spot where Meg had been standing only moments before. ''Maybe you don't know how much trouble you'd be getting yourself into.''

Diana raised an eyebrow and glanced from the spoon to the pint of cherry cordial ice cream.

Gabe got the message. ''Guess that one doesn't work, either.'' He scooped a spoonful of ice cream on top of everything else in the bowl, placed it on the floor and watched Diana dive in. ''Think she'd believe me if I just came right out and told her that if I got naked with her, *I'd* be the one getting into trouble?''

''Think maybe we should quit fooling around and find out?''

Gabe hadn't heard Meg come in, and when he realized she'd been listening, he spun toward the door. ''I was talking to Diana.'' He gave himself a mental slap. He sounded like a moron, like a kid caught with his hand in the cookie jar, or worse, like an adult who wanted a certain woman so bad, he could taste it. And who was too afraid to take the chance.

Maybe she didn't notice. Or maybe she didn't care who he was talking to.

Maybe she had her own agenda and little patience with Gabe's insecurities.

Meg let the door swing closed behind her. She was carrying a stack of brightly colored towels and she hugged them close and took a couple of slow steps in Gabe's direction.

"You were talking about me."

"I was." There was no use denying it, so Gabe didn't even try. He studied her still-dripping clothes and even though she was half hidden behind the towels, he remembered the way her T-shirt hugged her breasts. He looked at her wet hair, plastered to her head, and at her arms and the goose bumps that covered them, wrist to elbow and beyond. "I was thinking that you wouldn't want to give me a second chance. I mean, after what happened at the Love Shack this morning."

Meg set the stack of towels on the countertop. She took the top one in her hands, fluffed it and draped it over Gabe's shoulders.

Heat poured through him and he knew it had nothing to do with the soft, clean-smelling towel and everything to do with Meg. The warmth surged from his shoulders to his chest. It pooled in his groin and spread out again. It settled around his heart.

When she stroked the towel over his wet skin, the heat turned around on itself and rushed right back to his groin.

"What did happen in the Love Shack this morning?" Meg asked.

Gabe wasn't going to lie to her. Not about something this important. He gathered his thoughts and his words while he braced himself against the tingle of pure pleasure that rippled through him when she slowly scraped the towel down his spine and back up again. "What happened was that I wanted to kiss you. More than anything."

"And now?"

"And now..." He spun around and took her into his arms. "And now," he said, "I want to kiss you. More than anything."

The truth of that statement sang from his head to his toes, just as clearly as the music that played in his head the moment he touched her. He ignored it. Right here and right now, Meg was more important than the music. The feel of her mouth. The taste of her tongue. The impatience that trembled through her like the perfect vibrato brought to life by a musician with skill and flair.

When he heard a rumble, he wasn't sure if it was thunder or his own heartbeat.

When he heard it again, he knew it was Diana.

Grinning, Meg pulled away and grabbed Gabe's hand. "She's just jealous," she said. She tugged him away from the dog, who was staring at him as if she'd just lost her best friend, and led him into the dining room.

"Jealous?" Gabe wasn't so sure. By the time he closed the door and left Diana behind and saw that Meg had started a fire in the fireplace and tossed a quilt down on the floor in front of it, he didn't much care. "What does she have to be jealous about?"

"Don't you get it?" Meg poked him with one finger and he felt the same staggering jolt of energy rush that he'd felt out on the beach when he'd forgotten himself long enough to slap her a high-five. ''Diana adores you!''

It was news to Gabe. But now that he thought about it, he realized Diana had somehow wormed her smelly way into his heart.

At the moment, he didn't much care about that, either. He didn't much care about anything.

Not about anything or anyone except Meg.

He fitted his hands on her waist and back-stepped her toward the brightly colored quilt. When she went along for the ride with a smile on her face, his desire kicked up a notch.

It wasn't until they stood in front of the flickering fire that Gabe stopped. There was no other light in the room and the orange glow of the fire hugged Meg's body, outlining her hips and her nipples. Touching her face with color. Stroking her breasts.

He nudged her toward the couch.

''Oh, no!'' Meg placed one hand on his chest.

And Gabe refused to acknowledge the electrical jolt that rocketed through him.

''I might not mind mud on the kitchen floor,'' she told him. ''But there's no way you're getting on my couch in those filthy clothes. Everything off. Now.''

''Yes, ma'am.'' He wasn't about to argue. Gabe stripped off his wet jeans and lobbed them onto a towel Meg had set in the corner. His boxers were just a bit drier, and he slipped out of them and tossed them aside, too. It wasn't until he was standing in front of her stark naked that he realized Meg hadn't moved a muscle. She was looking him over as thoroughly as a horse trader examining the latest stock.

Looking him over and purring her approval.

Before she could ask to check out his teeth, he figured he should get things moving. ''This doesn't work really well unless you...'' He pointed one finger at her jeans and her T-shirt, but if there was one truth he should've learned about Meg, it was that she was single-minded. She shuffled closer. Her soggy T-shirt touched his chest. Her jeans were just starting to dry and they were stiff and scratchy. The fabric grated against his thighs.

And Gabe refused to acknowledge the Tasty Time burgers when they made their singing-and-dancing appearance, just as he'd known they would.

''Maybe you'd like to help.'' Her voice was no more than a throaty growl. It sent a similar vibration purring through Gabe. So did the fact that she tucked one of his legs between hers. That she worked her hips against his. That she skimmed her hands over his chest and down even further. That she reached for him, measuring, stroking, testing the length of him in her palm.

The music played louder.

The hamburgers danced faster.

Gabe closed his eyes. When he opened them again, he found Meg smiling up at him. Oblivious to the hamburgers, unaware of the tune that played in his head, she brushed her breasts against his chest. Her pupils were dark and wide. Her breathing was as quick as Gabe's. She flicked her tongue over her lips. ''So, what do you say? You want to start?''

Did he?

Gabe consigned the hamburgers to the back burner—literally and figuratively—and left them there to fry in the heat of the moment.

His heart doing a cha-cha in his chest and his blood racing like it was on the inside lane at Indianapolis, he gripped the hem of her shirt and pulled it over her head.

The second he touched her, Meg knew something

had changed. It was subtle and inexplicable. It wasn't bad. In fact, it was very, very good.

She felt the tension go out of Gabe's muscles. She felt the sigh that shivered along his body. As if he'd made some decision he was not only happy with but relieved about, a smile softened his lips. It traveled all the way to his eyes. When he tugged her shirt over her head, Meg stepped back to let him admire her.

"You're beautiful." He brought a finger to the hollow at the base of her throat and let it glide down ever so slowly to the shadowy place between her breasts. "You're also as cold as hell." He chuckled and pulled her close again. "Looks like you need some serious warming."

She glided her hands along his back. "Looks like I'm not the only one. You've got goose bumps on your goose bumps."

"And you…" He dipped his head long enough to press a kiss between her breasts. "You even taste cold."

"Then let's get warm." Meg glanced at the quilt lying on the floor in front of the fire. She unzipped her jeans.

"Guess you never got around to putting on that little black—" Gabe took one look at her white, French-cut panties and one look at the way Meg's mouth pulled into a thin line and thought better of the question. "No. I guess you didn't. Not that it matters." Her jeans were damp and they clung like wet tissue. Before she could tug them off, he slipped his hand behind the elastic band on her panties and Meg knew he was right. It didn't matter.

Her breath caught. Her eyes drifted shut. He kissed her neck and her ear. He reached around to her back and unfastened her bra and once she'd skimmed out of it and tossed it over her shoulder, he took her into his mouth.

Meg wrapped one arm around Gabe's neck and because it felt as if her legs still wouldn't hold her, she wrapped her other arm around him, too. His hair was damp and it tickled her skin, heightening the sensations that vibrated over her. When he pushed down her jeans, she knew they were too clammy for him to remove without help. As much as she hated to be too far away from him for too long, she moved back far enough to tug her jeans off and throw them aside.

She glanced down at her panties. "You want to..."

His smile was the only answer she needed. He grazed a hand up one of her hips and down again, tugging one side of the panties with him. He did the same thing on the other side and as they dropped even farther, Meg stepped out of them and kicked them out of the way.

He kissed her breasts and her stomach. He skimmed his hand between her legs and slid his fingers inside her. "You're beautiful," he whispered in her ear.

"You already said that." Meg's voice sounded as though it came from very far away. Her body trembling with anticipation, she looked at the quilt again. "Can we—"

"Oh, yeah." Gabe's grin lit up the room and ignited an answering fire inside her, and when Meg lay on the quilt and drew him down beside her she was smiling, too.

"You never let me tell you." He kissed her eyelids and her cheeks. He left a trail of kisses along her collarbone and over her hips and across her stomach. "You never let me explain. Why I was leaving this morning."

There was nothing she would have liked better than

to lie there and let him cover her with kisses from head to toe. But there were some things even more important than kisses. More important than the white-hot anticipation that poured through her like wine and made her head spin. She took Gabe's face in her hands and gazed into his eyes.

"Are you going to leave again?" she asked him. "Are you going to sneak away now?"

There was no hesitation in his eyes or in the kiss that made her feel as if she'd melt into the quilt. "No." He sealed the promise with a nip to the earlobe. "I'm not going anywhere. Not for a long, long time."

It was the only assurance Meg needed. She wrapped her arms around Gabe and pulled him on top of her and when he filled her, they rode together to mind-numbing bliss.

As Meg's breath caught over a tiny sob of perfect contentment, she heard Gabe growl her name.

Right before he said something else.

She couldn't be sure, of course. Couldn't be sure of anything more than the way her blood hummed and her heart sang with happiness.

She couldn't be sure.

But if she didn't know better, she would've said he mumbled something silly and so absolutely romantic it brought tears to her eyes.

Something about the perfect marriage between sweet and heat.

Chapter Twelve

"So..." Her hands laid comfortably across her belly, Laurel leaned against the kitchen countertop and watched Meg mixing up a batch of muffins for the guests who would be checking in later in the day. "You want to tell me what those phone calls were all about last night?"

"I told you. Yesterday." Meg added dried cranberries to the muffin batter and though she'd never tried the combination before, she decided white chocolate would be good, too. She went to the freezer where she'd stored some white chocolate chunks left over from a wedding cake. "When I called to tell you to stop calling, I told you what it was all about. You had to call me—"

"So you could find Diana. Yeah, I remember that part." Laurel was a firm believer in limiting her caffeine intake during her pregnancy, and she had refused coffee when Meg forgot and offered it. She sipped the orange juice Meg had squeezed for her instead. Since Laurel was a doctor, Meg figured she knew what she was talking about. And since Laurel would be a mother in just a couple of months...

Though she'd had plenty of time to get used to the thought of her older sister having a baby, Meg found herself in awe. Laurel and Noah would be perfect parents and there wasn't a shred of doubt in her mind that their baby would be perfect, too. Cute and cuddly and one-hundred-percent adorable. But while she'd had plenty of time to picture herself as the ideal aunt to her perfect little niece or nephew, Meg had never spent much time thinking of herself as a mother.

Until now.

Meg gulped down a feeling that was half-panic, half-joy. Though she and Gabe had made love three times the night before, they'd been in such a rush and so blinded by everything but their own need for each other that they'd never even thought to use protection.

Considering the time of the month, there really wasn't much chance that she could have gotten pregnant but…

Meg bobbled the bag of white-chocolate chunks and recovered just before it hit the floor.

A baby?

She turned the possibility over in her head. It would be nice. If not now, then sometime in the near future.

As long as Gabe was the father.

"You're grinning, Meg." Laurel carried her empty juice glass to the sink and rinsed it. She slipped into bedside-manner, tell-me-everything-I'm-your-doctor mode. "You expect me to believe that the only thing you were doing last night was searching for Diana and you're standing there grinning."

"Am not." Meg didn't even try to wipe the smile off her face. "If I was grinning—"

"I'll tell you who's grinning." Maisie pushed open the kitchen door and walked in, her smile as sunny as the sunshine outside the window. After the storm, the temperature had cooled considerably, and today Maisie was wearing a lightweight pink sweater along with stylish white slacks. "I just came in from outside," she said, firmly ignoring Meg and talking to Laurel. "Gabe is out there rinsing down the golf cart. Nice of him to offer, don't you think? Talk about grinning."

As if they'd planned the move (and for all she knew, they had), both Maisie and Laurel turned to Meg.

"All right. All right." Meg threw up her hands in surrender. "I'll admit it. I'm grinning."

"And Gabe is grinning," her grandmother reminded her.

"And yes, Gabe is grinning, too." It was nice to think she'd left him smiling. It was a turn-on, too. Meg promised herself an hour or so of making him smile again as soon as the muffins were finished baking. The thought sizzled over her skin and though she'd tried her best to play it cool with her sister and her grandmother, she knew that her best wasn't nearly good enough. Not when she was feeling like this. Meg grabbed her cup of coffee and pulled a chair up to the kitchen table. Sensing that they were in for a long story and plenty of juicy details, Laurel and Maisie sat down, too.

Meg grasped her coffee cup with both hands. "He's nice," she said.

"Nice?" Maisie wrinkled her nose. "Honey, Vern the mailman is nice, but I wouldn't want him in my bed. We *know* Gabe is nice. Tell us what we really want to know."

"He's more than nice." Remembering everything they'd said and done the night before made her cheeks hot and Meg fanned her face with one hand. "He's funny and kind, and anyone who can sing the Love Me Tenders commercial like that..." She sighed. "He pretends he doesn't like Diana, but he was willing to risk his life for her last night. And after we found her, he wrapped her in his own shirt and—''

''And this is sounding more like an episode of 'Lassie' than 'The View.' We want down and dirty. Come on, girl!'' Laurel poked her in the arm. ''We've got the message that Gabe is nice. And we know you found Diana. Now we want to know what happened *after* you found Diana.''

''Everything.'' It was Laurel and Maisie's turn to sigh, and Meg laughed. ''He's dreamy.''

''And hot,'' Maisie said. As if Meg needed the reminder.

''He's gentle and not at all boring and—''

''Hot,'' Maisie added.

''And he's got this ticklish spot right below his left shoulder blade and a scar on his knee from when he fell off a bike when he was ten.'' Meg knew she was getting carried away. She really didn't care. The way she figured it, a woman who'd spent the most special night of her life was entitled. ''And his eyes…'' Just thinking about their brandy color made her tingle all over. ''They're a soft, warm color in the firelight and he's—''

''Hot!''

''All right, he's hot!'' Meg sat back in her chair and laughed. After fourteen months of believing that the world was meant for other people and definitely not her, she was feeling remarkably connected and—not so remarkably—pretty satisfied with herself and the way things were going.

How could she not?

The last twenty-four hours had been incredible.

''And…well…'' Meg hesitated.

'''And…well…' That's all you're going to say?'' Laurel got up and put a hand to the small of her back.

''You're talking to a woman who's a walking hormone factory,'' she said, laughing. ''You're going to say 'And...well...'and leave it at that? I don't think so.''

Feeling as happy as she'd ever been, Meg joined in the fun. ''I don't want to make you two ladies jealous,'' she said. ''After all, Noah and Doc Ross are pretty nice guys.''

''Pretty nice?'' Laurel pretended to be offended.

''Pretty nice?'' Maisie sat up and tsk-tsked her opinion.

Meg laughed. ''Well, Gabe's a writer, after all. A songwriter. And a songwriter is the same as a poet.''

''He didn't!'' As if her legs wouldn't hold her, Laurel plopped down in her seat. She practically melted right in front of Meg's eyes. ''Don't tell me! He actually recited poetry to you?''

''Not exactly poetry. But pretty close.'' Meg leaned back, remembering the moment and the purr of Gabe's voice in her ear. ''It was when we were at my house,'' she said, smiling at the memory. ''And he kissed me. And then he said something so romantic. All about the perfect marriage between sweet and heat.''

''Sweet and heat? Oh, dear!'' The color drained from Maisie's face so fast, Meg was sure her grandmother was having a heart attack. She jumped out of her chair and grabbed Maisie's left hand but Laurel was already one step ahead of her. She was taking Maisie's pulse and peering into Maisie's eyes.

''Stop that, you two. I'm fine. I'm fine.'' Maisie brushed them aside, but in spite of her protests, she didn't sound fine.

She didn't look fine, either. After that one ashen moment, color raced back to her cheeks. It wasn't her usual rosy-pink color. This color was darker. And not nearly as pretty.

Trembling noticeably, Maisie stood and walked to

the other side of the room and Laurel and Meg exchanged worried glances.

"What's going on?" Meg asked.

"I'm not sure." Maisie turned and marched back the other way, her posture stiff and her expression clouded with concern. "I don't want to say anything I shouldn't," she mumbled, almost to herself. "I don't want to make judgments or jump to conclusions or..." She shook her head and her expression cleared. "I suppose you need to know," she told Meg.

Meg couldn't stand the suspense. She grabbed Maisie's arm in both hands and held on tight, determined that even if Maisie tried to turn around and head the other way again, she wasn't going to let go. Not until she heard the whole story. "I need to know what?" she asked Maisie.

"About the sweet. And the heat." Maisie's eyes darkened with worry again. Her forehead creased. She gave Meg's hand a squeeze. "You see, I saw something this morning. I went in to straighten up Gabe's room. Of course, I saw right away that I didn't need to straighten up. The bed hadn't been slept in and that's when I knew...well, never mind that right now. What I mean to say..."

The hesitation was so unlike Maisie, Meg knew she wasn't going to like whatever it was her grandmother was about to say. Her stomach tensed. Her palms got damp. For the first time since she and Gabe arrived had at her house the night before and he'd taken her in his arms and kissed her, the heat inside her chilled.

"It's hard to explain, dear." Maisie took Meg's hand and led her out of the kitchen. "It might be easier if I could just show you. It's upstairs. In Love Me Tender."

GABE COULDN'T GET the music out of his head. No big surprise there. Finally he felt in control. He had his jingle, and he hummed another few bars of it just to remind himself that it was catchy and easy on the ear. When Diana barked her approval, he grinned.

"You got it!" He gave the dog a thumbs-up. "That tune is going to send the folks at Tasty Time Burger into fast-food Nirvana."

He had his lyrics, too, and they were as clever as any he'd ever come up with. He put the finishing touch on the shine he was giving the roof of the golf cart. "They only need singing and dancing hamburgers to bring them to life."

He wound up the hose, hung the towels he'd used to wipe down the cart where Maisie'd said to put them, and headed back into the Hideaway, taking the steps two at a time. When he got to the top, he waited for Diana to catch up.

He was on top of the world.

And all because of Meg.

"Meg. Meg. Meg, Meg, Meg." He sang her name to the tune that would be sweeping the country in another few months, and it resonated through his heart.

Meg was terrific. She was warm and wonderful and every bit as sexy as he'd dreamed. Meg was giving and adventurous, and thinking about her…

Gabe pulled in a breath to calm himself and even before he slowly let it out, he realized there wasn't a chance. Just thinking about Meg made him want to sing at the top of his lungs.

And he wished his conscience didn't keep nudging him to fess up and tell her what happened every time he touched her.

One hand already on the back door, he hesitated and glanced inside.

"No sign of her," he told Diana. When a wave of relief swept over him, he told himself he was a fool.

Relieved at not seeing Meg? He might just as well be relieved at never taking another breath. Meg was everything that was right with his life.

"Which means that when I do get around to telling her she's my muse, she'll think it's as funny as I do. Ha-ha funny and bizarre funny," he added, in case Diana didn't get the subtle difference. "We'll share a laugh about it and that will be that, and then we're not going to talk about it again except maybe when I sweep her into my arms and she says, 'So, what are you feeling?'"

That possibility caused a wave of emotion to pour through Gabe and he gathered his wits and smiled down at Diana. He didn't even try to explain what would happen between him and Meg at times like that. Diana wouldn't understand, anyway. At times like that, what he'd be feeling would be so much more than simple inspiration, he didn't know how he'd ever explain it to Meg. Or even to himself.

The realization made him feel better, and Gabe opened the door and let Diana into the Hideaway ahead of him. He left her in the kitchen with a bowl of fresh water. He cut through the kitchen and into the lobby and walked up the winding stairway. In his heart of hearts, he knew he was right. Meg would think the whole you're-my-soul-and-my-life's-inspiration thing was hilarious. She'd think it was weird, too, just like he did. She'd tell him that needing her to kick-start his creativity didn't mean he had any reason to feel guilty.

Provided, of course, that he came clean and told her about the whole thing.

Knowing he'd have to face the music sooner or later

(although he hoped it would be much later), he pushed open the door of Love Me Tender and stopped cold.

Later had officially arrived.

Meg was standing by the piano, reading over the lyrics he'd scribbled on a legal pad the second he got back to the Hideaway that morning.

''We need to talk.'' Gabe congratulated himself. He managed to sound as if the whole, wonderful world that had opened up to him in the last twenty-four hours wasn't being threatened by some lines of lyrics and that musical notation on the pad in Meg's hands. He stepped into the room and closed the door behind him. She didn't seem surprised to see him and she didn't look upset, either. That would've been a good sign—if he was a complete idiot. Sure, Meg's hands were steady. Yes, her gaze was level.

It didn't mean she wasn't upset.

He could tell because the last time he'd seen her—just a couple hours before—there hadn't been anything separating them. Not clothing, that was for sure. Not shyness. Not hesitation or doubt. And now?

Gabe was a smart guy. He knew regret when he saw it. And it wasn't a pretty sight.

''I know how this looks,'' he told her.

''Really? Tell me, Gabe.'' As if he wasn't aware of exactly what she'd found and what she was reading, she turned the legal pad to face him. ''How does this look?''

He tried for the light and funny version of but-honey-you're-making-a-mountain-out-of-a-molehill and offered it to her along with a sunny smile. ''It looks like a Tasty Time Burger jingle to me.''

''Looks like one to me, too.'' Meg dropped the legal pad onto the piano bench and it landed with a slap. ''You want to explain how your singing and dancing hamburgers just happen to be singing and dancing to the sweet nothings you whispered in my ear last night?''

''Do I need to explain?'' Gabe shrugged and instantly recognized the gesture as ineffective. ''I mean, why do I need to explain? They're just words and—''

''They're just the same words you've been saying to me every time things start getting interesting between us.'' Meg picked up the pad and read from it. '''Dancing hamburgers. Tasty Time Burgers, what a treat. Tasty Time Burgers can't be beat.' And of course, the best of the best, the one you saved for the really interesting part. 'The perfect marriage of—'''

''Sweet and heat. Yeah. I know.'' Gabe took a step closer. Even from this far away, he could feel the anger that walled Meg off like a force field in a sci-fi flick. He stopped before he could slam into it.

''What were you doing, Gabe? Practicing on me?'' Meg shook her head and her hair twitched around her shoulders. ''Were you trying to see if your commercial was enough to distract me from—''

''Of course not!'' She was overreacting, that was for certain. But he supposed part of her anger was justified and part of that was his fault. Guilt swept through him, and the guilt only made him feel more defensive. ''You can't possibly believe that at a time like that I'd be thinking about—''

''Dancing hamburgers!'' Some version of the truth must have hit Meg like a two-ton truck. Her mouth dropped open and she sank down on the piano bench. She was winded, as if she'd just run a mile.

''It started with the dancing hamburgers. That day in the dining room.'' She looked up at him and though her eyes were filled with tears, she refused to let them fall. "You've been using me as your own personal test-market study!"

"No!" Force field or no force field, Gabe had to get closer. There was so much confusion on Meg's face, so much pain in her eyes, and he couldn't stand not trying to ease it away. Even if it took the truth to accomplish that.

He sat down on the bench next to her and when she automatically moved to put more distance between them and turned so that her back was to him, he knew better than to press his luck. As much as he wanted to take her in his arms, he didn't dare. She wouldn't let him and besides, he couldn't risk another visit from dancing hamburgers or anything else that smacked of jingles or clever ad campaigns.

Not when their short-lived happily-ever-after hung in the balance.

"You're not my test-market group," he told her, and he managed a voice that sounded far calmer than he felt. "You're my inspiration."

"Cut the poetry, Gabe." Her look told him she wasn't kidding. "I fell for the poetry once and it's not going to happen again. I'm too smart for that."

"You are. Smart, that is. You're smart and funny and you're wonderful and sexy, and Meg...I know this sounds crazy because it *is* crazy, but the truth of the matter is, you're my inspiration. Really. Literally."

Because he couldn't be that close to her without kissing her, Gabe got up and stepped away from the piano. "I know it's nuts," he told her. "I can't explain it. I don't understand it, but..." He went over to where he'd left his phone when he'd got back to the Hideaway a few hours earlier. He picked it up and showed it to her. As if she needed the reminder of how often it rang.

''You wondered why Dennis and Latoya are after me. It's because I owe the people at Tasty Time Burger an ad campaign. And not just any ad campaign. A really big, really important ad campaign. And I'm supposed to be meeting with them in New York next week to present them with my ideas.'' He tossed the phone down again and faced her.

''Except that I've had a major case of writer's block. For months. That's why I decided to drive to New York. I wasn't vacationing or on some sort of get-back-to-the-land experience. I was stalling for time. I was hoping an idea would come out of somewhere or out of nowhere or out of anywhere. But it didn't. No matter how hard I tried. And the phone kept ringing whether I liked it or not, and the clock kept ticking away. Big meeting in New York. And no idea whatsoever what I was going to say to these people.''

She didn't get up and walk out, and right about now, Gabe figured that was good. Instead, Meg's eyes were clouded with confusion. ''What does that have to do with me?'' she asked.

''Everything.'' He hurried back to where she was sitting and knelt on the floor in front of her and though he was tempted to take her hands in his, he stopped himself. ''Every time I touch you, Meg, I get a flash of inspiration. I'm not talking poetic, warm and fuzzy stuff here, though there's plenty of that going on, too. I'm talking about honest-to-gosh, this-is-going-to-sell-another-billion-burgers inspiration.''

''When you touch me?''

''When I touch you! First it was the dancing hamburgers and then yesterday in the Love Shack when I kissed you...'' He hauled in a deep breath. ''It was so overwhelming, I felt like I was going to explode. I pictured the whole ad campaign. The singing. The dancing. The costumes. The scenery. I couldn't stop it. Or the song. It zapped me. Right out of the blue. And I tried to fight it but I couldn't, so I decided to leave. And then last night..." He hauled in another breath, this time to keep himself from melting at the memories.

"Last night when we were together, the final pieces fell into place. A little bit more each time we made love. When I got back here this morning, I wrote it all down."

He fingered the edge of the legal pad. "The good news is that it's not just an okay jingle, Meg. It's brilliant. This commercial will do wonders for the agency. We've got bills to pay and payroll to meet and if this account didn't materialize, our name was going to be mud in the industry."

"Well, congratulations." It was a wonder to Meg that she could sound so normal when the world had turned upside down. She managed to pull herself off the piano bench and stand, even though her knees felt as if they were made of jelly. She managed to look down at Gabe, still kneeling on the green shag carpet, even though all she wanted to do was run out of the room and away from the memories that tore at her heart. "Thanks to you, the agency can meet payroll. And all you had to do was go to bed with me."

"No! It wasn't like that." He stood and when he reached for her, she took a step away. "I wanted you, Meg. I still do. More than anything."

If she stood there a minute longer, she'd burst into tears, and Meg wasn't going to do that. She'd have plenty of time for tears later. Plenty of days and months and maybe even years to relive this scene and torture herself with all the things she could have said and done differently. She knew it. But for now, all she could think was that she had to get out of there. As fast as she could. She marched to the door.

"You know, this whole story..." She tossed the comment over her shoulder at Gabe. "This is all sounding pretty familiar to me." At the door, she whirled and faced him. "You and Ben must go to the same school of excuses."

"Ben?" It took a second for Gabe to remember who she was talking about, but it didn't take long after that to catch on to what she meant. His chin came up and his shoulders went back. "No way," he said. "You're telling me that I've got something in common with that low-life chef who wanted you for your recipes and your cooking techniques? Come on, Meg! This isn't anything like that."

"This is exactly like that. You used me, Gabe. Ben wanted my recipes and you wanted me so you could get your commercial written. And don't tell me you didn't know you were a Ben clone. You knew, all right. That's why you decided to turn tail and run after I told you about Ben yesterday in the Love Shack. You felt guilty as hell. Otherwise, you would've told me what was going on."

Meg watched a moment's hesitation register in his eyes.

Damn, but she hated when she was right! Especially when she was right about something she didn't want to be right about.

"No." He was a lousy liar. Gabe rejected the idea with a sharp gesture. "Ben used you. He was a cold, calculating guy with his eye on nothing but a five-star rating from some snooty gourmet magazine."

"And you're what? Looking for the advertising equivalent of an Oscar? Sounds like the same sort of five-star rating to me."

"Absolutely not. It's not like it was with Ben. I didn't do this on purpose, Meg. It's just something that happened. I never intended it. I didn't even want it. Do you think I'm happy about the fact that I need you?"

Of all the things he'd said and all the hamburgers he thought about when she'd been thinking about nothing but him, this was what hurt the most.

"That pretty much sums it up, doesn't it?" Meg's words caught on the end of a sob. "You figure you don't have to feel guilty about doing what Ben did because something magical was going on. That means you're off the hook. But you're missing the big picture here, Gabe. You don't feel bad because you used me. You feel bad because you need me. You want to do it all yourself. You want to be your own man, without anybody's help. Just like back in Boston when you walked away from your family."

She'd hit a nerve. Gabe's eyes flashed and this time the color reminded her of brandy when it was touched with flame. "I didn't walk. They kicked me out. And I didn't tell you any of that so you'd feel sorry for me."

"Good. Because I don't. Don't you get it? I don't feel sorry for you, I feel sorry for *them.* Because you're so pig-headed, so convinced you have to prove that you don't need anyone or anything, you were willing to walk away without a fight. Just like you were willing to run out on me yesterday."

Meg opened the door. Even she was surprised at how calm she was. Surprised, but not fooled. Her stillness was like the eye of a hurricane, and storm winds blew all around her. Sooner or later, she'd get snatched up by them and tossed on her head. She promised herself it wouldn't be until Gabe was out of sight.

"You're not getting any of this, are you, Gabe?"

she asked him, even though she already knew the answer. "Your problem isn't writer's block. It's not your family, either. It's not Diana and it sure isn't me. Your problem is that you won't admit you need anyone's help to accomplish anything. And you know what?" She stepped out into the hall because if she didn't do it right then and there, she'd never have the strength to walk away from him.

"You can't accomplish everything on your own. You'd better come to grips with that. Otherwise, you're going to spend the rest of your life being a very lonely man."

Chapter Thirteen

Meg wasn't at home. Or, to be more precise, she didn't answer the door when Gabe knocked.

She didn't show up at the Hideaway again that day, either, and when Gabe walked over to Laurel and Noah's downtown medical clinic, they told him they hadn't seen her. While he was out and about, he checked the carousel, the marina, the park and the downtown restaurants. He stopped at the clinic again. No sign of her.

She didn't answer her phone, and, when questioned, Maisie swore she hadn't seen or talked to Meg since she'd stepped out of Love Me Tender, walked directly to the front door and left the Hideaway.

By the next morning, Gabe was ready to take drastic measures. He waited in the kitchen for Meg, convinced that when she arrived to make breakfast for the two newest guest couples, they'd have a chance to talk. But if he thought that would solve all his problems, he was in for a ruder awakening than getting up extra bright and extra early.

"There are muffins in the pantry."

That was what the note on the refrigerator said. A note written by Meg and addressed to Maisie.

"There is fresh-squeezed juice in the fridge. There

is a quiche all set and ready to go and all you have to do is heat it, slice it and serve it along with the fruit compote that's already mixed and chilling.''

''Do-it-yourself breakfast,'' Gabe mumbled. It only made him feel worse to think that it wasn't her breakfast duties Meg was trying to avoid.

He replaced the note where he'd found it and considered his options. It was nearly dawn, and it might be a good time to try and catch Meg at home.

Then again, it might not.

When he heard the door from the dining room swing open and then swing shut, he didn't need to turn around to know who'd come in.

He could feel the beady little eyes boring right through his back.

''Don't look at me that way.'' There was a cool breeze off the lake and the sky was clear. He opened the back door. ''I know. I know,'' he grumbled, finally giving up and turning around to face her. ''I blew it. Big-time.''

Diana was exactly where he knew she'd be. Sitting smack-dab in the middle of the kitchen floor, her brown eyes trained on Gabe. She wasn't dancing around in front of the refrigerator and that said something about her mood. So did the fact that her tail wasn't wagging.

Gabe knew how she felt.

''I tried to explain,'' he told her, going over every word of his last conversation with Meg, the way he'd gone over it a few hundred times in the hours after it happened and a few hundred more times during the night. ''I told her about my whole muse theory and she didn't get it.''

Apparently, Diana didn't, either. Her ears dropped.

''So what was I supposed to do?'' Gabe asked her. ''And what am I supposed to do now?''

Predictably, Diana offered no advice.

''I even went down to both ferry docks and talked to the captains,'' Gabe told the dog, simply to prove to her and to himself that he'd done everything possible. ''They both thought I was nuts when I asked if they'd seen Meg. Like I was some kind of stalker or something. And, by the way, neither one of them had seen her. That means she hasn't escaped to the mainland.'' As long as Gabe was up and in the kitchen, he figured he might as well make himself useful. He got out the quiche and set the oven to preheat. He poked through the cupboards and found the juice glasses and four pink cut-glass bowls that looked as though they'd be just right for compote. Whatever compote was.

Busywork was good, he told himself. Especially for a guy who couldn't keep his mind from running in circles. Busywork would've been even better if everything he touched didn't remind him of Meg.

Gabe sighed. ''I admit I screwed up when it came to explaining the whole muse thing.''

This, apparently, was something Diana knew about. She yipped her agreement.

''But she shouldn't have brought up all that other stuff.''

The muffins were where Meg had said they'd be, and Gabe rummaged through the pantry until he found the basket he'd seen her use to carry breads and muffins to the table. He searched through the drawers for one of the dainty tea towels she spread in the baskets and when he found one embroidered with tiny pink rosebuds and purple butterflies, he laid it out in the basket and set the muffins on top of it. He kept one muffin for Diana who, in spite of her mood, knew a good thing when she saw it. When he broke off bits of muffin and tossed them to her, she gulped them down and gave him her full attention, waiting for more.

"Just for the record, I don't think it's true," Gabe said, and he popped one of the chunks of muffin into his own mouth instead of giving it to Diana. "What she said about me not wanting to depend on anyone but myself." The dog barked, and he wasn't sure if it was because of what he'd said or because she was waiting for more muffin.

"I mean—yes, well...part of it's true. I *have* had to depend on myself. After all, that's the only way you can make a go of it in a business as tough as advertising. There's nothing wrong with being self-sufficient, is there?"

Diana knew nothing about self-sufficiency. She did, however, know quite a bit about food. She drooled and danced in place, waiting for another bite.

"And just because I didn't tell her about the muse thing right away—that doesn't prove anything, does it? I mean, about me not wanting to admit I need anyone's help. All it proves is that it's crazy that one person could be another person's muse and I knew it was crazy from the start and I knew she wouldn't believe it even if I told her. And, from the way she looked at me, I don't think she did." Gabe broke off another bit of muffin and ate it. "Besides, now that I'm back on track, I'll bet the music and the lyrics will keep right on coming. The way they always have. And that means this whole business about her being my muse is just some sort of anomaly. You know, like the Bermuda Triangle and the ghosts of Gettysburg and—"

"Dancing hamburgers?"

Gabe was so startled to hear another voice that he froze with a piece of muffin halfway to his mouth. He knew it wasn't possible, but that didn't stop him from looking down at Diana. He half expected to find her looking up at him, ready to continue.

He twitched away the fantasy and turned toward Maisie, who'd come in the door that led directly into the kitchen from her office. "You sound very sure of yourself," Meg's grandmother said.

"I am." He finished the muffin and brushed his hands together and Diana got to work hoovering the crumbs. "I wasn't," he murmured. He checked the oven and seeing that the temperature was just right, he put in the quiche. "I've spent the last day feeling very unsure. I figured I really made a big mistake."

"Did you?" Even this early in the morning, Maisie could be fluffy and sphinx-like all at the same time. She got to work brewing coffee but Gabe didn't fail to notice the glance she shot his way. It was part grandmotherly concern, part friendly curiosity and part flat-out snooping. As the coffeemaker began to drip, she turned her bright-blue gaze on him. "Did you make a big mistake, Gabe?"

"I thought I did." He wasn't embarrassed to admit it. What good would it do to deny the truth? Maisie knew everything that happened inside the walls of the Hideaway. Which meant that even though Meg had left soon after they'd argued, Maisie knew exactly what had gone on up in Love Me Tender and exactly what they'd said to each other. "She said—"

"That you're a Philistine, yes. Well..." She slid him a look that told him she just might agree. "Not in so many words, right?"

"She thinks I won't admit I need help. Not from anyone. For anything."

"Is it true?" Maisie got out cups and a crystal creamer. She poured the coffee and handed a cup to

Gabe. "Are you willing to admit you need Meg's help?"

"I don't." He set the coffee down untouched. "I can't need her help. It's crazy. And besides, I've never needed it before. I've done Okay for myself. All these years, I never needed anyone to inspire me."

"That was before you met Meg."

"Sure it was." Even though he'd just put it in the oven, Gabe checked the quiche. Checking the quiche gave him something to do. Something besides going over a situation he'd gone over so many times before, it was taking on the consistency of Diana's favorite beef jerky. He closed the oven door and set down the potholder shaped like a cupid. "Of course it was before I met Meg. Everything was fine before I met Meg."

"Was it?"

She was full of questions. Questions Gabe didn't want to answer. He decided that maybe coffee was a good idea, drank his down and poured another cup. Even by the time he'd finished doing that, Maisie was still stirring her silver spoon in her coffee and looking at him thoughtfully.

"You told me once that you followed your heart in order to become a songwriter."

"That's right." Gabe nodded.

"Then maybe it's time to follow your heart again."

"I've tried." He paced back and forth in front of the sink. "I've called her. I went to her house. I've looked all over the island for her. She's disappeared."

"Oh, I don't think so, dear." She gave him a grandmother's smile. "Meg is a lot of things, but a magician isn't one of them. Except with food, of course. You know, she comes across as breezy and carefree, but she's really quite sensitive. Maybe you know that.

She's also generous and loving. Not an easy thing, considering that she's had her heart broken once.''

''What I did was nothing like what he did.'' Gabe was sure of it. So sure, he slammed his cup on the counter. Coffee splattered everywhere and because he couldn't stand the thought of Maisie cleaning up his mess, he grabbed a dishcloth and got to work. ''I didn't do it on purpose,'' he said, and he wasn't talking about the spill.

''She knows that.'' Maisie sounded so certain, Gabe had to look at her. Just to see if she knew something he didn't. ''Actually, she's a very uncomplicated woman.'' Maisie got a big bowl of mixed fruit out of the refrigerator and started ladling some into each of the pink glass bowls Gabe had gotten down from the cupboard. ''To me, that indicates that what you really need is an uncomplicated solution to your problem.''

''Or it might indicate that I don't have a problem.'' His mind made up—even though the stab in his gut told him that maybe it wasn't made up in the best way—he rinsed out the dishcloth and draped it over the divider in the sink. ''Maybe the best course of action is pack up and get out of here. Because maybe Meg's the one with the problem.''

''Oh, she has a problem, all right. She just doesn't know it yet. Not completely. You see, she's fallen in love with you.''

Love?

The word echoed off the kitchen walls and created a racket in Gabe's head. Before he'd arrived at the Hideaway, he would have cringed at the thought. Now, thinking about it and everything it meant—and almost meant—made him feel as if there was a hole exactly where his heart used to be.

The heart he'd told Maisie he was used to following.

He was reluctant to ask the question but he knew he had to, or he'd wonder about it for the rest of his life. "You really think—"

"Well, I'm not a magician, either, dear. Or a mind reader. But I'd say, given the chance and a little reason to believe, Meg might come around and things might work out quite nicely."

"If I can convince her I'm not as proud as she thinks I am. That I'm perfectly open to help. From her or anybody else." Now that the idea had taken hold, Gabe felt as if he was on fire from it. He paced the length of the kitchen and back again, his mind working furiously. "Got any suggestions?" he asked Maisie.

"No, I don't." When he zoomed by, she stopped him, one hand on his arm. She smiled up at him, all pink and twinkly in the early-morning light. "But that's a start, dear. That's a start."

"YOU CAN'T STAY HERE forever, you know." Dylan O'Connell did his best to sound like the take-charge kind of guy he was. It might have been convincing if not for the fact that the police chief was carrying a cup of tea in one hand and a ham sandwich in the other. The cell door was pushed open and he walked in and handed dinner to Meg. "You know," he said, "sooner or later I'm going to have to arrest somebody. I'm going to need this cell and you'll have to get out of here."

"With any luck, it will be later." It was already late in the afternoon, and now that she thought about it, she hadn't eaten a bite since the day before when she'd had it out with Gabe. Meg grabbed the sandwich. One bite was all she needed to realize that her stomach was not in the mood for ham or anything else. She handed it back to Dylan. "No thanks," she said. "But I'll take the tea."

''You can't live on tea.''

''Who says I want to live?''

He barked out a laugh and dropped to sit next to her on the built-into-the-wall bed. ''You've got it bad, don't you?''

''Do not.'' Meg popped the plastic lid off the foam cup and blew away the steam that gathered over her tea. ''I'm simply stating a fact. That's all.''

''A fact that has something to do with you and Gabe being—''

''We aren't anything.''

''That in itself is a fact.'' Dylan crossed his arms over his chest and crossed his legs at the ankles. ''You want to try to work this out?''

''There's nothing to work out.'' The tea was watery and too sugary. Meg sipped it anyway.

''I can't keep taking you home at night and bringing you back to work with me in the morning. Not forever. You'll have to do something about going back home, Meg. If it bothers you that this guy has been around looking for you—''

''No. It's not that.'' Bless his heart, Dylan was a cop through and through. ''No restraining orders necessary, officer,'' she told him. ''And I will go back home. I promise.'' She looked at him over the rim of her cup. ''Only, until I do, you're not going to call Maisie, are you? You said you wouldn't. I don't want her or anyone else to know where I am.''

''I'm not going to call. I haven't called. Just like I promised. But Meg...she'll get worried if she doesn't hear from you. And you know Gabe must be worried, too.''

''I doubt that.'' Just thinking about Gabe sent her mind into the loop it had been playing and replaying since the day before. Disbelief, amazement, anger, back to disbelief. ''Can you believe he honestly thinks I'm some sort of muse?''

There was no other logical reaction, so she had no choice but to laugh. It was apparently not a sound heard very often in the Put-in-Bay jail. Jack, the sergeant who mostly handled rowdy college students and stolen bicycles, came from the office down the hall to see what was going on.

Dylan waved him away. He leaned back and was so quiet for so long, Meg thought he'd dozed off. She was about to give him a shake when she saw him open one eye and look at her. ''Maybe you are,'' he said.

''Maybe I am—his muse?'' Just thinking about it was enough to throw Meg back into the loop. Doubt sparred with bewilderment, which bumped into anger, and the chain reaction started all over again. ''You've been reading too many books. A person can't be another person's muse.''

''Who says?'' Dylan didn't seem totally convinced himself. He was still sitting back, still had his eyes closed and if Meg didn't know him better, she'd guess he was only half interested in what was going on.

But she knew him better than that.

He was not only a cop, he was her best friend. He had the instincts of both. ''So, if you are his muse...'' Dylan opened his eyes. He sat up and propped his elbows on his knees. ''It would bother you, huh?''

''Bother me?'' Meg stood and walked as far as the opposite wall. It wasn't very far. She turned around at the tiny window that overlooked a long line of garages. ''Something can't bother me if it isn't real,'' she said and even to her own ears, it seemed she was trying a little too hard to sound as if she believed it. ''I can't be a muse.'' She spun around. ''Do I look like a muse?''

''Sort of.'' Dylan let his gaze slide from the top of her head, along her yellow shirt and her khaki shorts, down to her sandals. ''But the question isn't do you look like one. The question is *are* you one. And since you're dodging, I'll ask again. Why does it bother you to think of yourself as Gabe's muse?''

''Because...'' Meg threw her hands in the air and screeched her frustration. ''Because I can't be,'' she said. ''Because if I am—''

''Because if you are, it's just like it was with Ben. That's what you're not saying. And you don't want things to be like they were with Ben, do you?''

''You know the answer.'' She came back to the bed and flopped down next to him. ''I never want to feel that way again, Dylan. I never want to think a guy's using me to get something he wants. I don't care if it's cooking techniques or dancing hamburgers.''

Dylan shook his head. ''That's not it,'' he said. ''I think you're afraid to share yourself. And I'm not saying you don't have the right.'' He held up one hand to stop her when it looked as if she was about to tell him he was way out in left field. ''What Ben did to you was wrong. He hurt you and of course you felt betrayed. But Gabe laid it on the line. He told you what was going on.''

''And I didn't believe him.''

''And you didn't believe him.'' Dylan stood. When he saw that Meg was finished with her tea, he took the cup from her and tossed it in the plastic garbage can outside the cell door. ''And you didn't want to believe him, either, did you?''

It wasn't easy hearing the truth. As she thought about it, Meg got up, too, and stepped out into the long, tiled hallway. Her head throbbed and her insides felt empty. ''You're right,'' she said, leaning against the cool-cement block wall. ''With Ben, I was young and stupid and blind. I had no idea what was going on. I didn't know what he was up to and that means he was stealing from me. He was stealing my recipes and my techniques, sure. But he was also draining away my creativity. And after Ben, I decided that was something I was never going to share with anyone. Not ever again. And now...''

''Now if you admit you're helping Gabe, it means you're sharing more than just a few laughs or your body.'' How he knew they'd been lovers, Meg had no idea, but Dylan didn't hesitate to say it. And he obviously wasn't surprised when she didn't tell him he was wrong. ''It means you're really giving yourself to him, Meg. All of you. Is that the part that really scares you?''

''Yeah.'' It felt good to admit it, and for the first time in what seemed like forever, Meg took a deep breath and felt some of the weight around her heart lifting. ''I guess I was holding back. I guess I didn't want to admit I need him as much as he needs me.''

''That's a good thing.'' Dylan grinned.

''That's a very good thing.'' She hugged him quickly, then combed her fingers through her hair. ''So I guess I'd better tell him, huh?''

''Tell him?'' He cocked his head and looked at her a little oddly.

Meg poked him in the arm. ''Yeah. Tell him. What I just figured out. All right, so it doesn't make things perfect. There's still this whole business about him thinking he can take on the world on his own. If I can admit the truth, then so can he. He's got to get over it. But at least I can talk to him. At least I can let him know that I finally understand why I was so upset when he told me about me being his muse. I'll just go over to the Hideaway and—''

''Ah, Meg...'' Dylan wasn't the type who displayed a lot of emotion. It was a great attribute for a cop, but there were times it was a frustrating characteristic for a friend. When his face went a little pale, it was enough to warn Meg that something was up. He frowned at her uncertainly. ''Gabe's not at the Hideaway.''

''Not at—'' Already at the door, Meg stopped and turned to him. ''What do you mean, not at the Hideaway? Sure he is. He spent yesterday trying to track me down and—''

''And that was yesterday. Today...'' Dylan looked up at the ceiling and down at the floor. Everywhere but at Meg. ''Today,'' he said, ''Jack says that when he was doing a drive around the island this afternoon, well...Jack says he saw the Porsche. Just as it was pulling onto the ferry.''

THERE DIDN'T SEEM TO BE much point in going over to the Hideaway once Meg called Maisie and had the news confirmed: Gabe had left on the three o'clock ferry.

She glanced at her kitchen clock. ''Nine o'clock,'' she told herself. ''Exactly five minutes later than last time you looked.''

Which meant that by now, Gabe was five minutes farther away.

Meg scooped a portion of cherry cordial ice cream into a bowl and carried it out to the patio. It was a perfect summer night, starlit and warm, and she settled down at the picnic table, her chin in her hands.

''Just as well,'' she muttered. ''Even if Dylan's right and I was just afraid to share myself...'' She sighed and poked her spoon into the ice cream. ''That doesn't change a thing. Not if Gabe was never willing to accept that he needed my help.''

Like all good epiphanies, this one was full of wisdom that would take some getting used to.

She just didn't think getting used to anything could make her feel this bad.

She mashed her spoon through the ice cream. Twirled it. Stirred it. The night was warm and the ice cream quickly melted. She swirled it around, then pushed it away. She wasn't very hungry, anyway.

''If you're not going to eat that, I've got somebody here who might be interested.''

Meg nearly jumped out of her seat when she heard the voice. She turned and saw Laurel and Noah standing at the gate that led into her back garden. They had Felix and Diana with them.

''He left her behind.'' Meg could tell that her words sounded hollow. It was no surprise, of course. Diana didn't belong to Gabe and he'd never liked her that much. She shook herself out of her daze. ''What are you two doing with Diana?'' she asked.

''Ingrid and Travis called. Their Cleveland appearance got cancelled and they're taking a couple more days. You want to come to the park?'' Noah opened the gate and stepped aside, as if he already knew Meg would join them. ''There's sort of a party planned for Diana so folks can say an official goodbye.''

''I'm not much in the mood for a party.'' Meg stood and picked up her bowl, ready to take it—and herself—into the house. At the last minute she decided the disposal was a waste of very good ice cream and put the dish down in front of the dogs. They slurped it up, and though Felix was enough of a gentleman to merely sit back when it was all gone, manners weren't anything

Diana had ever been accused of having. She burped and sat back smiling.

''Come on.'' Laurel grabbed Meg's arm. ''Nobody says you have to sing and dance, but you should be there. Diana adores you and you should say goodbye.''

''I can say goodbye right here.'' Meg looked down at the dog. ''Goodbye, Diana.'' She looked at her sister and brother-in-law. ''Goodbye, Laurel and Noah. Have fun. I'm going to bed.''

''Oh, no, you're not!'' If there was one thing she knew about Noah, it was that he was a perfect match for Laurel. They were both smart and they were both stubborn. He took Meg's arm and gently nudged her out of the gate. ''You've got to come with us,'' he said. ''Maisie's already on her way over and we promised her you'd be there. And you know how Maisie is.''

''Worried,'' Laurel added. She got on one side of Meg and Noah got on the other. They marched her down the walkway. ''She's worried about you. She hasn't seen you, she hasn't talked to you, and—''

''And she knows I'm fine.'' Meg resisted, but only for a moment. There was no use fighting, not when Maisie was involved. As much as she would rather have crawled into bed and stayed there for the duration, she couldn't stand Maisie being worried. Not that she thought her grandmother was frail or susceptible to fainting. It was just that Meg knew if she didn't show up at the park, Maisie would take things into her own hands. She'd show up at Meg's front door. Probably with an entourage of family, friends and well-meaning island residents. Maybe with some complete strangers thrown in for good measure.

An entourage was something Meg couldn't handle.

''All right. All right.'' Out on the sidewalk, she

shrugged off Laurel and Noah's hands. "I'll go quietly," she promised. "Only promise me one thing, Okay? Let's make this short and snappy."

"Short and snappy," Noah said.

"Short and snappy," Laurel echoed.

And if Meg had been feeling a little more like herself and a little less miserable, she would've noticed that neither one of them promised.

Chapter Fourteen

It paid to have connections.

When Meg, Laurel and Noah were almost at the park, Jack, the police sergeant, flashed the lights on his cruiser to signal Dylan. Dylan, who was leaning against a lamppost on the outskirts of the park, waved to Maisie. Maisie gave Gabe the high sign.

And Gabe touched a torch to the bonfire pile that had been set up in the middle of DeRivera Park.

The flames sprang to life, and Gabe gave Maisie the high sign. As if to say he had everything under control. Too bad he didn't feel that way.

And he wondered what was going to happen after that.

''Steady, boy,'' he told himself. ''You'll get through this just fine, but you've got to keep your head—provided she doesn't rip it off for you.''

''They're coming!'' he heard Maisie call before she disappeared into the place where the orange firelight met the Ohio night, and Gabe gulped down a breath for courage. Across the park, he saw Noah. He heard Diana bark. The next second, Meg came around the corner.

And Gabe swore his heart stopped right then and there.

She looked stunning in the moonlight.

Meg's hair was loose around her shoulders and she was wearing a flowing dress that just about glowed in the dark. It might have been silver. Or it might have been white. Whatever the color, it made her look delicate and ethereal, like a fairy from a storybook. She had on her favorite sandals and though Gabe couldn't tell what kind of earrings she was wearing, he saw them glint in the light, as if the embers behind him had leaped across the park and touched them with fire.

Whatever she'd been expecting, it obviously wasn't a bonfire. She stopped, and even at this distance, Gabe couldn't fail to notice that there were smudges of sleeplessness under her eyes or that though Laurel and Noah were doing their best to drag her into a conversation, Meg wasn't biting.

She didn't look just down and out. Down and out, Gabe could have dealt with. Meg looked lost and lonely. Even worse, she was quiet. For a woman who wasn't afraid to sing out her feelings for the world to hear (even if she didn't sing them on key), it was the ultimate sign that she was hurting. That, more than anything else, told Gabe he'd broken her heart.

Suddenly, what had seemed like such a good idea only a few short hours ago was sounding dumber by the moment. Gabe watched Meg get closer. Because of where he was standing in the shadows, she hadn't seen him yet and a part of him was glad. Another part of him wished it would just happen and be over with. So he could start breathing again.

WHEN MEG WALKED around the corner and saw the bonfire blazing in the center of the park, she didn't think much of it. The local chamber of commerce was always coming up with ways to make tourists feel home on the island.

It didn't, however, explain why no one was gathered around the fire.

"Told you it was a party." As if it was the most natural thing in the world, Laurel grabbed Meg's arm and tugged her across the street and into the park. "Just forgot to mention that it's a private party."

Nervous—and not sure why—Meg reached down and scooped Diana into her arms. She weighted a ton but there was something comforting in her bulk and in the little murmur that rumbled through the bulldog's chest. When Diana licked her cheek, Meg managed a fragile smile. She couldn't quite bring herself to laugh.

Even though she was getting closer and closer to the fire, a shiver skittered over Meg's shoulder. As if she was expecting something to happen. She twitched away the sensation. Just a couple of days ago she'd been expecting nothing less of life than everything. And now...

Meg saw a movement in the shadows to her right. The next second, she found herself face to face with Gabe. Her breath caught and she stopped dead.

She held on to Diana a little tighter, and the dog seemed to sense the emotions that were tumbling through Meg like the waves hitting the dock across the street. She barked a quiet greeting, but she didn't budge.

Gabe took a step nearer. "We need to talk," he said.

Meg stroked Diana's head. "You said that once before. Remember? Yesterday in Love Me Tender. You said we needed to talk."

"Yeah, I remember." Gabe's hair was inky in the firelight. His eyes were smoky. "But yesterday, we didn't talk. At least not to each other. That was more like *at* each other. And it sure didn't accomplish much."

"What *are* we trying to accomplish?" she asked him. "If you're waiting for me to admit that the muse thing is a possibility—"

"No. That's not it at all." He stepped even nearer. "I had to talk to you again, Meg, and when I couldn't find you—"

"I heard you left." It probably wasn't smart to lay her cards on the table this early in the game, but at this point, Meg didn't much care. She knew her voice trembled, and she knew Gabe noticed because when he turned to her, his expression was so tender, it made her ache inside. "Dylan told me you left."

"Dylan is a great guy. He's also a great liar."

"Liar?" Meg looked around, but there was no sign of Dylan—or anyone else. She turned back to Gabe. "You didn't leave?"

"I didn't. And I'm not going to. Not until I see what happens after I make a phone call."

Gabe reached into his pocket and pulled out his cell phone. He reached into another pocket and pulled out some pieces of paper and when he unfolded them, Meg recognized them as the ones on which he'd written the lyrics and music for the Tasty Time Burger jingle. He punched in a number and while it was connecting, he glanced at Meg.

"It wasn't easy getting all of them to agree to be there," he told her, but before she could ask who he was talking about and what they'd agreed to, Gabe was talking into the phone.

"Latoya, you there?" Obviously, she answered in the affirmative. Gabe nodded. "Dennis, too? Okay, stay on the line and I'll get the Tasty Time Burger folks. Then we can conference call."

She stood and watched in wonder while he dialed another number, checked to see if the people who were supposed to be there were all present, then connected the two calls.

"So what do you think?" he said into the phone. "One big happy family, huh?" There was a brief pause. "I suppose you're all wondering what this phone call is all about." Gabe continued to talk into the phone, loud enough for the people in New York and LA to hear. "It's about the jingle, of course. The Tasty Time Burger jingle. What's that?" he asked when someone shot him a question. "Is it good?"

He glanced down at the papers in his hand and Meg expected him to sing the lyrics that were all about the marriage of sweet and heat to the tune that had flowed from his fingers so effortlessly that night their hands had touched over the piano keys.

"No." The single word from Gabe was so quick and full of confidence, it startled Meg. "No," he said again. "It isn't good. Truth be told, it isn't even a jingle. I've got news for you folks and I suppose I should've told you sooner, but I've been thinking there might be some way out of this little dilemma. There isn't, and it's about time you knew. There is no jingle. There's not going to be a jingle. I've got writer's block, and I'm not talking about a little case of not being able to put two words together. This is the real McCoy, and it's not going anywhere. And just for the record, even if I could make it go away..." His gaze flickered to Meg. "I wouldn't do it. Not if it meant hurting someone I love very much."

Gabe was silent and Meg could only imagine what he was hearing from the other end of the phone. Whatever it was, it didn't keep him from smiling.

"That's right," he said. "I've been hiding out.

Dodging you. Even you, Latoya. But it hasn't been a complete waste of time. While I've been here, I've found out that there are more important things in life than jingles. And that I can't do everything on my own. Sometimes you need family and sometimes you need friends. Sometimes you need the help of absolute strangers. And I've learned that sometimes, inspiration—even my inspiration—needs a whole lot of assistance. I've also learned that none of it really matters. Not if a man doesn't have a woman to love. So you see…'' The phone in one hand, he used his other hand to crumple the lyrics and music into a tight ball. ''No jingle!'' he said, and he threw the ball of paper into the bonfire.

Meg was shocked that she could move so fast. She darted forward and caught the paper right before it fell into the heart of the flames. While Gabe was still too stunned to stop her, she grabbed the phone out of his hands.

''He's kidding,'' she said, and she didn't bother to introduce herself because she figured it wasn't important. ''About the jingle not being ready? He's kidding. In fact, it's not only ready, it's brilliant. I can sing the chorus for you if you—''

''Oh, no!'' Gabe plucked the phone out of her hands and though she couldn't hear the conversation on the other end, she could pretty much fill in the blanks. ''I'll talk to you in the morning,'' he said into the phone and though she distinctly heard the sound of a voice still talking on the other end, he closed the phone to disconnect the call. He slapped his thigh and Meg put Diana down, and the dog came running. Gabe put the phone in Diana's mouth, pointed her to the lake and told her he wasn't taking any more calls.

Side by side, Gabe and Meg watched the dog toddle

onto the dock at the marina across the street. A couple of seconds later, they heard the distinct plunk of the phone hitting the water.

"So." Gabe turned his attention back to her, the emotion in his eyes so warm and loving, it nearly knocked Meg off her feet. "You want to come to New York with me?" he asked.

"Nope." Meg laughed when his expression fell like a bad soufflé. "You need to go to New York on your own," she told him. "You need to prove to yourself that you can handle this. All on your own. But hey, I'll be here when you get back. And if you ever run out of ideas..."

MAISIE HAD NEVER been one to listen at keyholes. It wasn't fair, and it was downright ill-mannered. That didn't stop her from pausing outside the door of Love Me Tender. Just for a moment.

After luring Meg to the park and coming back to the Hideaway and opening a bottle of champagne to toast what was looking more and more like the happily-ever-after she'd been hoping for, she was just a little tired. But Doc Ross was waiting downstairs and there was a box of scented candles she needed to deliver to the nice folks who'd checked into Close to the Heart.

She spent a moment listening to the purr of contented voices from the other side of the door of Love Me Tender, then, deciding that her work was done—at least for now—she went downstairs humming the new Tasty Time Burger jingle.

ON THE OTHER SIDE of the Love Me Tender door, things were humming, too. Gabe had just finished kissing Meg and he propped himself on his elbows and smiled down into her eyes.

''I love you, Meg.''

''I know.'' She couldn't help herself. There was so much joy inside her, she had to smile.

''You'll marry me?''

She considered the question. For about a heartbeat. And the kiss she gave Gabe was the only answer he would ever need.

When she was done, she burrowed into the pillows piled at one end of the pink Cadillac. ''So....'' She skimmed one finger over Gabe's neck and across his chest. ''Here we are. And I'm touching you. And you...'' She glanced down to where he was trailing lazy circles over her stomach and breasts. ''You are touching me. So tell me, Gabe, you getting any ideas?''

''Oh, yeah.'' His smile was the last thing she saw before he kissed her. ''I'm getting plenty of ideas and something tells me I'm never going to run out.''

Epilogue

December 24

Within days of its initial airing that autumn, the Tasty Time Burger commercial took on a life of its own. The jingle was easy to remember and fun to sing along with and the dancing hamburgers became popular enough to generate their own line of greeting cards, men's silk ties and action figures, which were top sellers for the holidays. But it was the *sweet and heat* line that really hit it big. The words became a tag-line for everything from picture-perfect basketball shots to kisses, and hardly a day went by when Meg didn't hear the words uttered by disc jockeys on the radio or late-night TV talk-show hosts.

Every time she did, she couldn't help smiling.

Then again, she was doing a lot of that these days.

She brushed flour off her hands and sang the words of the now-famous commercial at the top of her lungs. Her singing had the expected results. Half laughing, half cringing, Gabe pushed open the door between Meg's dining room and the kitchen.

"You're not going to sing all the time, are you?"

"Hey, you asked for it." She dance-stepped her way over to him and kissed him on the cheek. "You're the one who agreed to the better or worse part."

"Yeah, but nobody said anything about the worse part meaning the worst singing!" He breathed in the aroma that filled the kitchen. "Making cinnamon bread?"

"Maisie's favorite." She smiled up at her husband. "Thought I'd put some under her tree, signed from Santa Claus. Didn't want to leave for LA without giving her some to put in the freezer. I told her when we come back to stay on the island every summer, I'd make her enough to last, and if she runs out, I promised I'd courier her more."

"I suppose that's the least we can do for her. She's a special lady. And she's not the only one." Though he was never quite sure what would happen when he took her into his arms, Gabe pulled Meg tight against him, her back to his chest.

She purred her approval. "Getting ideas?" she asked.

"You bet!" He kissed her ear and her neck and her cheek. "There's that jingle I need to write for the new account. You know, the breakfast cereal shaped like little stars." He nuzzled his lips against her neck and twirling her around, he held her at arm's length. "I've got it!"

Meg laughed. "The jingle?"

"Nope. A better idea. We don't have to be at the Hideaway for Christmas Eve dinner for a couple of hours and while we're waiting..."

She could well imagine what he was planning and it sounded good to her, too. Too bad they were interrupted. The door swung open and Diana came scuffling into the room followed by six of the ugliest puppies anyone on South Bass Island had ever seen. They had their father's chocolate lab coloring and their mother's shape, tough as tanks and round as beachballs. They also had her appetite.

''All right. All right.'' Gabe settled the dogs with a look. ''Corn chips and ice cream for everyone, and then you head over to Laurel and Noah's for the duration. And you—'' He looked down at Diana, and Meg noticed that even though he tried, he wasn't a good enough actor to hide a smile. ''You're coming with us.''

He scratched Diana's ears. ''Back to La-La Land and the limelight!''

Diana barked.

''First a stop in Boston.'' Gabe tried not to let on, but Meg knew he was anxious—not to mention a bit nervous—about seeing his family again. He was thrilled to be introducing his wife to them, too, and happy that when he sent a Christmas card, his grandfather had responded with the invitation. It wasn't perfect, but it was a start, a new beginning both he—and his family—deserved.

Diana barked again.

''I can't believe I own a dog.'' Gabe sighed, but there was more contentment than resignation in the sound. ''I can't believe they sold her to me when I asked, either.''

''Probably saved them a fortune in grocery bills.''

''Probably?'' He finished fixing snacks for the dogs and set their bowls on the floor and while they dug in, he wrapped his arm around Meg's shoulders.

''So, as I was saying…'' He urged her toward the dining room.

The bread was in the oven, the dogs were busy and Meg knew a good idea when she heard one.

She bent her head and gave him a smile. ''What a treat?''

''Can't be beat.'' He closed the dining-room door and taking her hand, led her into the living room. Most of what Meg owned had already been packed. The pint-size aluminum tree from Love Me Tender stood on the mantel. The candle-shaped lights bubbled merrily, bathing the room in soft shades of red and yellow. There was a quilt laid out on the floor in front of the fireplace and he tugged her down onto it and took her in his arms.

''Forget the pepper bacon and the honey butter.'' When he trailed a series of kisses from her mouth to her neck, Meg's breath caught over a sigh of pure happiness. *''This,''* she said, ''is the perfect marriage of sweet and heat.''

Your opinion is important to us! Please take a few moments to share your thoughts with us about your experiences with Harlequin and Silhouette books. Your comments will be very useful in ensuring that we deliver books you love to read.
Please take a few minutes to complete the questionnaire, then send it to us at the address below.

Send your completed questionnaires to:
Harlequin/Silhouette Reader Survey, P.O. Box 9046, Buffalo, NY 14269-9046

1. As you may know, there are many different lines under the Harlequin and Silhouette brands. Each of the lines is listed below. Please check the box that most represents your reading habit for each line.

Line	Currently read this line	Do not read this line	Not sure if I read this line
Harlequin American Romance	❑	❑	❑
Harlequin Duets	❑	❑	❑
Harlequin Romance	❑	❑	❑
Harlequin Historicals	❑	❑	❑
Harlequin Superromance	❑	❑	❑
Harlequin Intrigue	❑	❑	❑
Harlequin Presents	❑	❑	❑
Harlequin Temptation	❑	❑	❑
Harlequin Blaze	❑	❑	❑
Silhouette Special Edition	❑	❑	❑
Silhouette Romance	❑	❑	❑
Silhouette Intimate Moments	❑	❑	❑
Silhouette Desire	❑	❑	❑

2. Which of the following best describes why you bought *this book?* One answer only, please.

- the picture on the cover ❑
- the author ❑
- part of a miniseries ❑
- saw an ad in a magazine/newsletter ❑
- I borrowed/was given this book ❑
- the title ❑
- the line is one I read often ❑
- saw an ad in another book ❑
- a friend told me about it ❑
- other: ________________ ❑

3. Where did you buy *this book?* One answer only, please.

- at Barnes & Noble ❑
- at Waldenbooks ❑
- at Borders ❑
- at another bookstore ❑
- at Wal-Mart ❑
- at Target ❑
- at Kmart ❑
- at another department store or mass merchandiser ❑
- at a grocery store ❑
- at a drugstore ❑
- on eHarlequin.com Web site ❑
- from another Web site ❑
- Harlequin/Silhouette Reader Service/through the mail ❑
- used books from anywhere ❑
- I borrowed/was given this book ❑

4. On average, how many Harlequin and Silhouette books do you buy at one time?

- I buy ______ books at one time ❑
- I rarely buy a book ❑

MRQ403HAR-1A

5. How many times per month do you shop for any *Harlequin and/or Silhouette* books? One answer only, please.

1 or more times a week	❑	a few times per year	❑
1 to 3 times per month	❑	less often than once a year	❑
1 to 2 times every 3 months	❑	never	❑

6. When you think of your ideal heroine, which *one* statement describes her the best? One answer only, please.

She's a woman who is strong-willed	❑	She's a desirable woman	❑
She's a woman who is needed by others	❑	She's a powerful woman	❑
She's a woman who is taken care of	❑	She's a passionate woman	❑
She's an adventurous woman	❑	She's a sensitive woman	❑

7. The following statements describe types or genres of books that you may be interested in reading. Pick *up to 2 types* of books that you are most interested in.

I like to read about truly romantic relationships ❑
I like to read stories that are sexy romances ❑
I like to read romantic comedies ❑
I like to read a romantic mystery/suspense ❑
I like to read about romantic adventures ❑
I like to read romance stories that involve family ❑
I like to read about a romance in times or places that I have never seen ❑
Other: ______________________________ ❑

The following questions help us to group your answers with those readers who are similar to you. Your answers will remain confidential.

8. Please record your year of birth below.

19 ____

9. What is your marital status?

single ❑ married ❑ common-law ❑ widowed ❑
divorced/separated ❑

10. Do you have children 18 years of age or younger currently living at home?

yes ❑ no ❑

11. Which of the following best describes your employment status?

employed full-time or part-time ❑ homemaker ❑ student ❑
retired ❑ unemployed ❑

12. Do you have access to the Internet from either home or work?

yes ❑ no ❑

13. Have you ever visited eHarlequin.com?

yes ❑ no ❑

14. What state do you live in?

____

15. Are you a member of Harlequin/Silhouette Reader Service?

yes ❑ Account # ____________ no ❑ MRQ403HAR-1B